HOME OF THE VSIIR,
NIGHTMARE OF MAN—

He lies on a broad white slab in a scorched desert. It's getting hard to breathe. A terrible pull, bending and breaking him, ripping bones apart. Hooded figures pointing, laughing, exchanging blurred comments in an unknown language. Porcupine quills sprouting inside his flesh and forcing their way upward. Points of fire all over him. A thin scarlet hand, withered fingers like crab-claws, hovering in front of his face. Scratching. Scratching. Scratching. His blood runs among the quills, thick and sluggish. He shivers, struggling to sit up —lifts a hand, leaving pieces of quivering flesh stuck to the slab—sits up— screaming . . .

From "Something Wild Is Loose"

Earth's
Other Shadow

Nine Science Fiction Stories

by

Robert Silverberg

A SIGNET BOOK from

NEW AMERICAN LIBRARY

TIMES MIRROR

SIGNET TRADEMARK REG. U.S. PAT. OFF. AND FOREIGN COUNTRIES
REGISTERED TRADEMARK—MARCA REGISTRADA
HECHO EN CHICAGO, U.S.A.

SIGNET, SIGNET CLASSICS, SIGNETTE, MENTOR AND PLUME BOOKS
are published by The New American Library, Inc.,
1301 Avenue of the Americas, New York, New York 10019
FIRST PRINTING, JUNE, 1973

2 3 4 5 6 7 8 9

PRINTED IN THE UNITED STATES OF AMERICA

Contents

Something Wild
Is Loose

1.

The Vsiir got aboard the Earthbound ship by accident.
It had absolutely no plans for taking a holiday on a wet,
grimy planet like Earth. But it was in its metamorphic
phase, undergoing the period of undisciplined change that
began as winter came on, and it had shifted so far
up-spectrum that Earthborn eyes couldn't see it. Oh, a
really skilled observer might notice a slippery little purple
flicker once in a while, a kind of snore, as the Vsiir
momentarily dropped down out of the ultra-violet; but
he'd have to know where to look, and when. The crewman
who was responsible for putting the Vsiir on the ship
never even considered the possibility that there might be
something invisible sleeping atop one of the crates of
cargo being hoisted into the ship's hold. He simply went
down the row, slapping a floater-node on each crate and
sending it gliding up the gravity well toward the open
hatch. The fifth crate to go inside was the one on which
the Vsiir had decided to take its nap. The spaceman didn't
know that he had inadvertently given an alien organism a
free ride to Earth. The Vsiir didn't know it, either,
until the hatch was sealed and an oxygen-nitrogen atmosphere began to hiss from the vents. The Vsiir did not
happen to breathe those gases, but, because it was in its
time of metamorphosis, it was able to adapt itself quickly
and nicely to the sour, prickly vapors seeping into its
metabolic cells. The next step was to fashion a set of
full-spectrum scanners and learn something about its sur-
roundings. Within a few minutes, the Vsiir was aware—
—that it was in a large, dark place that held a great
many boxes containing various mineral and vegetable

7

products of its world, mainly branches of the greenfire tree but also some other things of no comprehensible value to a Vsiir—

—that a double wall of curved metal enclosed this place—

—that just beyond this wall was a null-atmosphere zone, such as is found between one planet and another—

—that this entire closed system was undergoing acceleration—

—that this therefore was a spaceship, heading rapidly away from the world of Vsiirs and in fact already some ten planetary diameters distant, with the gap growing alarmingly moment by moment—

—that it would be impossible, even for a Vsiir in metamorphosis, to escape from the spaceship at this point—

—and that, unless it could persuade the crew of the ship to halt and go back, it would be compelled to undertake a long and dreary voyage to a strange and probably loathsome world, where life would at best be highly inconvenient, and might present great dangers. It would find itself cut off painfully from the rhythm of its own civilization. It would miss the Festival of Changing. It would miss the Holy Eclipse. It would not be able to take part in next spring's Rising of the Sea. It would suffer in a thousand ways.

There were six human beings aboard the ship. Extending its perceptors, the Vsiir tried to reach their minds. Though humans had been coming to its planet for many years, it had never bothered making contact with them before; but it had never been in this much trouble before, either. It sent a foggy tendril of thought roving the corridors, looking for traces of human intelligence. Here? A glow of electrical activity within a sphere of bone: a mind, a mind! A busy mind. But surrounded by a wall, apparently; the Vsiir rammed up against it and was thrust back. That was startling and disturbing. What kind of beings were these, whose minds were closed to ordinary contact? The Vsiir went on, hunting through the ship. Another mind: again closed. Another. Another. The Vsiir felt panic rising. Its mantle fluttered; its energy radiations dropped far down into the visible spectrum, then shot nervously toward much shorter waves. Even its physical form experienced a series of quick involuntary metamorphoses, to the Vsiir's intense embarassment. It did not get control of its body until it had passed from spherical to cubical to chaotic, and had become a grid-work of fibrous threads held together only by a pulsing strand of ego. Fiercely it forced itself back to the spherical form and resumed its search of the ship, dismally realizing that by this time its native world was half a stellar unit away. It was without hope now, but it continued to probe the minds of the crew, if only for the sake of thoroughness. Even if it made contact, though, how could it communicate the nature of its plight, and even if it communicated, why would the humans be disposed to help it? Yet it went on through the ship. And—

Here: an open mind. No wall at all. A miracle! The Vsiir rushed into close contact, overcome with joy and surprise, pouring out its predicament. *Please listen. Unfortunate non-human organism accidentally transported into this vessel during loading of cargo. Metabolically and psychologically unsuited for prolonged life on Earth. Begs pardon for inconvenience, wishes prompt return to home planet recently left, regrets disturbance in shipping schedule but hopes that this large favor will not prove impossible to grant. Do you comprehend my sending? Unfortunate non-human organism accidentally transported—*

2.

Lieutenant Falkirk had drawn the first sleep-shift after floatoff. It was only fair; Falkirk had knocked himself out processing the cargo during the loading stage, slapping the floater-nodes on every crate and feeding the transit manifests to the computer. Now that the ship was space-borne he could grab some rest while the other crewmen were handling the floatoff chores. So he settled down for six hours in the cradle as soon as they were on their way. Below him, the ship's six gravity-drinkers spun on their axes, gobbling inertia and pushing up the acceleration, and the ship floated Earthward at a velocity that would reach the galactic level before Falkirk woke. He drifted into drowsiness. A good trip: enough greenfire bark in the hold to see Earth through a dozen fits of the molecule plague, and plenty of other potential medicinals besides, along with a load of interesting mineral samples, and—Falkirk slept. For half an hour he enjoyed sweet slumber, his mind disengaged, his body loose.

Until a dark dream bubbled through his skull.

Deep purple sunlight, hot and somber. Something slippery tickling the edges of his brain. He lies on a broad white slab in a scorched desert. Unable to move. Getting harder to breathe. The gravity—a terrible pull, bending and breaking him, ripping his bones apart. Hooded figures moving around him, pointing, laughing, exchanging blurred comments in an unknown language. His skin melting and taking on a new texture: porcupine quills sprouting inside his flesh and forcing their way upward, poking out through every pore. Points of fire all over him. A thin scarlet hand, withered fingers like crab-claws, hovering in front of his face. Scratching. Scratching. Scratching. His blood running among the quills, thick and sluggish. He shivers, struggling to sit up—lifts a hand, leaving pieces of quivering flesh stuck to the slab—sits up—

Wakes, trembling, screaming.

Falkirk's shout still sounded in his own ears as his eyes adjusted to the light. Lieutenant Commander Rodriguez was holding his shoulders and shaking him.

"You all right?"

Falkirk tried to reply. Words wouldn't come. Hallucinatory shock, he realized, as part of his mind attempted to convince the other part that the dream was over. He was trained to handle crises; he ran through a quick disciplinary countdown and calmed himself, though he was still badly shaken. "Nightmare," he said hoarsely. "A beauty. Never had a dream with that kind of intensity before."

Rodriguez relaxed. Obviously he couldn't get very upset over a mere nightmare. "You want a pill?"

Falkirk shook his head. "I'll manage, thanks."

But the impact of the dream lingered. It was more than an hour before he got back to sleep, and then he fell into a light, restless doze, as if his mind were on guard against a return of those chilling fantasies. Fifty minutes before his programmed wake-up time, he was awakened by a ghastly shriek from the far side of the cabin.

Lieutenant Commander Rodriguez was having a nightmare.

3.

When the ship made floatdown on Earth a month later it was, of course, put through the usual decontamination procedures before anyone or anything aboard it was allowed out of the starport. The outer hull got squirted with sealants designed to trap and smother any microorganism that might have hitchhiked from another world; the crewmen emerged through the safety pouch and went straight into a quarantine chamber without being exposed to the air; the ship's atmosphere was cycled into withdrawal chambers, where it underwent a thorough purification, and the entire interior of the vessel received a six-phase sterilization, beginning with fifteen minutes of hard vacuum and ending with an hour of neutron bombardment.

These procedures caused a certain degree of inconvenience for the Vsiir. It was already at the low end of its energy phase, due mainly to the repeated discouragements it had suffered in its attempts to communicate with the six humans. Now it was forced to adapt to a variety of unpleasant environments with no chance to rest between changes. Even the most adaptable of organisms can get tired. By the time the starport's decontamination team was ready to certify that the ship was wholly free of alien life-forms, the Vsiir was very, very tired indeed.

The oxygen-nitrogen atmosphere entered the hold once more. The Vsiir found it quite welcome, at least in contrast to all that had just been thrown at it. The hatch was open; stevedores were muscling the cargo crates into position to be floated across the field to the handling dome. The Vsiir took advantage of this moment to extrude some legs and scramble out of the ship. It found itself on a broad concrete apron, rimmed by massive buildings. A yellow sun was shining in a blue sky; infrared was bouncing all over the place, but the Vsiir speedily made arrangements to deflect the excess. It also compensated immediately for the tinge of ugly hydrocarbons in the atmosphere, for the frightening noise level, and for the leaden feeling of homesickness that suddenly threatened its organic stability at the first sight of this unfamiliar, disheartening world. How to get home again? How to make contact, even? The Vsiir sensed nothing but closed minds—sealed like seeds in their shells. True, from time to time the minds of these humans opened, but even then they seemed unwilling to let the Vsiir's message get through.

Perhaps it would be different here. Perhaps those six were poor communicators, for some reason, and there would be more receptive minds available in this place. Perhaps. Perhaps. Close to despair, the Vsiir hurried across the field and slipped into the first building in which it sensed open minds. There were hundreds of humans in it, occupying many levels, and the open minds were widely scattered. The Vsiir located the nearest one and, worriedly, earnestly, hopefully, touched the tip of its mind to the human's. *Please listen. I mean no harm. Am non-human organism arrived on your planet through unhappy circumstances, wishing only quick going back to own world—*

4.

The cardiac wing of Long Island Starport Hospital was on the ground floor, in the rear, where the patients could be given floater therapy without upsetting the gravitational ratios of the rest of the building. As always, the hospital was full—people were always coming in sick off starliners, and most of them were hospitalized right at the starport for their own safety—and the cardiac wing had more than its share. At the moment it held a dozen infarcts awaiting implant, nine post-implant recupes, five coronaries in emergency stasis, three ventricle-regrowth projects, an aortal patch job, and nine or ten assorted other cases. Most of the patients were floating, to keep down the gravitational strain on their damaged tissues—all but the regrowth people, who were under full Earthnorm gravity so that their new hearts would come in with the proper resilience and toughness. The hospital had a fine reputation and one of the lowest mortality rates in the hemisphere.

Losing two patients the same morning was a shock to the entire staff.

At 0917 the monitor flashed the red light for Mrs. Maldonado, 87, post-implant and thus far doing fine. She had developed acute endocarditis coming back from a tour of the Jupiter system; at her age there wasn't enough vitality to sustain her through the slow business of growing a new heart with a genetic prod, but they'd given her a synthetic implant and for two weeks it had worked quite well. Suddenly, though, the hospital's control center was getting a load of grim telemetry from Mrs. Maldonado's bed: valve action zero, blood pressure zero, respiration zero, pulse zero, everything zero, zero, zero. The EEG tape showed a violent lurch—as though she had received some abrupt and intense shock—followed by a minute or two of irregular action, followed by termination of brain activity. Long before any hospital personnel had reached her bedside, automatic revival equipment, both chemical and electrical, had gone to work on the patient, but she was beyond reach: a massive cerebral hemorrhage, coming totally without warning, had done irreversible damage.

At 0928 came the second loss: Mr. Guinness, 51, three days past surgery for a coronary embolism. The same series of events. A severe jolt to the nervous system, an immediate and fatal physiological response. Resuscitation procedures negative. No one on the staff had any plausible explanation for Mr. Guinness' death. Like Mrs. Maldonado, he had been sleeping peacefully, all vital signs good, until the moment of the fatal seizure.

"As though someone had come up and yelled *boo* in their ears," one doctor muttered, puzzling over the charts. He pointed to the wild EEG track. "Or as if they'd had unbearably vivid nightmares and couldn't take the sensory overload. But no one was making noise in the ward. And nightmares aren't contagious."

5.

Dr. Peter Mookherji, resident in neuropathology, was beginning his morning rounds on the hospital's sixth level when the soft voice of his annunciator, taped behind his left ear, asked him to report to the quarantine building immediately. Dr. Mookherji scowled. "Can't it wait? This is my busiest time of day, and—"

"You are asked to come at once."

"Look, I've got a girl in a coma here, due for her teletherapy session in fifteen minutes, and she's counting on seeing me. I'm her only link to the world. If I'm not there when—"

"You are asked to come at once, Dr. Mookherji."

"Why do the quarantine people need a neuropathologist in such a hurry? Let me take care of the girl, at least, and in forty-five minutes they can have me."

"Dr. Mookherji—"

It didn't pay to argue with a machine. Mookherji forced his temper down. Short tempers ran in his family, along with a fondness for torrid curries and a talent for telepathy. Glowering, he grabbed a data terminal, identified himself, and told the hospital's control center to reprogram his entire morning schedule. "Build in a half-hour postponement somehow," he snapped. "I can't help it—see for yourself. I've been requisitioned by the quarantine staff." The computer was thoughtful enough to have a rollerbuggy waiting for him when he emerged from the hospital. It whisked him across the starport to the quarantine building in three minutes, but he was still angry when he got there. The scanner at the door ticked off his badge and one of the control center's innumerable voice-outputs told him solemnly, "You are expected in Room 403, Dr. Mookherji."

Room 403 turned out to be a two-sector interrogation office. The rear sector of the room was part of the building's central quarantine core, and the front sector belonged to the public-access part of the building, with a thick glass wall in between. Six haggard-looking spacemen were slouched on sofas behind the wall, and three members of the starport's quarantine staff paced about in the front. Mookherji's irritation ebbed when he saw that one of the quarantine men was an old medical-school friend, Lee Nakadai. The slender Japanese was a year older than Mookherji—29 to 28; they met for lunch occasionally at the starport commissary, and they had double-dated a pair of Filipina twins earlier in the year, but the pressure of work had kept them apart for months. Nakadai got down to business quickly now: "Pete, have you ever heard of an epidemic of nightmares?"

"Eh?"

Indicating the men behind the quarantine wall, Nakadai said, "These fellows came in a couple of hours ago from Norton's Star. Brought back a cargo of greenfire bark. Physically they check out to five decimal places, and I'd release them except for one funny thing. They're all in a bad state of nervous exhaustion, which they say is the result of having had practically no sleep during their whole month-long return trip. And the reason for that is that they were having nightmares—every one of them—real mind-wrecking dreams, whenever they tried to sleep. It sounded so peculiar that I thought we'd better run a neuropath checkup, in case they've picked up some kind of cerebral infection."

Mookherji frowned. "For this you got me out of my ward on emergency requisition, Lee?"

"Talk to them," Nakadai said. "Maybe it'll scare you a little."

Mookherji glanced at the spacemen. "All right," he said. "What about these nightmares?"

A tall, bony-looking officer who introduced himself as Lieutenant Falkirk said, "I was the first victim—right after floatoff. I almost flipped. It was like, well, something touching my mind, filling it with weird thoughts. And everything absolutely real while it was going on—I thought I was choking, I thought my body was changing into something alien, I felt my blood running out my pores—" Falkirk shrugged. "Like any sort of bad dream, I guess, only ten times as vivid. Fifty times. A few hours later Lieutenant Commander Rodriguez had the same kind of dream. Different images, same effect. And then, one by one, as the others took their sleep-shifts, they started to wake up screaming. Two of us ended up spending three weeks on happy-pills. We're pretty stable men, doctor—we're trained to take almost anything. But I think a civilian would have cracked up for good with dreams like those. Not so much the images as the intensity, the realness of them."

"And these dreams recurred throughout the voyage?" Mookherji asked.

"Every shift. It got so we were afraid to doze off, because we knew the devils would start crawling through our heads when we did. Or we'd put ourselves real down on sleeper-tabs. And even so we'd have the dreams, with our minds doped to a level where you wouldn't imagine dreams would happen. A plague of nightmares, doctor. An epidemic."

"When was the last episode?"

"The final sleep-shift before floatdown."

"You haven't gone to sleep, any of you, since leaving the ship?"

"No," Falkirk said.

One of the other spacemen said, "Maybe he didn't make it clear to you, doctor. These were killer dreams. They were mind-crackers. We were lucky to get home sane. If we did."

Mookherji drummed his fingertips together, rummaging through his experience for some parallel case. He couldn't find any. He knew of mass hallucinations, plenty of them, episodes in which whole mobs had persuaded themselves they had seen gods, demons, miracles, the dead walking, fiery symbols in the sky. But a series of hallucinations coming in sequence, shift after shift, to an entire crew of tough, pragmatic spacemen? It didn't make sense.

Nakadai said, "Pete, the men had a guess about what might have done it to them. Just a wild idea, but maybe—"

"What is it?"

Falkirk laughed uneasily. "Actually, it's pretty fantastic, doctor."

"Go ahead."

"Well, that something from the planet came aboard the ship with us. Something, well, telepathic. Which fiddled around with our minds whenever we went to sleep. What we felt as nightmares was maybe this thing inside our heads."

"Possibly it rode all the way back to Earth with us," another spaceman said. "It could still be aboard the ship. Or loose in the city by now."

"The Invisible Nightmare Menace?" Mookherji said, with a faint smile. "I doubt that I can buy that."

"There *are* telepathic creatures," Falkirk pointed out.

"I know," Mookherji said sharply. "I happen to be one myself."

"I'm sorry, doctor, if—"

"But that doesn't lead me to look for telepaths under every bush. I'm not ruling out your alien menace, mind you. But I think it's a lot more likely that you picked up some kind of inflammation of the brain out there. A virus disease, a type of encephalitis that shows itself in the form of chronic hallucinations." The spacemen looked troubled. Obviously they would rather be victims of an unknown monster preying on them from outside than of an unknown virus lodged in their brains. Mookherji went on, "I'm not saying that's what it is, either. I'm just tossing around hypotheses. We'll know more after we've run some tests." Checking his watch, he said to Nakadai, "Lee, there's not much more I can find out right now, and I've got to get back to my patients. I want these fellows plugged in for the full series of neuropsychological check-outs. Have the outputs relayed to my office as they come in. Run the tests in staggered series and start letting the men go to sleep, two at a time, after each series—I'll send over a technician to help you rig the telemetry. I want to be notified immediately if there's any nightmare experience."

"Right."

"And get them to sign telepathy releases. I'll give them a preliminary mind-probe this evening after I've had a chance to study the clinical findings. Maintain absolute quarantine, of course. This thing might just be infectious. Play it very safe."

Nakadai nodded. Mookherji flashed a professional smile at the six somber spacemen and went out, brooding. A nightmare virus? Or a mind-meddling alien organism that no one can see? He wasn't sure which notion he liked less. Probably, though, there was some prosaic and unstartling explanation for that month of bad dreams—contaminated food supplies, or something funny in the atmosphere recycler. A simple, mundane explanation.

Probably.

6.

The first time it happened, the Vsiir was not sure what had actually taken place. It had touched a human mind; there had been an immediate vehement reaction; the Vsiir had pulled back, alarmed by the surging fury of the response, and then, a moment later, had been unable to locate the mind at all. Possibly it was some defense mechanism, the Vsiir thought, by which the humans guarded their minds against intruders. But that seemed unlikely since the humans' minds were quite effectively guarded most of the time anyway. Aboard the ship, whenever the Vsiir had managed to slip past the walls that shielded the minds of the crewmen, it had always encountered a great deal of turbulence—plainly these humans did not enjoy mental contact with a Vsiir—but never this complete shutdown, this total cutoff of signal. Puzzled, the Vsiir tried again, reaching toward an open mind situated not far from where the one that had vanished had been. *Kindly attention, a moment of consideration for confused other-worldly individual, victim of unhappy circumstances, who—*

Again the violent response: a sudden tremendous flare of mental energy, a churning blaze of fear and pain and shock. And again, moments later, complete silence, as though the human had retreated behind an impermeable barrier. *Where are you? Where did you go?* The Vsiir, troubled, took the risk of creating an optical receptor that worked in the visible spectrum—and that therefore would itself be visible to humans—and surveyed the scene. It saw a human on a bed, completely surrounded by intricate machinery. Colored lights were flashing. Other humans, looking agitated, were rushing toward the bed. The human on the bed lay quite still, not even moving when a metal arm descended and jabbed a long bright needle into his chest.

Suddenly the Vsiir understood.

The two humans must have experienced termination of existence!

Hastily the Vsiir dissolved its visible-spectrum receptor and retreated to a sheltered corner to consider what had happened. *Datum*: two humans had died. *Datum*: each had undergone termination immediately after receiving a mental transmission from the Vsiir. *Problem*: had the mental transmission brought about the terminations?

The possibility that the Vsiir might have destroyed two lives was shocking and appalling, and such a chill went through its body that it shrank into a tight, hard ball, with all thought-processes snarled. It needed several minutes to return to a fully functional state. If its attempts at communicating with these humans produced such terrible effects, the Vsiir realized, then its prospects of finding help on this planet were slim. How could it dare risk trying to contact other humans, if—

A comforting thought surfaced. The Vsiir realized that it was jumping to a hasty conclusion on the basis of sketchy evidence, while overlooking some powerful arguments against that conclusion. All during the voyage to this world the Vsiir had been making contact with humans, the six crewmen, and none of *them* had terminated. That was ample evidence that humans could withstand contact with a Vsiir mind. Therefore contact alone could not have caused these two deaths.

Possibly it was only coincidental that the Vsiir had approached two humans in succession that were on the verge of termination. Was this the place where humans were brought when their time of termination was near? Would the terminations have happened even if the Vsiir had not tried to make contact? Was the attempt at contact just enough of a drain on dwindling energies to push the two over the edge into termination? The Vsiir did not know. It was uncomfortably conscious of how many important facts it lacked. Only one thing was certain: its time was running short. If it did not find help soon, metabolic decay was going to set in, followed by metamorphic rigidity, followed by a fatal loss in adaptability, followed by . . . termination.

The Vsiir had no choice. Continuing its quest for contact with a human was its only hope of survival. Cautiously, timidly, the Vsiir again began to send out its probes, looking for a properly receptive mind. This one was walled. So was this. And all these: no entrance, no entrance! The Vsiir wondered if the barriers these humans possessed were designed merely to keep out intruding non-human consciousnesses, or actually shielded each human against mental contact of all kinds, including contact with other humans. If any human-to-human contact existed, the Vsiir had not detected it, either in this building or aboard the spaceship. What a strange race!

Perhaps it would be best to try a different level of this building. The Vsiir flowed easily under a closed door and up a service staircase to a higher floor. Once more it sent forth its probes. A closed mind here. And here. And here. And then a receptive one. The Vsiir prepared to send its message. For safety's sake it stepped down the power of its transmission, letting a mere wisp of thought curl forth. *Do you hear? Stranded extraterrestrial being is calling. Seeks aid. Wishes—*

From the human came a sharp, stinging displeasure-response, wordless but unmistakably hostile. The Vsiir at once withdrew. It waited, terrified, fearing that it had caused another termination. No: the human mind continued to function, although it was no longer open, but now surrounded by the sort of barrier humans normally wore. Drooping, dejected, the Vsiir crept away. Failure, again.

Not even a moment of meaningful mind-to-mind contact. Was there no way to reach these people? Dismally, the Vsiir resumed its search for a receptive mind. What else could it do?

7.

The visit to the quarantine building had taken forty minutes out of Dr. Mookherji's morning schedule. That bothered him. He couldn't blame the quarantine people for getting upset over the six spacemen's tale of chronic hallucinations, but he didn't think the situation, mysterious as it was, was grave enough to warrant calling him in on an emergency basis. Whatever was troubling the spacemen would eventually come to light; meanwhile they were safely isolated from the rest of the starport. Nakadai should have run more tests before asking for him. And he resented having to steal time from his patients.

But as he began his belated morning rounds, Mookherji calmed himself with a deliberate effort: it wouldn't do him or his patients any good if he visited them while still loaded with tensions and irritations. He was supposed to be a healer, not a spreader of anxieties. He spent a moment going through a deescalation routine, and by the time he entered the first patient's room—that of Satina Ransom—he was convincingly relaxed and amiable.

Satina lay on her left side, eyes closed, a slender girl of sixteen with a fragile-looking face and long, soft straw-colored hair. A spidery network of monitoring systems surrounded her. She had been unconscious for fourteen months, twelve of them here in the starport's neuropathology ward and the last six under Mookherji's care. As a holiday treat, her parents had taken her to one of the resorts on Titan during the best season for viewing Saturn's rings; with great difficulty they succeeded in booking reservations at Galileo Dome, and were there on the grim day when a violent Titanquake ruptured the dome and exposed a thousand tourists to the icy moon's poisonous methane atmosphere. Satina was one of the lucky ones: she got no more than a couple of whiffs of the stuff before a dome guide with whom she'd been talking managed to slap a breathing mask over her face. She survived. Her mother, father, and younger brother didn't. But she had never regained consciousness after collapsing

at the moment of the disaster. Months of examination on
Earth had shown that her brief methane inhalation hadn't
caused any major brain damage; organically there seemed
to be nothing wrong with her, but she refused to wake up.
A shock reaction, Mookherji believed: she would rather
go on dreaming forever than return to the living nightmare that consciousness had become. He had been able
to reach her mind telepathically, but so far he had been
unable to cleanse her of the trauma of that catastrophe
and bring her back to the waking world.

Now he prepared to make contact. There was nothing
easy or automatic about his telepathy; "reading" minds
was strenuous work for him, as difficult and as taxing as
running a cross-country race or memorizing a lengthy part
in *Hamlet*. Despite the fears of laymen, he had no way of
scanning anyone's intimate thoughts with a casual glance.
To enter another mind, he had to go through an elaborate
procedure of warming up and reaching out, and even so it
was a slow business to tune in on somebody's "wavelength," with little coherent information coming across
until the ninth or tenth attempt. The gift had been in the
Mookherji family for at least a dozen generations, helped
along by shrewdly planned marriages designed to conserve
the precious gene; he was more adept than any of his
ancestors, yet it might take another century or two of
Mookherjis to produce a really potent telepath. At least he
was able to make good use of such talent for mind-contact
as he had. He knew that many members of his family in
earlier times had been forced to hide their gift from those
about them, back in India, lest they be classed with
vampires and werewolves and cast out of society.

Gently he placed his dark hand on Satina's pale wrist.
Physical contact was necessary to attain the mental link-
age. He concentrated on reaching her. After months of
teletherapy, her mind was sensitized to his; he was able to
skip the intermediate steps, and, once he was warmed up,
could plunge straight into her troubled soul. His eyes were
closed. He saw a swirl of pearl-gray fog before him:
Satina's mind. He thrust himself into it, entering easily. Up
from the depths of her spirit swam a question mark.

—*Who is it? Doctor?*
—*Me, yes. How are you today, Satina?*
—*Fine. Just fine.*
—*Been sleeping well?*

—*It's so peaceful here, doctor.*

—*Yes. Yes, I imagine it is. But you ought to see how it is here. A wonderful summer day. The sun in the blue sky. Everything in bloom. A perfect day for swimming, eh? Wouldn't you like a swim?* He puts all the force of his concentration into images of swimming: a cold mountain stream, a deep pool at the base of a creamy waterfall, the sudden delightful shock of diving in, the crystal flow tingling against her warm skin, the laughter of her friends, the splashing, the swift powerful strokes carrying her to the far shore—

—*I'd rather stay where I am,* she tells him.

—*Maybe you'd like to go floating instead?* He summons the sensations of free flight: a floater-node fastened to her belt, lifting her serenely to an altitude of a hundred feet, and off she goes, drifting over fields and valleys, her friends beside her, her body totally relaxed, weightless, soaring on the updrafts, rising until the ground is a checkerboard of brown and green, looking down on the tiny houses and the comical cars, now crossing a shimmering silvery lake, now hovering over a dark, somber forest of thick-packed spruce, now simply lying on her back, legs crossed, hands clasped behind her head, the sunlight on her cheeks, three hundred feet of nothingness underneath her—

But Satina doesn't take his bait. She prefers to stay where she is. The temptations of floating are not strong enough.

Mookherji does not have enough energy left to try a third attempt at luring her out of her coma. Instead he shifts to a purely medical function and tries to probe for the source of the trauma that has cut her off from the world. The fright, no doubt; and the terrible crack in the dome, spelling the end to all security; and the sight of her parents and brother dying before her eyes; and the swampy reek of Titan's atmosphere hitting her nostrils— all of those things, no doubt. But people have rebounded from worse calamities. Why does she insist on withdrawing from life? Why not come to terms with the dreadful past, and accept existence again?

She fights him. Her defenses are fierce; she does not want him meddling with her mind. All of their sessions have ended this way: Satina clinging to her retreat, Satina blocking any shot at knocking her free of her self-imposed prison. He has gone on hoping that one day she will lower her guard. But this is not to be the day. Wearily, he pulls back from the core of her mind and talks to her on a shallower level.

—*You ought to be getting back to school, Satina.*

—*Not yet. It's been such a short vacation!*

—*Do you know how long?*

—*About three weeks, isn't it?*

—*Fourteen months so far,* he tells her.

—*That's impossible. We just went away to Titan a little while ago—the week before Christmas, wasn't it, and—*

—*Satina, how old are you?*

—*I'll be fifteen in April.*

—*Wrong,* he tells her. *That April's been here and gone, and so has the next one. You were sixteen two months ago. Sixteen, Satina.*

—*That can't be true, doctor. A girl's sixteenth birthday is something special, don't you know that? My parents are going to give me a big party. All my friends invited. And a nine-piece robot orchestra with synthesizers. And I know that that hasn't happened yet, so how can I be sixteen?*

His reservoir of strength is almost drained. His mental signal is weak. He cannot find the energy to tell her that she is blocking reality again, that her parents are dead, that time is passing while she lies here, that it is too late for a Sweet Sixteen party.

—*We'll talk about it . . . another time, Satina. I'll . . . see . . . you . . . again . . . tomorrow. . . . Tomorrow . . . morning. . . .*

—*Don't go so soon, doctor!* But he can no longer hold the contact, and lets it break.

Releasing her, Mookherji stood up, shaking his head. A shame, he thought. A damned shame. He went out of the room on trembling legs and paused a moment in the hall, propping himself against a closed door and mopping his sweaty forehead. He was getting nowhere with Satina. After the initial encouraging period of contact, he had failed entirely to lessen the intensity of her coma. She had settled quite comfortably into her delusive world of withdrawal, and, telepathy or no, he could find no way to blast her loose.

He took a deep breath. Fighting back a growing mood of bleak discouragement, he went toward the next patient's room.

8.

The operation was going smoothly. The dozen third-year medical students occupied the observation deck of the surgical gallery on the starport hospital's third floor, studying Dr. Hammond's expert technique by direct viewing and by simultaneous microamplified relay to their individual desk-screens. The patient, a brain-tumor victim in his late sixties, was visible only as a head and shoulders protruding from a life-support chamber. His scalp had been shaved; blue lines and dark red dots were painted on it to indicate the inner contours of the skull, as previously determined by short-range sonar-bounces; the surgeon had finished the job of positioning the lasers that would excise the tumor. The hard part was over. Nothing remained except to bring the lasers to full power and send their fierce, precise bolts of light slicing into the patient's brain. Cranial surgery of this kind was entirely bloodless; there was no need to cut through skin and bone to expose the tumor, for the beams of the lasers, calibrated to a millionth of an inch, would penetrate through minute openings and, playing on the tumor from different sides, would destroy the malignant growth without harming a bit of the surrounding healthy brain tissue. Planning was everything in an operation like this. Once the exact outlines of the tumor were determined, and the surgical lasers were mounted at the correct angles, any interne could finish the job.

For Dr. Hammond it was a routine procedure. He had performed a hundred operations of this kind in the past year alone. He gave the signal; the warning light glowed on the laser rack; the students in the gallery leaned forth expectantly—

And, just as the lasers' glittering fire leaped toward the operating table, the face of the anesthetized patient contorted weirdly, as though some terrifying dream had come drifting up out of the caverns of the man's drugged mind. His nostrils flared; his lips drew back; his eyes opened wide; he seemed to be trying to scream; he moved convulsively, twisting his head to one side. The lasers bit deep into the patient's left temple, far from the indicated zone of the tumor. The right side of his face began to sag, all muscles paralyzed. The medical students looked at each other in bewilderment. Dr. Hammond, stunned, retained enough presence of mind to kill the lasers with a quick swipe of his hand. Then, gripping the operating table with both hands in his agitation, he peered at the dials and meters that told him the details of the botched operation. The tumor remained intact; a vast sector of the patient's brain had been devastated. "Impossible," Hammond muttered. What could goad a patient under anesthesia into jumping around like that? "Impossible. Impossible." He strode to the end of the table and checked the readings on the life-support chamber. The question now was not whether the brain tumor would be successfully removed; the immediate question was whether the patient was going to survive.

9.

By four that afternoon Mookherji had finished most of his chores. He had seen every patient; he had brought his progress charts up to date; he had fed a prognosis digest to the master computer that was the starport hospital's control center; he had even found time for a gulped lunch. Ordinarily, now, he could take the next four hours off, going back to his spartan room in the residents' building at the edge of the starport complex for a nap, or dropping in at the recreation center to have a couple of rounds of floater-tennis, or looking in at the latest cube-show, or whatever. His next round of patient-visiting didn't begin until eight in the evening. But he couldn't relax: there was that business of the quarantined spacemen to worry about. Nakadai had been sending test outputs over since two o'clock, and now they were stacked deep in Mookherji's data terminal. Nothing had carried an *urgent* flag, so Mookherji had simply let the reports pile up; but now he felt he ought to have a look. He tapped the keys of the terminal, requesting printouts, and Nakadai's outputs began to slide from the slot.

Mookherji ruffled through the yellow sheets. Reflexes, synapse charge, degree of neural ionization, endocrine balances, visual response, respiratory and circulatory, cerebral molecular exchange, sensory percepts, EEG both enhanced and minimated. . . . No, nothing unusual here. It was plain from the tests that the six men who had been to Norton's Star were badly in need of a vacation—frayed nerves, blurred reflexes—but there was no indication of anything more serious than chronic loss of sleep. He couldn't detect signs of brain lesions, infection, nerve damage, or other organic disabilities.

Why the nightmares, then?

He tapped out the phone number of Nakadai's office. "Quarantine," a crisp voice said almost at once, and moments later Nakadai's lean, tawny face appeared on the screen. "Hello, Pete. I was just going to call you."

Mookherji said, "I didn't finish up until a little while ago. But I've been through the outputs you sent over. Lee, there's nothing here."

"As I thought."

"What about the men? You were supposed to call me if any of them went into nightmares."

"None of them have," Nakadai said. "Falkirk and Rodriguez have been sleeping since eleven. Like lambs. Schmidt and Carroll were allowed to conk out at half past one. Webster and Schiavone hit the cots at three. All six are still snoring away, sleeping like they haven't slept in years. I've got them loaded with equipment and everything's reading perfectly normal. You want me to shunt the data to you?"

"Why bother? If they aren't hallucinating, what'll I learn?"

"Does that mean you plan to skip the mind-probes tonight?"

"I don't know," Mookherji said, shrugging. "I suspect there's no point in it, but let's leave that part open. I'll be finishing my evening rounds about eleven, and if there's some reason to get into the heads of those spacemen then, I will." He frowned. "But look—didn't they say that each one of them went into the nightmares on *every single sleep-shift?*"

"Right."

"And here they are, sleeping outside the ship for the first time since the nightmares started, and none of them having any trouble at all. And no sign of possible hallucinogenic brain lesions. You know something, Lee? I'm starting to come around to a very silly hypothesis that those men proposed this morning."

"That the hallucinations were caused by some unseen alien being?" Nakadai asked.

"Something like that. Lee, what's the status of the ship they came in on?"

"It's been through all the routine purification checks, and now it's sitting in an isolation vector until we have some idea of what's going on."

"Would I be able to get aboard it?" Mookherji asked.

"I suppose so, yes, but—why—?"

"On the wild shot that something external caused those nightmares, and that that something may still be aboard the ship. And perhaps a low-level telepath like myself will be able to detect its presence. Can you set up clearance fast?"

"Within ten minutes," Nakadai said. "I'll pick you up."

Nakadai came by shortly in a rollerbuggy. As they headed out toward the landing field, he handed Mookherji a crumpled spacesuit and told him to put it on.

"What for?"

"You may want to breathe inside the ship. Right now it's full of vacuum—we decided it wasn't safe to leave it under atmosphere. Also it's still loaded with radiation from the decontamination process. Okay?"

Mookherji struggled into the suit.

They reached the ship: a standard interstellar null-gravity-drive job, looking small and lonely in its corner of the field. A robot cordon kept it under isolation, but, tipped off by the control center, the robots let the two doctors pass. Nakadai remained outside; Mookherji crawled into the safety pouch and, after the hatch had gone through its admission cycle, entered the ship. He moved cautiously from cabin to cabin, like a man walking in a forest that was said to have a jaguar in every tree. While looking about, he brought himself as quickly as possible up to full telepathic receptivity, and, wide open, awaited telepathic contact with anything that might be lurking in the ship.

—*Go on. Do your worst.*

Complete silence on all mental wavelengths. Mookherji prowled everywhere: the cargo hold, the crew cabins, the drive compartment. Everything empty, everything still. Surely he would have been able to detect the presence of a telepathic creature in here, no matter how alien; if it was capable of reaching the mind of a sleeping spaceman, it should be able to reach the mind of a waking telepath as well. After fifteen minutes he left the ship, satisfied.

"Nothing there," he told Nakadai. "We're still no-where."

10.

The Vsiir was growing desperate. It had been roaming this building all day; judging by the quality of the solar radiation coming through the windows, night was begin-ning to fall now. And, though there were open minds on every level of the structure, the Vsiir had had no luck in making contact. At least there had been no more termina-tions. But it was the same story here as on the ship: whenever the Vsiir touched a human mind, the reaction was so negative as to make communication impossible. And yet the Vsiir went on and on and on, to mind after mind, unable to believe that this whole planet did not hold a single human to whom it could tell its story. It hoped it was not doing severe damage to these minds it was approaching; but it had its own fate to consider.

Perhaps this mind would be the one. The Vsiir started once more to tell its tale—

11.

Half past nine at night. Dr. Peter Mookherji, blood-shot, tense, hauled himself through his neuropathological responsibilities. The ward was full: a schizoid collapse, a catatonic freeze, Satina in her coma, half a dozen routine hysterias, a couple of paralysis cases, an aphasic, and plenty more, enough to keep him going for sixteen hours a day and strain his telepathic powers, not to mention his conventional medical skills, to their limits. Some day the ordeal of residency would be over; some day he'd be quit of this hospital, and would set up private practice on some sweet tropical isle, and commute to Bombay on weekends to see his family, and spend his holidays on planets of distant stars, like any prosperous medical specialist. . . . Some day. He tried to banish such lavish fantasies from his mind. If you're going to look forward to anything, he told himself, look forward to midnight. To sleep. Beauti-ful, beautiful sleep. And then in the morning it all begins again, Satina and the coma, the schizoid, the catatonic, the aphasic. . . .

As he stepped into the hall, going from patient to

patient, his annunciator said, "Dr. Mookherji, please report at once to Dr. Bailey's office."

Bailey? The head of the neuropathology department, still hitting the desk this late. What now? But of course there was no ignoring such a summons. Mookherji notified the control center that he had been called off his rounds, and made his way quickly down the corridor to the frosted-glass door marked SAMUEL F. BAILEY, M.D.

He found at least half the neuropath staff there already: four of the other senior residents, most of the internes, even a few of the high-level doctors. Bailey, a puffy-faced, sandy-haired, fiftyish man of formidable professional standing, was thumbing a sheaf of outputs and scowling. He gave Mookherji a faint nod by way of greeting. They were not on the best of terms; Bailey, somewhat old-school in his attitudes, had not made a good adjustment to the advent of telepathy as a tool in the treatment of mental disturbance. "As I was just saying," Bailey began, "these reports have been accumulating all day, and they've all been dumped on me, God knows why. Listen: two cardiac patients under sedation undergo sudden violent shocks, described by one doctor as sensory overloads. One reacts with cardiac arrest, the other with cerebral hemorrhage. Both die. A patient being treated for endocrine restabilization develops a runaway adrenalin flow while asleep, and gets a six-month setback. A patient undergoing brain surgery starts lurching around on the operating table, despite adequate anesthesia, and gets badly carved up by the lasers. Et cetera. Serious problems like this all over the hospital today. Computer check of general EEG patterns shows that fourteen patients, other than those mentioned, have experienced exceptionally severe episodes of nightmare in the last eleven hours, nearly all of them of such impact that the patient has sustained some degree of psychic damage and often actual physiological harm. Control center reports no case histories of previous epidemics of bad dreams. No reason to suspect a widespread dietary imbalance or similar cause for the outbreak. Nevertheless, sleeping patients are continuing to suffer, and those whose condition is particularly critical may be exposed to grave risks. Effective immediately, sedation of critical patients has been interrupted where feasible, and sleep schedules of other patients have been rearranged, but this is obviously not an expedient that is going to do

much good if this outbreak continues into tomorrow."
Bailey paused, glanced around the room, let his gaze rest
on Mookherji. "Control center has offered one hypothesis:
that a psychopathic individual with strong telepathic
powers is at large in the hospital, preying on sleeping
patients and transmitting images to them that take the
form of horrifying nightmares. Mookherji, what do you
make of that idea?"

Mookherji said, "It's perfectly feasible, I suppose, although I can't imagine why any telepath would want to
go around distributing nightmares. But has control center
correlated any of this with the business over at the quarantine building?"

Bailey stared at his output slips. "What business is
that?"

"Six spacemen who came in early this morning, reporting that they'd all suffered chronic nightmares on their
voyage homeward. Dr. Lee Nakadai's been testing them;
he called me in as a consultant, but I couldn't discover
anything useful. I imagine there are some late reports
from Nakadai in my office, but—"

Bailey said, "Control center seems only to be concerned
about events in the hospital, not in the starport complex
as a whole. And if your six spacemen had their nightmares during their voyage, there's no chance that their
symptoms are going to find their way onto—"

"That's just it!" Mookherji cut in. "They had their
nightmares in space. But they've been asleep since morning,
and Nakadai says they're resting peacefully. Meanwhile
an outbreak of hallucinations has started over here. Which
means that whatever was bothering them during their
voyage has somehow got loose in the hospital today—
some sort of entity capable of stirring up such ghastly
dreams that they bring veteran spacemen to the edge of
nervous breakdowns and can seriously injure or even kill
someone in poor health." He realized that Bailey was looking at him strangely, and that Bailey was not the only one.
In a more restrained tone, Mookherji said, "I'm sorry if
this sounds fantastic to you. I've been checking it out all
day, so I've had some time to get used to the concept. And
things began to fit together for me just now. I'm not saying that my idea is necessarily correct. I'm simply saying
that it's a reasonable notion, that it links up with the
spacemen's own idea of what was bothering them, that

it corresponds to the shape of the situation—and that it
deserves a decent investigation, if we're going to stop this
stuff before we lose some more patients."

"All right, doctor," Bailey said. "How do you propose
to conduct the investigation?"

Mookherji was shaken by that. He had been on the go
all day; he was ready to fold. Here was Bailey abruptly
putting him in charge of this snark-hunt, without even
asking! But he saw there was no way to refuse. He was the
only telepath on the staff. And, if the supposed creature
really was at large in the hospital, how could it be tracked
except by a telepath?

Fighting back his fatigue, Mookherji said rigidly, "Well,
I'd want a chart of all the nightmare cases, to begin with,
a chart showing the location of each victim and the ap-
proximate time of onset of hallucination—"

12.

They would be preparing for the Festival of Changing,
now, the grand climax of the winter. Thousands of
Vsiirs in the metamorphic phase would be on their way
toward the Valley of Sand, toward that great natural
amphitheater where the holiest rituals were performed. By
now the firstcomers would already have taken up their
positions, facing the west, waiting for the sunrise. Gradually the rows would fill as Vsiirs came in from every part
of the planet, until the golden valley was thick with them,
Vsiirs that constantly shifted their energy-levels, dimen-
sional extensions, and inner resonances, shuttling glorious-
ly through the final joyous moments of the season of
metamorphosis, competing with one another in a gentle
way to display the greatest variety of form, the most
dynamic cycle of physical changes—and, when the first
red rays of the sun crept past the Needle, the celebrants
would grow even more frenzied, dancing and leaping and
transforming themselves with total abandon, purging themselves of the winter's flamboyance as the season of stability
swept across the world. And finally, in the full blaze of
sunlight, they would turn to one another in renewed kin-
ship, embracing, and—

The Vsiir tried not to think about it. But it was hard
to repress that sense of loss, that pang of nostalgia. The
pain grew more intense with every moment. No imaginable

miracle would get the Vsiir home in time for the Festival
of Changing, it knew, and yet it could not really believe
that such a calamity had befallen it.

Trying to touch minds with humans was useless. Perhaps
if it assumed a form visible to them, and let itself be
noticed, and *then* tried to open verbal communication—

But the Vsiir was so small, and these humans were so
large. The dangers were great. The Vsiir, clinging to a
wall and carefully keeping its wavelength well beyond the
ultra-violet, weighed one risk against another, and, for the
moment, did nothing.

13.

"All right," Mookherji said foggily, a little before midnight. "I think we've got the trail clear now." He sat before
a wall-sized screen on which the control center had thrown
a three-dimensional schematic plan of the hospital. Bright
red dots marked the place of each nightmare incident,
yellow dashes the probable path of the unseen alien
creature. "It came in the side way, probably, straight off
the ship, and went into the cardiac wing first. Mrs. Maldonado's bed here, Mr. Guinness' over here, eh? Then it
went up to the second level, coming around to the front
wing and impinging on the minds of patients here and
here and here between ten and eleven in the morning.
There were no reported episodes of hallucination in the
next hour and ten minutes, but then came that nasty
business in the third-level surgical gallery, and after that—"
Mookherji's aching eyes closed a moment; it seemed to
him that he could still see the red dots and yellow dashes.
He forced himself to go on, tracing the rest of the intru-
der's route for his audience of doctors and hospital
security personnel. At last he said, "That's it. I figure
that the thing must be somewhere between the fifth and
eighth levels by now. It's moving much more slowly than
it did this morning, possibly running out of energy. What
we have to do is keep the hospital's wings tightly sealed to
prevent its free movement, if that can be done, and attempt to narrow down the number of places where it
might be found."

One of the security men said, a little belligerently,
"Doctor, just how are we supposed to find an invisible
entity?"

Mookherji struggled to keep impatience out of his voice. "The visible spectrum isn't the only sort of electromagnetic energy in the universe. If this thing is alive, it's got to be radiating *somewhere* along the line. You've got a master computer with a million sensory pickups mounted all over the hospital. Can't you have the sensors scan for a point-source of infra-red or ultra-violet moving through a room? Or even x Rays, for God's sake: we don't know where the radiation's likely to be. Maybe it's a gamma emitter, even. Look, something wild is loose in this building, and we can't see it, but the computer can. Make it search."

Dr. Bailey said, "Perhaps the energy we ought to be trying to trace it by is, ah, telepathic energy, doctor."

Mookherji shrugged. "As far as anybody knows, telepathic impulses propagate somewhere outside the electromagnetic spectrum. But of course you're right that I might be able to pick up some kind of output, and I intend to make a floor-by-floor search as soon as this briefing session is over." He turned toward Nakadai. "Lee, what's the word from your quarantined spacemen?"

"All six went through eight-hour sleep periods today without any sign of a nightmare episode: there was some dreaming, but all of it normal. In the past couple of hours I've had them on the phone talking with some of the patients who had the nightmares, and everybody agrees that the kind of dreams people have been having here today are the same in tone, texture, and general level of horror as the ones the men had aboard the ship. Images of bodily destruction and alien landscapes, accompanied by an overwhelming, almost intolerable, feeling of isolation, loneliness, separation from one's own kind."

"Which would fit the hypothesis of an alien being as the cause," said Martinson of the psychology staff. "If it's wandering around trying to communicate with us, trying to tell us it doesn't want to be here, say, and its communications reach human minds only in the form of frightful nightmares—"

"Why does it communicate only with sleeping people?" an interne asked.

"Perhaps those are the only ones it can reach. Maybe a mind that's awake isn't receptive," Martinson suggested.

"Seems to me," a security man said, "that we're making a whole lot of guesses based on no evidence at all. You're all sitting around talking about an invisible telepathic thing that breathes nightmares in people's ears, and it might just as easily be a virus that attacks the brain, or something in yesterday's food, or—"

Mookherji said, "The ideas you're offering now have already been examined and discarded. We're working on this line of inquiry now because it seems to hold together, fantastic though it sounds, and because it's all we have. If you'll excuse me, I'd like to start checking the building for telepathic output, now." He went out, pressing his hands to his throbbing temples.

14.

Satina Ransom stirred, stretched, subsided. She looked up and saw the dazzling blaze of Saturn's rings overhead, glowing through the hotel's domed roof. She had never seen anything more beautiful in her life. This close to them, only about 750,000 miles out, she could clearly make out the different zones of the rings, each revolving about Saturn at its own speed, with the blackness of space visible through the open places. And Saturn itself, gleaming in the heavens, so bright, so huge—

What was that rumbling sound? Thunder? Not here, not on Titan. Again: louder. And the ground swaying. A crack in the dome! Oh, no, no, no, feel the air rushing out, look at that cold greenish mist pouring in—people falling down all over the place—what's happening, what's happening, what's happening? Saturn seems to be falling toward us. That taste in my mouth—oh—oh—oh—

Satina screamed. And screamed. And went on screaming as she slipped down into darkness, and pulled the soft blanket of unconsciousness over her, and shivered, and gave thanks for finding a safe place to hide.

15.

Mookherji had plodded through the whole building, accompanied by three security men and a couple of internes. He had seen whole sectors of the hospital that he didn't know existed. He had toured basements and sub-basements and sub-sub-basements; he had been through laboratories and computer rooms and wards and exercise chambers. He had kept himself in a state of complete telepathic receptivity throughout the trek, but he had detected nothing, not even a flicker of mental current anywhere. Somehow that came as no surprise to him. Now, with dawn near, he wanted nothing more than sixteen hours or so of sleep. Even with nightmares. He was tired beyond all comprehension of the meaning of tiredness.

Yet something wild was loose, still, and the nightmares still were going on. Three incidents, ninety minutes apart, had occurred during the night: two patients on the fifth level and one on the sixth had awakened in states of terror. It had been possible to calm them quickly, and apparently no lasting harm had been done; but now the stranger was close to Mookherji's neuropathology ward, and he didn't like the thought of exposing a bunch of mentally unstable patients to that kind of stimulus. By this time, the control center had reprogrammed all patient-monitoring systems to watch for the early stages of nightmare—hormone changes, EEG tremors, respiration rate rise, and so forth—in the hope of awakening a victim before the full impact could be felt. Even so, Mookherji wanted to see that thing caught and out of the hospital before it got to any of his own people.

But how?

As he trudged back to his sixth-level office, he considered some of the ideas people had tossed around in that midnight briefing session. *Wandering around trying to communicate with us,* Martinson had said. *Its communications reach human minds only in the form of frightful nightmares. Maybe a mind that's awake isn't receptive.* Even the mind of a human telepath, it seemed, wasn't receptive while awake. Mookherji wondered if he should go to sleep and hope the alien would reach him, and then try to deal with it, lead it into a trap of some kind—but no. He wasn't that different from other people. If he slept, and the alien did open contact, he'd simply have a hell of a nightmare and wake up, with nothing gained. That wasn't the answer. Suppose, though, he managed to make contact with the alien through the mind of a nightmare victim—someone he could use as a kind of telepathic loudspeaker—someone who wasn't likely to wake up while the dream was going on—

Satina.

Perhaps. Perhaps. Of course, he'd have to make sure

the girl was shielded from possible harm. She had enough horrors running free in her head as it was. But if he lent her his strength, drained off the poison of the nightmare, took the impact himself via their telepathic link, and was able to stand the strain and still speak to the alien mind—that might just work. Might.

He went to her room. He clasped her hand between his.

—*Satina?*

—*Morning so soon, doctor?*

—*It's still early, Satina. But things are a little unusual here today. We need your help. You don't have to if you don't want to, but I think you can be of great value to us, and maybe even to yourself. Listen to me very carefully, and think it over before you say yes or no—*

God help me if I'm wrong, Mookherji thought, far below the level of telepathic transmission.

16.

Chilled, alone, growing groggy with dismay and hopelessness, the Vsiir had made no attempts at contact for several hours now. What was the use? The results were always the same when it touched a human mind; it was exhausting itself and apparently bothering the humans, to no purpose. Now the sun had risen. The Vsiir contemplated slipping out of the building and exposing itself to the yellow solar radiation while dropping all defenses; it would be a quick death, an end to all this misery and longing. It was folly to dream of seeing the home planet again. And—

What was that?

A call. Clear, intelligible, unmistakable. *Come to me.* An open mind somewhere on this level, speaking neither the human language nor the Vsiir language, but using the wordless, universally comprehensible communion that occurs when mind speaks directly to mind. *Come to me. Tell me everything. How can I help you?*

In its excitement the Vsiir slid up and down the spectrum, emitting a blast of infra-red, a jagged blurt of ultra-violet, a lively blaze of visible light, before getting control. Quickly it took a fix on the direction of the call. Not far away: down this corridor, under this door, through this passage. *Come to me.* Yes. Yes. Extending its mind-probes ahead of it, groping for contact with the beckoning mind, the Vsiir hastened forward.

17.

Mookherji, his mind locked to Satina's, felt the sudden crashing shock of the nightmare moving in, and even at second remove the effect was stunning in its power. He perceived a clicking sensation of mind touching mind. And then, into Satina's receptive spirit, there poured—

A wall higher than Everest. Satina trying to climb it, scrambling up a smooth white face, digging fingertips into minute crevices. Slipping back one yard for every two gained. Below, a roiling pit, flames shooting up, foul gases rising, monsters with needle-sharp fangs waiting for her to fall. The wall grows taller. The air is so thin—she can barely breathe, her eyes are dimming, a greasy hand is squeezing her heart, she can feel her veins pulling free of her flesh like wires coming out of a broken plaster ceiling, and the gravitational pull is growing constantly—pain, her lungs crumbling, her face sagging hideously—a river of terror surging through her skull—

—*None of it is real, Satina. They're just illusions. None of it is really happening.*

—*Yes,* she says, *yes, I know,* but still she resonates with fright, her muscles jerking at random, her face flushed and sweating, her eyes fluttering beneath the lids. The dream continues. How much more can she stand?

—*Give it to me,* he tells her. *Give me the dream!*

She does not understand. No matter. Mookherji knows how to do it. He is so tired that fatigue is unimportant; somewhere in the realm beyond collapse he finds unexpected strength, and reaches into her numbed soul, and pulls the hallucinations forth as though they were cobwebs. They engulf him. No longer does he experience them indirectly; now all the phantoms are loose in his skull, and, even as he feels Satina relax, he braces himself against the onslaught of unreality that he has summoned into himself. And he copes. He drains the excess of irrationality out of her and winds it about his consciousness, and adapts, learning to live with the appalling flood of images. He and Satina share what is coming forth. Together they can bear the burden; he carries more of it than she does, but she does her part, and now neither of them is overwhelmed by the parade of bogeys. They can laugh at the dream-monsters; they can even admire them for being so richly fantastic. That beast with a hundred heads, that bundle of living copper wires, that pit of dragons, that coiling mass of spiky teeth—who can fear what does not exist?

Over the clatter of bizarre images Mookherji sends a coherent thought, pushing it through Satina's mind to the *alien:*

—*Can you turn off the nightmares?*

—*No,* something replies. *They are in you, not in me. I only provide the liberating stimulus. You generate the images.*

—*All right. Who are you, and what do you want here?*

—*I am a Vsiir.*

—*A what?*

—*Native lifeform of the planet where you collect the greenfire branches. Through my own carelessness I was transported to your planet.* Accompanying the message is an overriding impulse of sadness, a mixture of pathos, self-pity, discomfort, exhaustion. Above this the nightmares still flow, but they are insignificant now. The Vsiir says, *I wish only to be sent home. I did not want to come here.*

And this is our alien monster? Mookherji thinks. This is our fearsome nightmare-spreading beast from the stars?

—*Why do you spread hallucinations?*

—*This was not my intention. I was merely trying to make mental contact. Some defect in the human receptive system, perhaps—I do not know. I do not know. I am so tired, though. Can you help me?*

—*We'll send you home, yes,* Mookherji promises. *Where are you? Can you show yourself to me? Let me know how to find you, and I'll notify the starport authorities, and they'll arrange for your passage home on the first ship out.*

Hesitation. Silence. Contact wavers and perhaps breaks.

—*Well?* Mookherji says, after a moment. *What's happening? Where are you?*

From the Vsiir an uneasy response:

—*How can I trust you? Perhaps you merely wish to destroy me. If I reveal myself—*

Mookherji bites his lip in sudden fury. His reserve of strength is almost gone; he can barely sustain the contact at all. And if he now has to find some way of persuading a suspicious alien to surrender itself, he may run out of steam before he can settle things. The situation calls for desperate measures.

—Listen, Vsiir. I'm not strong enough to talk much longer, and neither is this girl I'm using. I invite you into my head. I'll drop all defensess if you can look at who I am, look hard, and decide for yourself whether you can trust me. After that it's up to you. I can help you get home, but only if you produce yourself right away.

He opens his mind wide. He stands mentally naked.

The Vsiir rushes into Mookherji's brain.

18.

A hand touched Mookherji's shoulder. He snapped awake instantly, blinking, trying to get his bearings. Lee Nakadai stood above him. They were in—where?—Satina Ransom's room. The pale light of early morning was coming through the window; he must have dozed only a minute or so. His head was splitting.

"We've been looking all over for you, Pete," Nakadai said.

"It's all right now," Mookherji murmured. "It's all all right." He shook his head to clear it. He remembered things. Yes. On the floor, next to Satina's bed, squatted something about the size of a frog, but very different in shape, color, and texture from any frog Mookherji had ever seen. He showed it to Nakadai. "That's the Vsiir," Mookherji said. "The alien terror. Satina and I made friends with it. We talked it into showing itself. Listen, it isn't happy here, so will you get hold of a starport official fast, and explain that we've got an organism here that has to be shipped back to Norton's Star at once, and—"

Satina said, "Are you Dr. Mookherji?"

"That's right. I suppose I should have introduced myself when—*you're awake?*"

"It's morning, isn't it?" The girl sat up, grinning. "You're younger than I thought you were. And so serious-looking. And I *love* that color of skin. I—"

"You're awake?"

"I had a bad dream," she said. "Or maybe a bad dream within a bad dream—I don't know. Whatever it was, it was pretty awful, but I felt so much better when it went away—I just felt that if I slept any longer I was going to miss a lot of good things, that I had to get up and see what was happening in the world—do you understand any of this, doctor?"

Mookherji realized his knees were shaking. "Shock therapy," he muttered. "We blasted her loose from the coma—without even knowing what we were doing." He moved toward the bed. "Listen, Satina, I've been up for about a million years, and I'm ready to burn out from overload. And I've got a thousand things to talk about with you, only not now. Is that okay? Not now. I'll send Dr. Bailey in—he's my boss—and after I've had some sleep I'll come back and we'll go over everything together, okay? Say, five, six this evening. All right?"

"Well, of course, all right," Satina said, with a twinkling smile. "If you feel you really have to run off, just when I've—sure. Go. Go. You look awfully tired, doctor."

Mookherji blew her a kiss. Then, taking Nakadai by the elbow, he headed for the door. When he was outside he said, "Get the Vsiir over to your quarantine place pronto and try to put it in an atmosphere it finds comfortable. And arrange for its trip home. And I guess you can let your six spacemen out. I'll go talk to Bailey—and then I'm going to drop."

Nakadai nodded. "You get some rest, Pete. I'll handle things."

Mookherji shuffled slowly down the hall toward Dr. Bailey's office, thinking of the smile on Satina's face, thinking of the sad little Vsiir, thinking of nightmares—

"Pleasant dreams, Pete," Nakadai called.

To See the Invisible Man

And then they found me guilty, and then they pro-nounced me invisible, for a span of one year beginning on the eleventh of May in the year of Grace 2104, and they took me to a dark room beneath the courthouse to affix the mark to my forehead before turning me loose.

Two municipally paid ruffians did the job. One flung me into a chair and the other lifted the brand.

"This won't hurt a bit," the slab-jawed ape said, and thrust the brand against my forehead, and there was a moment of coolness, and that was all.

"What happens now?" I asked.

But there was no answer, and they turned away from me and left the room without a word. The door remained open. I was free to leave, or to stay and rot, as I chose. No one would speak to me, or look at me more than once, long enough to see the sign on my forehead. I was invisible.

You must understand that my invisibility was strictly metaphorical. I still had corporeal solidity. People *could* see me—but they *would not* see me.

An absurd punishment? Perhaps. But then, the crime was absurd too. The crime of coldness. Refusal to unbur-den myself for my fellow man. I was a four-time offender. The penalty for that was a year's invisibility. The com-plaint had been duly sworn, the trial held, the brand duly affixed.

I was invisible.

I went out, out into the world of warmth.

They had already had the afternoon rain. The streets of the city were drying, and there was the smell of growth in the Hanging Gardens. Men and women went about their

41

business. I walked among them, but they took no notice of me.

The penalty for speaking to an invisible man is invisibility, a month to a year or more, depending on the seriousness of the offense. On this the whole concept depends. I wondered how rigidly the rule was observed.

I soon found out.

I stepped into a liftshaft and let myself be spiraled up toward the nearest of the Hanging Gardens. It was Eleven, the cactus garden, and those gnarled, bizarre shapes suited my mood. I emerged on the landing stage and advanced toward the admissions counter to buy my token. A pasty-faced, empty-eyed woman sat back of the counter.

I laid down my coin. Something like fright entered her eyes, quickly faded.

"One admission," I said.

No answer. People were queuing up behind me. I repeated my demand. The woman looked up helplessly, then stared over my left shoulder. A hand extended itself, another coin was placed down. She took it, and handed the man his token. He dropped it in the slot and went in.

"Let me have a token," I said crisply.

Others were jostling me out of the way. Not a word of apology. I began to sense some of the meaning of my invisibility. They were literally treating me as though they could not see me.

There are countervailing advantages. I walked around behind the counter and helped myself to a token without paying for it. Since I was invisible, I could not be stopped. I thrust the token in the slot and entered the garden.

But the cacti bored me. An inexpressible malaise slipped over me, and I felt no desire to stay. On my way out I pressed my finger against a jutting thorn and drew blood. The cactus, at least, still recognized my existence. But only to draw blood.

I returned to my apartment. My books awaited me, but I felt no interest in them. I sprawled out on my narrow bed and activated the energizer to combat the strange lassitude that was afflicting me. I thought about my invisibility.

It would not be such a hardship, I told myself. I had never depended overly on other human beings. Indeed, had I not been sentenced in the first place for my coldness toward my fellow creatures? So what need did I have of them now? *Let* them ignore me!

It would be restful. I had a year's respite from work, after all. Invisible men did not work. How could they? Who would go to an invisible doctor for a consultation, or hire an invisible lawyer to represent him, or give a document to an invisible clerk to file? No work, then. No income, of course, either. But landlords did not take rent from invisible men. Invisible men went where they pleased, at no cost. I had just demonstrated that at the Hanging Gardens.

Invisibility would be a great joke on society, I felt. They had sentenced me to nothing more dreadful than a year's rest cure. I was certain I would enjoy it.

But there were certain practical disadvantages. On the first night of my invisibility I went to the city's finest restaurant. I would order their most lavish dishes, a hundred-unit meal, and then conveniently vanish at the presentation of the bill.

My thinking was muddy. I never got seated. I stood in the entrance half an hour, bypassed again and again by a maître d'hotel who had clearly been through all this many times before. Walking to a seat, I realized, would gain me nothing. No waiter would take my order.

I could go into the kitchen. I could help myself to anything I pleased. I could disrupt the workings of the restaurant. But I decided against it. Society had its ways of protecting itself against invisible ones. There could be no direct retaliation, of course, no intentional defense. But who could say no to a chef's claim that he had seen no one in the way when he hurled a pot of scalding water toward the wall? Invisibility was invisibility, a two-edged sword.

I left the restaurant.

I ate at an automated restaurant nearby. Then I took an autocab home. Machines, like cacti, did not discriminate against my sort. I sensed that they would make poor companions for a year, though.

I slept poorly.

The second day of my invisibility was a day of further testing and discovery.

I went for a long walk, careful to stay on the pedestrian paths. I had heard all about the boys who enjoy running down those who carry the mark of invisibility on their foreheads. Again, there is no recourse, no punishment for them. My condition has its little hazards by intention.

I walked the streets, seeing how the throngs parted for me. I cut through them like a microtome passing between cells. They were well trained. At midday I saw my first fellow Invisible. He was a tall man of middle years, stocky and dignified, bearing the mark of shame on a domelike forehead. His eyes met mine only for a moment. Then he passed on. An invisible man, naturally, cannot see another of his kind.

I was amused, nothing more. I was still savoring the novelty of this way of life. No slight could hurt me. Not yet.

Late in the day I came to one of those bathhouses where working girls can cleanse themselves for a couple of small coins. I smiled wickedly and went up the steps. The attendant at the door gave me the flicker of a startled look—it was a small triumph for me—but did not dare to stop me.

I went in.

An overpowering smell of soap and sweat struck me. I persevered inward. I passed cloakrooms where long rows of gray smocks were hanging, and it occurred to me that I could rifle those smocks of every unit they contained, but I did not. Theft loses meaning when it becomes too easy, as the clever ones who devised invisibility were aware.

I passed on, into the bath chambers themselves.

Hundreds of women were there. Nubile girls, weary wenches, old crones. Some blushed. A few smiled. Many turned their backs on me. But they were careful not to show any real reaction to my presence. Supervisory matrons stood guard, and who knew but that she might be reported for taking undue cognizance of the existence of an Invisible?

So I watched them bathe, watched five hundred pairs of bobbing breasts, watched naked bodies glistening under the spray, watched this vast mass of bare feminine flesh. My reaction was a mixed one, a sense of wicked achievement at having penetrated this sanctum sanctorum unhalted, and then, welling up slowly within me, a sensation of—was it sorrow? Boredom? Revulsion?

I was unable to analyze it. But it felt as though a clammy hand had seized my throat. I left quickly. The smell of soapy water stung my nostrils for hours afterward, and the sight of pink flesh haunted my dreams that night. I ate alone, in one of the automatics. I began to see that the novelty of this punishment was soon lost.

In the third week I fell ill. It began with a high fever, then pains of the stomach, vomiting, the rest of the ugly symptomatology. By midnight I was certain I was dying. The cramps were intolerable, and when I dragged myself to the toilet cubicle I caught sight of my face in the mirror, distorted, greenish, beaded with sweat. The mark of invisibility stood out like a beacon in my pale forehead.

For a long time I lay on the tiled floor, limply absorbing the coolness of it. Then I thought: What if it's my appendix? That ridiculous, obsolete, obscure prehistoric survival? Inflamed, ready to burst?

I needed a doctor.

The phone was covered with dust. They had not bothered to disconnect it, but I had not called anyone since my arrest, and no one had dared call me. The penalty for knowingly telephoning an invisible man is invisibility. My friends, such as they were, had stayed far away.

I grasped the phone, thumbed the panel. It lit up and the directory robot said, "With whom do you wish to speak, sir?"

"Doctor," I gasped.

"Certainly, sir." Bland, smug mechanical words! No way to pronounce a robot invisible, so it was free to talk to me!

The screen glowed. A doctorly voice said, "What seems to be the trouble?"

"Stomach pains. Maybe appendicitis."

"We'll have a man over in—" He stopped. I had made the mistake of upturning my agonized face. His eyes lit on my forehead mark. The screen winked into blackness as rapidly as though I had extended a leprous hand for him to kiss.

"Doctor," I groaned.

He was gone. I buried my face in my hands. This was carrying things too far, I thought. Did the Hippocratic Oath allow things like this? Could a doctor ignore a sick man's plea for help?

Hippocrates had not known anything about invisible

men. A doctor was not required to minister to an invisible man. To society at large I simply was not there. Doctors could not diagnose diseases in nonexistent individuals.

I was left to suffer.

It was one of invisibility's less attractive features. You enter a bathhouse unhindered, if that pleases you—but you writhe on a bed of pain equally unhindered. The one with the other, and if your appendix happens to rupture, why, it is all the greater deterrent to others who might perhaps have gone your lawless way!

My appendix did not rupture. I survived, though badly shaken. A man can survive without human conversation for a year. He can travel on automated cars and eat at automated restaurants. But there are no automated doctors. For the first time, I felt truly beyond the pale. A convict in a prison is given a doctor when he falls ill. My crime had not been serious enough to merit prison, and so no doctor would treat me if I suffered. It was unfair. I cursed the devils who had invented my punishment. I faced each bleak dawn alone, as alone as Crusoe on his island, here in the midst of a city of twelve million souls.

How can I describe my shifts of mood, my many tacks before the changing winds of the passing months?

There were times when invisibility was a joy, a delight, a treasure. In those paranoid moments I gloried in my exemption from the rules that bound ordinary men.

I stole. I entered small stores and seized the receipts while the cowering merchant feared to stop me, lest in crying out he make himself liable to my invisibility. If I had known that the State reimbursed all such losses, I might have taken less pleasure in it. But I stole.

I invaded. The bathhouse never tempted me again, but I breached other sanctuaries. I entered hotels and walked down the corridors, opening doors at random. Most rooms were empty. Some were not.

Godlike, I observed all. I toughened. My disdain for society—the crime that had earned me invisibility in the first place—heightened.

I stood in the empty streets during the periods of rain, and railed at the gleaming faces of the towering buildings on every side. "Who needs you?" I roared. "Not I! Who needs you in the slightest?"

I jeered and mocked and railed. It was a kind of

insanity, brought on, I suppose, by the loneliness. I entered theaters—where the happy lotus eaters sat slumped in their massage chairs, transfixed by the glowing tridim images—and capered down the aisles. No one grumbled at me. The luminescence of my forehead told them to keep their complaints to themselves, and they did.

Those were the mad moments, the good moments, the moments when I towered twenty feet high and strode among the visible clods with contempt oozing from every pore. Those were insane moments—I admit that freely. A man who has been in a condition of involuntary invisibility for several months is not likely to be well balanced.

Did I call them paranoid moments? Manic depressive might be more to the point. The pendulum swung dizzily. The days when I felt only contempt for the visible fools all around me were balanced by days when the isolation pressed in tangibly on me. I would walk the endless streets, pass through the gleaming arcades, stare down at the highways with their streaking bullets of gay colors. Not even a beggar would come up to me. Did you know we had beggars, in our shining century? Not till I was pronounced invisible did I know it, for then my long walks took me to the slums, where the shine has worn thin, and where shuffling stubble-faced old men beg for small coins.

No one begged for coins from me. Once a blind man came up to me.

"For the love of God," he wheezed, "help me to buy new eyes from the eye bank."

They were the first direct words any human being had spoken to me in months. I started to reach into my tunic for money, planning to give him every unit on me in gratitude. Why not? I could get more simply by taking it. But before I could draw the money out, a nightmare figure hobbled on crutches between us. I caught the whispered word, "Invisible," and then the two of them scuttled away like frightened crabs. I stood there stupidly holding my money.

Not even the beggars. Devils, to have invented this torment!

So I softened again. My arrogance ebbed away. I was lonely, now. Who could accuse me of coldness? I was spongy soft, pathetically eager for a word, a smile, a clasping hand. It was the sixth month of my invisibility.

I loathed it entirely, now. Its pleasures were hollow ones and its torment was unbearable. I wondered how I would survive the remaining six months. Believe me, suicide was not far from my mind in those dark hours.

And finally I committed an act of foolishness. On one of my endless walks I encountered another Invisible, no more than the third or the fourth such creature I had seen in my six months. As in the previous encounters, our eyes met, warily, only for a moment. Then he dropped his to the pavement, and he sidestepped me and walked on. He was a slim young man, no more than forty, with touseled brown hair and a narrow, pinched face. He had a look of scholarship about him, and I wondered what he might have done to merit his punishment, and I was seized with the desire to run after him and ask him, and to learn his name, and talk to him, and embrace him.

All these things are forbidden to mankind. No one shall have any contact whatsoever with an Invisible—not even a fellow Invisible. Especially not a fellow Invisible. There is no wish on society's part to foster a secret bond of fellowship among its pariahs.

I knew all this.

I turned and followed him, all the same.

For three blocks I moved along behind him, remaining twenty to fifty paces to the rear. Security robots seemed to be everywhere, their scanners quick to detect an infraction, and I did not dare make my move. Then he turned down a side street, a gray, dusty street five centuries old, and began to stroll, with the ambling, going-nowhere gait of the Invisible. I came up behind him.

"Please," I said softly. "No one will see us here. We can talk. My name is—"

He whirled on me, horror in his eyes. His face was pale. He looked at me in amazement for a moment, then darted forward as though to go around me.

I blocked him.

"Wait," I said. "Don't be afraid. Please—"

He burst past me. I put my hand on his shoulder, and he wriggled free.

"Just a word," I begged.

Not even a word. Not even a hoarsely uttered, "Leave me alone!" He sidestepped me and ran down the empty street, his steps diminishing from a clatter to a murmur as he reached the corner and rounded it. I looked after him, feeling a great loneliness well up in me.

And then a fear. *He* hadn't breached the rules of Invisibility, but I had. I had seen him. That left me subject to punishment, an extension of my term of invisibility, perhaps. I looked around anxiously, but there were no security robots in sight, no one at all.

I was alone.

Turning, calming myself, I continued down the street. Gradually I regained control over myself. I saw that I had done something unpardonably foolish. The stupidity of my action troubled me, but even more the sentimentality of it. To reach out in that panicky way to another Invisible—to admit openly my loneliness, my need—no. It meant that society was winning. I couldn't have that.

I found that I was near the cactus garden once again. I rode the liftshaft, grabbed a token from the attendant, and bought my way in. I searched for a moment, then found a twisted, elaborately ornate cactus eight feet high, a spiny monster. I wrenched it from its pot and broke the angular limbs to fragments, filling my hands with a thousand needles. People pretended not to watch. I plucked the spines from my hands and, palms bleeding, rode the liftshaft down, once again sublimely aloof in my invisibility.

The eighth month passed, the ninth, the tenth. The seasonal round had made nearly a complete turn. Spring had given way to a mild summer, summer to a crisp autumn, autumn to winter with its fortnightly snowfalls, still permitted for esthetic reasons. Winter had ended, now. In the parks, the trees sprouted green buds. The weather control people stepped up the rainfall to thrice daily.

My term was drawing to its end.

In the final months of my invisibility I had slipped into a kind of torpor. My mind, forced back on its own resources, no longer cared to consider the implications of my condition, and I slid in a blurred haze from day to day. I read compulsively but unselectively, Aristotle one day, the Bible the next, a handbook of mechanics the next. I retained nothing; as I turned a fresh page, its predecessor slipped from my memory.

I no longer bothered to enjoy the few advantages of

invisibility, the voyeuristic thrills, the minute throb of power that comes from being able to commit any act with only limited fear of retaliation. I say *limited* because the passage of the Invisibility Act had not been accompanied by an act repealing human nature; few men would not risk invisibility to protect their wives or children from an invisible one's molestations; no one would coolly allow an Invisible to jab out his eyes; no one would tolerate an Invisible's invasion of his home. There were ways of coping with such infringements without appearing to recognize the existence of the Invisible, as I have mentioned.

Still, it was possible to get away with a great deal. I declined to try. Somewhere Dostoevski has written, "Without God, all things are possible." I can amend that. "To the invisible man, all things are possible—and uninteresting." So it was.

The weary months passed.

I did not count the minutes till my release. To be precise, I wholly forgot that my term was due to end. On the day itself, I was reading in my room, morosely turning page after page, when the annunciator chimed.

It had not chimed for a full year. I had almost forgotten the meaning of the sound.

But I opened the door. There they stood, the men of the law. Wordlessly, they broke the seal that held the mark to my forehead. The emblem dropped away and shattered.

"Hello, citizen," they said to me.

I nodded gravely. "Yes. Hello."

"May 11, 2105. Your term is up. You are restored to society. You have paid your debt."

"Thank you. Yes."

"Come for a drink with us."

"I'd sooner not."

"It's the tradition. Come along."

I went with them. My forehead felt strangely naked now, and I glanced in a mirror to see that there was a pale spot where the emblem had been. They took me to a bar nearby, and treated me to synthetic whiskey, raw, powerful. The bartender grinned at me. Someone on the next stool clapped me on the shoulder and asked me who I liked in tomorrow's jet races. I had no idea, and I said so.

"You mean it? I'm backing Kelso. Four to one, but he's got terrific spurt power."

"I'm sorry," I said.

"He's been away for a while," one of the government men said softly.

The euphemism was unmistakable. My neighbor glanced at my forehead and nodded at the pale spot. He offered to buy me a drink too. I accepted, though I was already feeling the effects of the first one. I was a human being again. I was visible.

I did not dare snub him, anyway. It might have been construed as the crime of coldness once again. My fifth offense would have meant five years of Invisibility. I had learned humility.

Returning to visibility involved an awkward transition, of course. Old friends to meet, lame conversations to hold, shattered relationships to renew. I had been an exile in my own city for a year, and coming back was not easy.

No one referred to my time of invisibility, naturally. It was treated as an affliction best left unmentioned. Hypocrisy, I thought, but I accepted it. Doubtless they were all trying to spare my feelings. Does one tell a man whose cancerous stomach has been replaced, "I hear you had a narrow escape just now?" Does one say to a man whose aged father has tottered off toward a euthanasia house, "Well, he was getting pretty feeble anyway, wasn't he?"

No. Of course not.

So there was this hole in our shared experience, this void, this blankness. Which left me little to talk about with my friends, in particular since I had lost the knack of conversation entirely. The period of readjustment was a trying one.

But I persevered, for I was no longer the same haughty, aloof person I had been before my conviction. I had learned humility in the hardest of schools.

Now and then I noticed an Invisible on the streets, of course. It was impossible to avoid them. But, trained as I had been trained, I quickly glanced away, as though my eyes had come momentarily to rest on some shambling, festering horror from another world.

It was in the fourth month of my return to visibility that the ultimate lesson of my sentence struck home, though. I was in the vicinity of the City Tower, having returned to my old job in the documents division of the municipal government. I had left work for the day and was walking toward the tubes when a hand emerged from the crowd, caught my arm.

"Please," the soft voice said. "Wait a minute. Don't be afraid."

I looked up, startled. In our city strangers do not accost strangers.

I saw the gleaming emblem of invisibility on the man's forehead. Then I recognized him—the slim boy I had accosted more than half a year before on that deserted street. He had grown haggard; his eyes were wild, his brown hair flecked with gray. He must have been at the beginning of his term, then. Now he must have been near its end.

He held my arm. I trembled. This was no deserted street. This was the most crowded square of the city. I pulled my arm away from his grasp and started to turn away.

"No—don't go," he cried. "Can't you pity me? You've been there yourself."

I took a faltering step. Then I remembered how I had cried out to him, how I had begged him not to spurn me. I remembered my own miserable loneliness.

I took another step away from him.

"Coward!" he shrieked after me. "Talk to me! I dare you! Talk to me, coward!"

It was too much. I was touched. Sudden tears stung my eyes, and I turned to him, stretched out a hand to his. I caught his thin wrist. The contact seemed to electrify him. A moment later, I held him in my arms, trying to draw some of the misery from his frame to mine.

The security robots closed in, surrounding us. He was hurled to one side, I was taken into custody. They will try me again—not for the crime of coldness, this time, but for a crime of warmth. Perhaps they will find extenuating circumstances and release me; perhaps not.

I do not care. If they condemn me, this time I will wear my invisibility like a shield of glory.

Ishmael in Love

Call me Ishmael. All human beings who know me do. My own kind does not make use of the unit-structural designation ("name") to distinguish individuals, but this is the name the humans gave to me, and it will do. I was named by Miss Lisabeth Calkins, for whom I feel protective-chivalrous-sexual emotions ("love"). Throughout my narrative it is understood that the designation "Ishmael" refers only to myself.

I am a member of an intelligent aquatic mammalian non-primate non-human species, *Tursiops truncatus,* a bottle-nosed dolphin. I am eleven years old, which is to say that I am fully mature in all respects. My weight is 175 kilograms, and my total length is 2.9 meters. I am employed at Gerard-Worzel Seawater Recovery Station, St. Croix, Virgin Islands, in a maintenance capacity, having commenced there on your date of August 14, 1994. To my own species I am sexually desirable and also highly regarded for my mental development. I have a large vocabulary. I communicate well with members of *H. sapiens.* I have considerable mechanical ability, as you can see by my success in switching on the electronic-acoustic device through which I am dictating this memoir.

I am a lonely mammalian organism who has committed acts of heroism on behalf of your species and wishes only the reward of a more intimate relationship ("love") with Miss Lisabeth Calkins. I beseech compassionate members of *H. sapiens* to speak favorably of me to her. I am loyal, trustworthy, reliable, devoted, and extremely intelligent. I would endeavor to give her stimulating companionship and emotional fulfillment ("happiness") in all respects within my power.

Permit me to explain the pertinent circumstances.

Category 1: My Employment.

Gerard-Worzel Seawater Recovery Station occupies a prominent position on the north shore of the island of St. Croix, in the West Indies. It operates on the atmospheric-condensation principle. All this I know from Miss Calkins ("Lisabeth") who has described its workings to me in great detail. The purpose of our installation is to recover some of the fresh water, estimated at two hundred million gallons per day, carried as vapor in the lower hundred meters of air sweeping over each kilometer of the windward side of the island.

A pipe .9 meters in diameter takes in cold seawater at depths of up to 900 meters and carries it approximately 2 kilometers to our station. The pipe delivers some 30 million gallons of water a day at a temperature of 5°C. This is pumped toward our condenser, which intercepts approximately 1 billion cubic meters of warm tropical air each day. This air has a temperature of 25°C. and a relative humidity of 70 to 80 per cent. Upon exposure to the cold seawater in the condenser the air cools to 10°C. and reaches a humidity of 100 per cent, permitting us to extract approximately 16 gallons of water per cubic meter of air. This salt-free ("fresh") water is delivered to the main water system of the island, for St. Croix is deficient in a natural supply of water suitable for consumption by human beings. It is frequently said by government officials who visit our installation on various ceremonial occasions that without our plant the great industrial expansion of St. Croix would have been wholly impossible.

For reasons of economy we operate in conjunction with an aquicultural enterprise ("the fish farm") that puts our wastes to work. Once our seawater has been pumped through the condenser it must be discarded; however, because it originates in a low-level ocean area, its content of dissolved phosphates and nitrates is 1500 per cent greater than at the surface. This nutrient-rich water is pumped from our condenser into an adjoining circular lagoon of natural origin ("the coral corral") which is stocked with fish. In such an enhanced environment the fish are highly productive, and the yield of food is great enough to offset the costs of operating our pumps.

(Misguided human beings sometimes question the morality of using dolphins to help maintain fish farms. They believe it is degrading to compel us to produce fellow aquatic creatures to be eaten by man. May I simply point out, first, that none of us works here under compulsion, and second, that my species sees nothing immoral about feeding on aquatic creatures. We eat fish ourselves.)

My role in the functioning of the Gerard-Worzel Sea-water Recovery Station is an important one. I ("Ishmael") serve as foreman of the Intake Maintenance Squad. I lead nine members of my species. Our assignment is to monitor the intake valves of the main seawater pipe; these valves frequently become fouled through the presence on them of low-phylum organisms, such as starfish or algae, hampering the efficiency of the installation. Our task is to descend at periodic intervals and clear the obstruction. Normally this can be achieved without the need for manipulative organs ("fingers") with which we are unfortunately not equipped.

(Certain individuals among you have objected that it is improper to make use of dolphins in the labor force when members of *H. sapiens* are out of work. The intelligent reply to this is that, first, we are designed by evolution to function superbly underwater without special breathing equipment, and second, that only a highly skilled human being could perform our function, and such human beings are themselves in short supply in the labor force.)

I have held my post for two years and four months. In that time there has been no significant interruption in intake capacity of the valves I maintain.

As compensation for my work ("salary") I receive an ample supply of food. One could hire a mere shark for such pay, of course; but above and beyond my daily pails of fish I also receive such intangibles as the companionship of human beings and the opportunity to develop my latent intelligence through access to reference spools, vocabulary expanders, and various training devices. As you can see, I have made the most of my opportunities.

Category 2: Miss Lisabeth Calkins.

Her dossier is on file here. I have had access to it through the spool-reader mounted at the edge of the dolphin exercise tank. By spoken instruction I can bring into view anything in the station files, although I doubt that it was anticipated by any one that a dolphin should want to read the personnel dossiers.

She is twenty-seven years old. Thus she is of the same generation as my genetic predecessors ("parents"). However, I do not share the prevailing cultural taboo of many *H. sapiens* against emotional relationships with older women. Besides, after compensating for differences in species it will be seen that Miss Lisabeth and I are of the same age. She reached sexual maturity approximately half her lifetime ago. So did I.

(I must admit that she is considered slightly past the optimum age at which human females take a permanent mate. I assume she does not engage in the practice of temporary mating, since her dossier shows no indication that she has reproduced. It is possible that humans do not necessarily produce offspring at each yearly mating, or even that matings take place at random, unpredictable times not related to the reproductive process at all. This seems strange and somehow perverse to me, yet I infer from some data I have seen that it may be the case. There is little information on human mating habits in the material accessible to me. I must learn more.)

Lisabeth, as I allow myself privately to call her, stands 1.8 meters tall (humans do not measure themselves by "length") and weighs 52 kilograms. Her hair is golden ("blonde") and is worn long. Her skin, though darkened by exposure to the sun, is quite fair. The irises of her eyes are blue. From my conversations with humans I have learned that she is considered quite beautiful. From words I have overheard while at surface level I realize that most males at the station feel intense sexual desires toward her. I regard her as beautiful also, inasmuch as I am capable of responding to human beauty. (I think I am.) I am not sure if I feel actual sexual desire for Lisabeth; more likely what troubles me is a generalized longing for her presence and her closeness, which I translate into sexual terms simply as a means of making it comprehensible to me.

Beyond doubt she does not have the traits I normally seek in a mate (prominent beak, sleek fins). Any attempt at our making love in the anatomical sense would certainly result in pain or injury to her. That is not my wish. The physical traits that make her so desirable to the males of her species (highly developed milk glands, shining hair, delicate features, long hind limbs or "legs," and so forth) have no particular importance to me, and in some instances actually have a negative value. As in the case of the two milk glands in her pectoral region, which jut forward from her body in such a fashion that they must surely slow her when she swims. This is poor design, and I am incapable of finding poor design beautiful in any way. Evidently Lisabeth regrets the size and placement of those glands herself, since she is careful to conceal them at all times by a narrow covering. The others at the station, who are all males and therefore have only rudimentary milk glands that in no way destroy the flow lines of their bodies, leave them bare.

What, then, is the cause of my attraction for Lisabeth?

It arises out of the need I feel for her companionship. I believe that she understands me as no member of my own species does. Hence I will be happier in her company than away from her. This impression dates from our earliest meeting. Lisabeth, who is a specialist in human-cetacean relations, came to St. Croix four months ago, and I was requested to bring my maintenance group to the surface to be introduced to her. I leaped high for a good view and saw instantly that she was of a finer sort than the humans I already knew; her body was more delicate, looking at once fragile and powerful, and her gracefulness was a welcome change from the thick awkwardness of the human males I knew. Nor was she covered with the coarse body hair that my kind finds so distressing. (I did not at first know that Lisabeth's difference from the others at the station was the result of her being female. I had never seen a human female before. But I quickly learned.)

I came forward, made contact with the acoustic transmitter, and said, "I am the foreman of the Intake Maintenance Squad. I have the unit-structural designation TT-66."

"Don't you have a name?" she asked.

"Meaning of term, name?"

"Your—your unit-structural designation—but not just TT-66. I mean, that's no good at all. For example, my name's Lisabeth Calkins. And I—" She shook her head and looked at the plant supervisor. "Don't these workers have *names*?"

The supervisor did not see why dolphins should have names. Lisabeth did—she was greatly concerned about it —and since she now was in charge of liaison with us, she gave us names on the spot. Thus I was dubbed Ishmael. It was, she told me, the name of a man who had gone to sea, had many wonderful experiences, and put them all down in a story-spool that every cultured person played. I have since had access to Ishmael's story—that *other* Ishmael—and I agree that it is remarkable. For a human being he had unusual insight into the ways of whales, who are, however, stupid creatures for whom I have little respect. I am proud to carry Ishmael's name.

After she had named us, Lisabeth leaped into the sea and swam with us. I must tell you that most of us feel a sort of contempt for you humans because you are such poor swimmers. Perhaps it is a mark of my above-normal intelligence or greater compassion that I have no such scorn in me. I admire you for the zeal and energy you give to swimming, and you are quite good at it, considering all your handicaps. As I remind my people, you manage far more ably in the water than we would on land. Anyway, Lisabeth swam well, by human standards, and we tolerantly adjusted our pace to hers. We frolicked in the water awhile. Then she seized my dorsal fin and said, "Take me for a ride, Ishmael!"

I tremble now to recollect the contact of her body with mine. She sat astride me, her legs gripping my body tightly, and off I sped at close to full velocity, soaring at surface level. Her laughter told of her delight as I launched myself again and again through the air. It was a purely physical display in which I made no use of my extraordinary mental capacity; I was, if you will, simply showing off my dolphinhood. Lisabeth's response was ecstatic. Even when I plunged, taking her so deep she might have feared harm from the pressure, she kept her grip and showed no alarm. When we breached the surface again she cried out in joy.

Through sheer animality I had made my first impact on her. I knew human beings well enough to be able to interpret her flushed, exhilarated expression as I returned her to shore. My challenge now was to expose her to my higher traits—to show her that even among dolphins I was unusually swift to learn, unusually capable of comprehending the universe.

I was already then in love with her.

During the weeks that followed we had many conversations. I am not flattering myself when I tell you that she quickly realized how extraordinary I am. My vocabulary, which was already large when she came to the station, grew rapidly under the stimulus of Lisabeth's presence. I learned from her; she gave me access to spools no dolphin was thought likely to wish to play; I developed insights into my environment that astonished even myself. In short order I reached my present peak of attainment. I think you will agree that I can express myself more eloquently than most human beings. I trust that the computer doing the printout on this memoir will not betray me by inserting inappropriate punctuation or deviating from the proper spellings of the words whose sounds I utter.

My love for Lisabeth deepened and grew more rich. I learned the meaning of jealousy for the first time when I saw her running arm in arm along the beach with Dr. Madison, the power-plant man. I knew anger when I overheard the lewd and vulgar remarks of the human males as Lisabeth walked by. My fascination with her led me to explore many avenues of human experience; I did not dare talk of such things with her, but from other personnel at the base who sometimes talked with me I learned certain aspects of the phenomenon humans call "love." I also obtained explanations of the vulgar words spoken by males here behind her back: most of them pertained to a wish to mate with Lisabeth (apparently on a temporary basis), but there were also highly favorable descriptions of her milk glands (why are humans so aggressively mammalian?) and even of the rounded area in back, just above the place where her body divides into the two hind limbs. I confess that that region fascinates me also. It seems so *alien* for one's body to split like that in the middle!

I never explicitly stated my feelings toward Lisabeth. I tried to lead her slowly toward an understanding that I loved her. Once she came overtly to that awareness, I thought, we might begin to plan some sort of future for ourselves together.

What a fool I was!

Category 3: The Conspiracy.

A male voice said, "How in hell are you going to bribe a dolphin?"

A different voice, deeper, more cultured, replied, "Leave it to me."

"What do you give him? Ten cans of sardines?"

"This one's special. Peculiar, even. He's scholarly. We can get to him."

They did not know that I could hear them. I was drifting near the surface in my rest tank, between shifts. Our hearing is acute, and I was well within auditory range. I sensed at once that something was amiss, but I kept my position, pretending I knew nothing.

"Ishmael!" one man called out. "Is that you, Ismael?"

I rose to the surface and came to the edge of the tank. Three male humans stood there. One was a technician at the station; the other two I had never seen before, and they wore body covering from their feet to their throats, marking them at once as strangers here. The technician I despised, for he was one of the ones who had made vulgar remarks about Lisabeth's milk glands.

He said, "Look at him, gentlemen. Worn out in his prime! A victim of human exploitation!" To me he said, "Ishmael, these gentlemen come from the League for the Prevention of Cruelty to Intelligent Species. You know about that?"

"No," I said.

"They're trying to put an end to dolphin exploitation. The criminal use of our planet's only other truly intelligent species in slave labor. They want to help you."

"I am no slave. I receive compensation for my work."

"A few stinking fish!" said the fully dressed man to the left of the technician. "They exploit you, Ishmael! They give you dangerous, dirty work and don't pay you worth a damn!"

His companion said, "It has to stop. We want to serve notice to the world that the age of enslaved dolphins is over. Help us, Ishmael. Help us help you!"

I need not say that I was hostile to their purported purposes. A more literal-minded dolphin than I might well have said so at once and spoiled their plot. But I shrewdly said, "What do you want me to do?"

"Foul the intakes," said the technician quickly.

Despite myself I snorted in anger and surprise. "Betray a sacred trust? How can I?"

"It's for your own sake, Ishmael. Here's how it works: you and your crew will plug up the intakes, and the water plant will stop working. The whole island will panic. Human maintenance crews will go down to see what's what, but as soon as they clear the valves, you go back and foul them again. Emergency water supplies will have to be rushed to St. Croix. It'll focus public attention on the fact that this island is dependent on dolphin labor—underpaid, overworked dolphin labor! During the crisis we'll step forward to tell the world your story. We'll get every human being to cry out in outrage against the way you're being treated."

I did not say that I felt no outrage myself. Instead I cleverly replied, "There could be dangers in this for me."

"Nonsense!"

"They will ask me why I have not cleared the valves. It is my responsibility. There will be trouble."

For a while we debated the point. Then the technician said, "Look, Ishmael, we know there are a few risks. But we're willing to offer extra payment if you'll handle the job."

"Such as?"

"Spools. Anything you'd like to hear, we'll get for you. I know you've got literary interests. Plays, poetry, novels, all that sort of stuff. After hours we'll feed literature to you by the bushel, if you'll help us."

I had to admire their slickness. They knew how to motivate me.

"It's a deal," I said.

"Just tell us what you'd like."

"Anything about love."

"*Love?*"

"Love. Man and woman. Bring me love poems. Bring me stories of famous lovers. Bring me descriptions of the sexual embrace. I must understand these things."

"He wants the *Kama Sutra*," said the one on the left.

"Then we bring him the *Kama Sutra*," said the one on the right.

Category 4: My Response to the Criminals.

They did not actually bring me the *Kama Sutra*. But they brought me a good many other things, including one spool that quoted at length from the *Kama Sutra*. For several weeks I devoted myself intensively to a study of human love literature. There were maddening gaps in the texts, and I still lack real comprehension of much that goes on between man and woman. The joining of body to body does not puzzle me; but I am baffled by the dialectic of the chase, in which the male must be predatory and the woman must pretend to be out of season; I am mystified by the morality of temporary mating as distinct from permanent ("marriage"); I have no grasp of the intricate systems of taboos and prohibitions that humans have invented. This has been my one intellectual failure: at the end of my studies I knew little more of how to conduct myself with Lisabeth than I had before the conspirators had begun slipping me spools in secret.

Now they called on me to do my part.

Naturally I could not betray the station. I knew that these men were not the enlightened foes of dolphin exploitation that they claimed to be; for some private reason they wished the station shut down, that was all, and they had used their supposed sympathies with my species to win my cooperation. I do not feel exploited.

Was it improper of me to accept spools from them if I had no intention of aiding them? I doubt it. They wished to use me; instead I used them. Sometimes a superior species must exploit its inferiors to gain knowledge.

They came to me and asked me to foul the valves that evening. I said, "I am not certain what you actually wish me to do. Will you instruct me again?"

Cunningly I had switched on a recording device used by Lisabeth in her study sessions with the station dolphins. So they told me again about how fouling the valves would throw the island into panic and cast a spotlight on dolphin abuse. I questioned them repeatedly, drawing out details and also giving each man a chance to place his voiceprints on record. When proper incrimination had been achieved, I said, "Very well. On the next shift I'll do as you say."

"And the rest of your maintenance squad?"

"I'll order them to leave the valves untended for the sake of our species."

They left the station, looking quite satisfied with themselves. When they were gone I beaked the switch that summoned Lisabeth. She came from her living quarters rapidly. I showed her the spool in the recording machine.

"Play it," I said grandly. "And then notify the island police!"

Category 5: The Reward of Heroism.

The arrests were made. The three men had no concern with dolphin exploitation whatever. They were members of a disruptive group ("revolutionaries") attempting to delude a naïve dolphin into helping them cause chaos on the island. Through my loyalty, courage, and intelligence I had thwarted them.

Afterward Lisabeth came to me at the rest tank and said, "You were wonderful, Ishmael. To play along with them like that, to make them record their own confession—marvelous! You're a wonder among dolphins, Ishmael."

I was in a transport of joy.

The moment had come. I blurted, "Lisabeth, I love you."

My words went booming around the walls of the tank as they burst from the speakers. Echoes amplified and modulated them into grotesque barking noises more worthy of some miserable moron of a seal. "Love you ... love you ... love you ..."

"Why, Ishmael!"

"I can't tell you how much you mean to me. Come live with me and be my love. Lisabeth, Lisabeth, Lisabeth!"

Torrents of poetry broke from me. Gales of passionate rhetoric escaped my beak. I begged her to come down into the tank and let me embrace her. She laughed and said she wasn't dressed for swimming. It was true: she had come from town after the arrests. I implored. I begged. She yielded. We were alone; she removed her garments and entered the tank; for an instant I looked upon beauty bare. The sight left me shaken—those ugly swinging milk glands normally so wisely concealed, the strips of sickly white skin where the sun had been unable to reach, that unexpected patch of additional body hair—but once she was in the water I forgot my love's imperfections and rushed toward her. "Love!" I cried "Blessed Love!" I wrapped my fins about her in what I imagined was the human embrace. "Lisabeth! Lisabeth!" We slid below the surface. For the first time in my life I knew true passion, the kind of which the poets sing, that overwhelms even the coldest mind. I crushed her to me. I was aware of her forelimb-ends ("fists") beating against my pectoral zone, and took it at first for a sign that my passion was being reciprocated; then it reached my love-hazed brain that she might be short of air. Hastily I surfaced. My darling Lisabeth, choking and gasping, sucked in breath and struggled to escape me. In shock I released her. She fled the tank and fell along its rim, exhausted, her pale body quivering. "Forgive me," I boomed. "I love you, Lisabeth! I saved the station out of love for you!" She managed to lift her lips as a sign that she did not feel anger for me (a "smile"). In a faint voice she said, "You almost drowned me, Ishmael!"

"I was carried away by my emotions. Come back into the tank. I'll be more gentle. I promise! To have you near me—"

"Oh, Ishmael! What are you saying?"

"I love you! I love you!"

I heard footsteps. The power-plant man, Dr. Madison, came running. Hastily Lisabeth cupped her hands over her milk glands and pulled her discarded garments over the lower half of her body. That pained me, for if she chose to hide such things from him, such ugly parts of herself, was that not an indication of her love for him?

"Are you all right, Liz?" he asked. "I heard yelling—"

"It's nothing, Jeff. Only Ishmael. He started hugging me in the tank. He's in love with me, Jeff, can you imagine? In *love* with me!"

They laughed together at the folly of the love-smitten dolphin.

Before dawn came I was far out to sea. I swam where dolphins swim, far from man and his things. Lisabeth's mocking laughter rang within me. She had not meant to be cruel. She who knows me better than anyone else had not been able to keep from laughing at my absurdity.

Nursing my wounds, I stayed at sea for several days, neglecting my duties at the station. Slowly, as the pain gave way to a dull ache, I headed back toward the island. In passing I met a female of my own kind. She was newly come into her season and offered herself to me, but I told her to follow me, and she did. Several times I was forced to warn off other males who wished to make use of her. I led her to the station, into the lagoon the dolphins use in their sport. A member of my crew came out to investigate—Mordred, it was—and I told him to summon Lisabeth and tell her I had returned.

Lisabeth appeared on the shore. She waved to me, smiled, called my name.

Before her eyes I frolicked with the female dolphin. We did the dance of mating; we broke the surface and lashed it with our flukes; we leaped, we soared, we bellowed.

Lisabeth watched us. And I prayed: *let her become jealous.*

I seized my companion and drew her to the depths and violently took her, and set her free to bear my child in some other place. I found Mordred again. "Tell Lisabeth," I instructed him, "that I have found another love, but that someday I may forgive her."

Mordred gave me a glassy look and swam to shore.

My tactic failed. Lisabeth sent word that I was welcome to come back to work, and that she was sorry if she had offended me; but there was no hint of jealousy in her message. My soul was turned to rotting seaweed within me. Once more I clear the intake valves, like the good beast I am, I, Ishmael, who has read Keats and Donne. Lisabeth! Lisabeth! Can you feel my pain?

Tonight by darkness I have spoken my story. You who hear this, whoever you may be, aid a lonely organism, mammalian and aquatic, who desires more intimate contact with a female of a different species. Speak kindly of me to Lisabeth. Praise my intelligence, my loyalty, and my devotion.

Tell her I give her one more chance. I offer a unique and exciting experience. I will wait for her, tomorrow night, by the edge of the reef. Let her swim to me. Let her embrace poor lonely Ishmael. Let her speak the words of love.

From the depths of my soul ... from the depths ... Lisabeth, the foolish beast bids you good night, in grunting tones of deepest love.

How It Was When the
Past Went Away

The day that an antisocial fiend dumped an amnesifacient drug into the city water supply was one of the finest that San Francisco had had in a long while. The damp cloud that had been hovering over everything for three weeks finally drifted across the bay into Berkeley that Wednesday, and the sun emerged, bright and warm, to give the old town its warmest day so far in 2003. The temperature climbed into the high twenties, and even those oldsters who hadn't managed to learn to convert to the centigrade thermometer knew it was hot. Air-conditioners hummed from the Golden Gate to the Embarcadero. Pacific Gas & Electric recorded its highest one-hour load in history between two and three in the afternoon. The parks were crowded. People drank a lot of water, some a good deal more than others. Toward nightfall, the thirstiest ones were already beginning to forget things. By the next morning, everybody in the city was in trouble, with a few exceptions. It had really been an ideal day for committing a monstrous crime.

On the day before the past went away, Paul Mueller had been thinking seriously about leaving the state and claiming refuge in one of the debtor sanctuaries—Reno, maybe, or Caracas. It wasn't altogether his fault, but he was close to a million in the red, and his creditors were getting unruly. It had reached the point where they were sending their robot bill collectors around to harass him in person, just about every three hours.

"Mr. Mueller? I am requested to notify you that the sum of $8,005.97 is overdue in your account with Modern Age Recreators, Inc. We have applied to your financial representative and have discovered your state of insolvency, and therefore, unless a payment of $395.61 is made by the eleventh of this month, we may find it necessary to begin confiscation procedures against your person. Thus I advise you—"

"—the amount of $11,554.97, payable on the ninth of August, 2002, has not yet been received by Luna Tours, Ltd. Under the Credit Laws of 1995 we have applied for injunctive relief against you and anticipate receiving a decree of personal service due, if no payment is received by—"

"—interest on the unpaid balance is accruing, as specified in your contract, at a rate of four percent per month—"

"—balloon payment now coming due, requiring the immediate payment of—"

Mueller was growing accustomed to the routine. The robots couldn't call him—Pacific Tel & Tel had cut him out of their data net months ago—and so they came around, polite blank-faced machines stenciled with corporate emblems, and in soft purring voices told him precisely how deep in the mire he was at the moment, how fast the penalty charges were piling up, and what they planned to do to him unless he settled his debts instantly. If he tried to duck them, they'd simply track him down in the streets like indefatigable process servers, and announce his shame to the whole city. So he didn't duck them. But fairly soon their threats would begin to materialize.

They could do awful things to him. The decree of personal service, for example, would turn him into a slave; he'd become an employee of his creditor, at a court-stipulated salary, but every cent he earned would be applied against his debt, while the creditor provided him with minimal food, shelter, and clothing. He might find himself compelled to do menial jobs that a robot would spit at, for two or three years, just to clear that one debt. Personal confiscation procedures were even worse; under that deal he might well end up as the actual servant of one of the executives of a creditor company, shining shoes and folding shirts. They might also get an open-ended garnishment on him, under which he and his descendants, if any, would pay a stated percentage of their annual income down through the ages until the debt, and the compounding interest thereon, was finally satisfied. There were other techniques for dealing with delinquents, too.

He had no recourse to bankruptcy. The states and the federal government had tossed out the bankruptcy laws in 1995, after the so-called Credit Epidemic of the 1980's, when for a while it was actually fashionable to go irretrievably into debt and throw yourself on the mercy of the courts. The haven of easy bankruptcy was no more; if you became insolvent, your creditors had you in their grip. The only way out was to jump to a debtor sanctuary, a place where local laws barred any extradition for a credit offense. There were about a dozen such sanctuaries, and you could live well there, provided you had some special skill that you could sell at a high price. You needed to make a good living, because in a debtor sanctuary everything was on a strictly cash basis—cash in advance, at that, even for a haircut. Mueller had a skill that he thought would see him through: he was an artist, a maker of sonic sculptures, and his work was always in good demand. All he needed was a few thousand dollars to purchase the basic tools of his trade—his last set of sculpting equipment had been repossessed a few weeks ago—and he could set up a studio in one of the sanctuaries, beyond the reach of the robot hounds. He imagined he could still find a friend who would lend him a few thousand dollars. In the name of art, so to speak. In a good cause.

If he stayed within the sanctuary area for ten consecutive years, he would be absolved of his debts and could come forth a free man. There was only one catch, not a small one. Once a man had taken the sanctuary route, he was forever barred from all credit channels when he returned to the outside world. He couldn't even get a post office credit card, let alone a bank loan. Mueller wasn't sure he could live that way, paying cash for everything all the rest of his life. It would be terribly cumbersome and dreary. Worse: it would be barbaric.

He made a note on his memo pad: *Call Freddy Munson in morning and borrow three bigs. Buy ticket to Caracas. Buy sculpting stuff.*

The die was cast—unless he changed his mind in the morning.

He peered moodily out at the row of glistening whitewashed just-post-Earthquake houses descending the steeply

inclined street that ran down Telegraph Hill toward
Fisherman's Wharf. They sparkled in the unfamiliar sunlight. A beautiful day, Mueller thought. A beautiful day to
drown yourself in the bay. Damn. Damn. Damn. He was
going to be forty years old soon. He had come into the
world on the same black day that President John Kennedy
had left it. Born in an evil hour, doomed to a dark fate.
Mueller scowled. He went to the tap and got a glass of
water. It was the only thing he could afford to drink, just
now. He asked himself how he had ever managed to get
into such a mess. Nearly a million in debt!

He lay down dismally to take a nap.

When he woke, toward midnight, he felt better than he
had felt for a long time. Some great cloud seemed to have
lifted from him, even as it had lifted from the city that
day. Mueller was actually in a cheerful mood. He couldn't
imagine why.

In an elegant townhouse on Marina Boulevard, the
Amazing Montini was rehearsing his act. The Amazing
Montini was a professional mnemonist: a small, dapper
man of sixty, who never forgot a thing. Deeply tanned, his
dark hair slicked back at a sharp angle, his small black
eyes glistening with confidence, his thin lips fastidiously
pursed. He drew a book from a shelf and let it drop open
at random. It was an old one-volume edition of Shakespeare, a familiar prop in his nightclub act. He skimmed
the page, nodded, looked briefly at another, then another,
and smiled his inward smile. Life was kind to The
Amazing Montini. He earned a comfortable $30,000 a
week on tour, having converted a freakish gift into a
profitable enterprise. Tomorrow night he'd open for a
week at Vegas; then on to Manila, Tokyo, Bangkok,
Cairo, on around the globe. In twelve weeks he'd earn his
year's take; then he'd relax once more.

It was all so easy. He knew so many good tricks. Let
them scream out a twenty-digit number; he'd scream it
right back. Let them bombard him with long strings of
nonsense syllables; he'd repeat the gibberish flawlessly. Let
them draw intricate mathematical formulas on the
computer screen; he'd reproduce them down to the last
exponent. His memory was perfect, both for visuals and
auditories, and for the other registers as well.

The Shakespeare thing, which was one of the simplest

routines he had, always awed the impressionable. It seemed so fantastic to most people that a man could memorize the complete works, page by page. He liked to use it as an opener.

He handed the book to Nadia, his assistant. Also his mistress; Montini liked to keep his circle of intimates close. She was twenty years old, taller than he was, with wide frost-gleamed eyes and a torrent of glowing, artificially radiant azure hair: up to the minute in every fashion. She wore a glass bodice, a nice container for the things contained. She was not very bright, but she did the things Montini expected her to do, and did them quite well. She would be replaced, he estimated, in about eighteen more months. He grew bored quickly with his women. His memory was too good.

"Let's start," he said.

She opened the book. "Page 537, left-hand column."

Instantly the page floated before Montini's eyes. "Henry VI, Part Two," he said. "King Henry: Say, man, were these thy words? Horner: An't shall please your majesty, I never said nor thought any such matter: God is my witness, I am falsely accused by the villain. Peter: By these ten bones, my lords, he did speak them to me in the garret one night, as we were scouring my Lord of York's armour. York: Base dunghill villain, and—"

"Page 778, right-hand column," Nadia said.

"Romeo and Juliet. Mercutio is speaking: ... an eye would spy out such a quarrel? Thy head is as full of quarrels as an egg is full of meat, and yet thy head hath been beaten as addle as an egg for quarreling. Thou hast quarreled with a man for coughing in the street, because he hath wakened thy dog that hath lain asleep in the sun. Didst thou not—"

"Page 307, starting fourteen lines down on the right side."

Montini smiled. He liked the passage. A screen would show it to his audience at the performance.

"Twelfth Night," he said. "The Duke speaks: Too old, by heaven. Let still the woman take an elder than herself, so wears she to him, so sways she level in her husband's heart: For, boy, however we do praise ourselves, our fancies are more giddy and unfirm—"

"Page 495, left-hand column."

"Wait a minute," Montini said. He poured himself a tall

glass of water and drank it in three quick gulps. "This work always makes me thirsty."

Taylor Braskett, Lt. Comdr., Ret., U.S. Space Service, strode with springy stride into his Oak Street home, just outside Golden Gate Park. At 71, Commander Braskett still managed to move in a jaunty way, and he was ready to step back into uniform at once if his country needed him. He believed his country did need him, more than ever, now that socialism was running like wildfire through half the nations of Europe. Guard the home front, at least. Protect what's left of traditional American liberty. What we ought to have, Commander Braskett believed, is a network of C-bombs in orbit, ready to rain hellish death on the enemies of democracy. No matter what the treaty says, we must be prepared to defend ourselves.

Commander Braskett's theories were not widely accepted. People respected him for having been one of the first Americans to land on Mars, of course, but he knew that they quietly regarded him as a crank, a crackpot, an antiquated Minute Man still fretting about the Redcoats. He had enough of a sense of humor to realize that he did cut an absurd figure to these young people. But he was sincere in his determination to help keep America free—to protect the youngsters from the lash of totalitarianism, whether they laughed at him or not. All this glorious sunny day he had been walking through the park, trying to talk to the young ones, attempting to explain his position. He was courteous, attentive, eager to find someone who would ask him questions. The trouble was that no one listened. And the young ones—stripped to the waist in the sunshine, girls as well as boys, taking drugs out in the open, using the foulest obscenities in casual speech—at times, Commander Braskett almost came to think that the battle for America had already been lost. Yet he never gave up all hope.

He had been in the park for hours. Now, at home, he walked past the trophy room, into the kitchen, opened the refrigerator, drew out a bottle of water. Commander Braskett had three bottles of mountain spring water delivered to his home every two days; it was a habit he had begun fifty years ago, when they had first started talking about putting fluorides in the water. He was not unaware of the little smiles they gave him when he

admitted that he drank only bottled spring water, but he
didn't mind; he had outlived many of the smilers already,
and attributed his perfect health to his refusal to touch the
polluted, contaminated water that most other people
drank. First chlorine, then fluorides—probably they were
putting in some other things by now, Commander Braskett
thought.

He drank deeply.

You have no way of telling what sort of dangerous
chemicals they might be putting in the municipal water
system these days, he told himself. Am I a crank? Then
I'm a crank. But a sane man drinks only water he can
trust.

Fetally curled, knees pressed almost to chin, trembling,
sweating, Nate Haldersen closed his eyes and tried to ease
himself of the pain of existence. Another day. A sweet,
sunny day. Happy people playing in the park. Fathers and
children. He bit his lip, hard, just short of laceration
intensity. He was an expert at punishing himself.

Sensors mounted in his bed in the Psychotrauma Ward
of Fletcher Memorial Hospital scanned him continuously,
sending a constant flow of reports to Dr. Bryce and his
team of shrinks. Nate Haldersen knew he was a man
without secrets. His hormone count, enzyme ratios, respiration, circulation, even the taste of bile in his mouth—it
all became instantaneously known to hospital personnel.
When the sensors discovered him slipping below the
depression line, ultrasonic snouts came nosing up from the
recesses of the mattress, proximity nozzles that sought him
out in the bed, found the proper veins, squirted him full of
dynajuice to cheer him up. Modern science was wonderful.
It could do everything for Haldersen except give him back
his family.

The door slid open. Dr. Bryce came in. The head shrink
looked his part: tall, solemn yet charming, gray at the
temples, clearly a wielder of power and an initiate of
mysteries. He sat down beside Haldersen's bed. As usual,
he made a big point of not looking at the row of
computer outputs next to the bed that gave the latest
details on Haldersen's condition.

"Nate?" he said. "How goes?"

"It goes," Haldersen muttered.

"Feel like talking a while?"

"Not specially. Get me a drink of water?"

"Sure," the shrink said. He fetched it and said, "It's a gorgeous day. How about a walk in the park?"

"I haven't left this room in two and a half years, Doctor. You know that."

"Always a time to break loose. There's nothing physically wrong with you, you know."

"I just don't feel like seeing people," Haldersen said. He handed back the empty glass. "More?"

"Want something stronger to drink?"

"Water's fine." Haldersen closed his eyes. Unwanted images danced behind the lids: the rocket liner blowing open over the pole, the passengers spilling out like autumn seeds erupting from a pod, Emily tumbling down, down, falling eighty thousand feet, her golden hair swept up by the thin cold wind, her short skirt flapping at her hips, her long lovely legs clawing at the sky for a place to stand. And the children falling beside her, angels dropping from heaven, down, down, down, toward the white soothing fleece of the polar ice. They sleep in peace, Haldersen thought, and I missed the plane, and I alone remain. And Job spake, and said, Let the day perish wherein I was born, and the night in which it was said, There is a man child conceived.

"It was eleven years ago," Dr. Bryce told him. "Won't you let go of it?"

"Stupid talk coming from a shrink. Why won't it let go of *me?*"

"You don't want it to. You're too fond of playing your role."

"Today is talking-tough day, eh? Get me some more water."

"Get up and get it yourself," said the shrink.

Haldersen smiled bitterly. He left the bed, crossing the room a little unsteadily, and filled his glass. He had had all sorts of therapy—sympathy therapy, antagonism therapy, drugs, shock, orthodox freuding, the works. They did nothing for him. He was left with the image of an opening pod, and falling figures against the iron-blue sky. The Lord gave, and the Lord hath taken away; blessed be the name of the Lord. My soul is weary of my life. He put the glass to his lips. Eleven years. I missed the plane. I sinned with Marie, and Emily died, and John, and Beth.

What did it feel like to fall so far? Was it like flying? Was there ecstasy in it? Haldersen filled the glass again.

"Thirsty today, eh?"

"Yes," Haldersen said.

"Sure you don't want to take a little walk?"

"You know I don't." Haldersen shivered. He turned and caught the psychiatrist by the forearm. "When does it end, Tim? How long do I have to carry this thing around?"

"Until you're willing to put it down."

"How can I make a conscious effort to forget something? Tim, Tim, isn't there some drug I can take, something to wash away a memory that's killing me?"

"Nothing effective."

"You're lying," Haldersen murmured. "I've read about the amnesifacients. The enzymes that eat memory-R.N.A The experiments with di-isopropyl fluorophosphate. Puromycin. The—"

Dr. Bryce said, "We have no control over their operations. We can't simply go after a single block of traumatic memories while leaving the rest of your mind unharmed. We'd have to bash about at random, hoping we got the trouble spot, but never knowing what else we were blotting out. You'd wake up without your trauma, but maybe without remembering anything else that happened to you between, say, the ages of 14 and 40. Maybe in fifty years we'll know enough to be able to direct the dosage at a specific—"

"I can't wait fifty years."

"I'm sorry, Nate."

"Give me the drug anyway. I'll take my chances on what I lose."

"We'll talk about that some other time, all right? The drugs are experimental. There'd be months of red tape before I could get authorization to try them on a human subject. You have to realize—"

Haldersen turned him off. He saw only with his inner eye, saw the tumbling bodies, reliving his bereavement for the billionth time, slipping easily back into his self-assumed role of Job. I am a brother to dragons, and a companion to owls. My skin is black upon me, and my bones are burned with heat. He hath destroyed me on every side, and I am gone: and mine hope hath he removed like a tree.

The shrink continued to speak. Haldersen continued not

to listen. He poured himself one more glass of water with a shaky hand.

It was close to midnight on Wednesday before Pierre Gerard, his wife, their two sons, and their daughter had a chance to have dinner. They were the proprietors, chefs, and total staff of the Petit Pois Restaurant on Sansome Street, and business had been extraordinary, exhaustingly good all evening. Usually they were able to eat about half past five, before the dinner rush began, but today people had begun coming in early—made more expansive by the good weather, no doubt—and there hadn't been a free moment for anybody since the cocktail hour. The Gerards were accustomed to brisk trade, for theirs was perhaps the most popular family-run bistro in the city, with a passionately devoted clientele. Still, a night like this was too much!

They dined modestly on the evening's miscalculations: an overdone rack of lamb, some faintly corky Château Beychevelle '97, a fallen soufflé, and such. They were thrifty people. Their one extravagance was the Évian water that they imported from France. Pierre Gerard had not set foot in his native Lyons for thirty years, but he preserved many of the customs of the motherland, including the traditional attitude toward water. A Frenchman does not drink much water; but what he does drink comes always from the bottle, never from the tap. To do otherwise is to risk a diseased liver. One must guard one's liver.

That night Freddy Munson picked up Helene at her flat on Geary and drove across the bridge to Sausalito for dinner, as usual, at Ondine. Ondine was one of only four restaurants, all of them famous old ones, at which Munson ate in fixed rotation. He was a man of firm habits. He awakened religiously at six each morning, and was at his desk in the brokerage house by seven, plugging himself into the data channels to learn what had happened in the European finance markets while he slept. At half past seven local time the New York exchanges opened and the real day's work began. By half past eleven, New York was through for the day, and Munson went around the corner for lunch, always at the Petit Pois, whose proprietor he had helped to make a millionaire by putting him into Consolidated Nucleonics' several components two and a half years before the big merger. At half past one, Munson was back in the office to transact business for his own account on the Pacific Coast exchange; three days a week he left at three, but on Tuesdays and Thursdays he stayed as late as five in order to catch some deals on the Honolulu and Tokyo exchanges. Afterwards, dinner, a play or concert, always a handsome female companion. He tried to get to sleep, or at least to bed, by midnight.

A man in Freddy Munson's position *had* to be orderly. At any given time, his thefts from his clients ranged from six to nine million dollars, and he kept all the details of his jugglings in his head. He couldn't trust putting them on paper, because there were scanner eyes everywhere; and he certainly didn't dare employ the data net, since it was well known that anything you confided to one computer was bound to be accessible to some other computer somewhere, no matter how tight a privacy seal you slapped on it. So Munson had to remember the intricacies of fifty or more illicit transactions, a constantly changing chain of embezzlements, and a man who practices such necessary disciplines of memory soon gets into the habit of extending discipline to every phase of his life.

Helene snuggled close. Her faintly psychedelic perfume drifted toward his nostrils. He locked the car into the Sausalito circuit and leaned back comfortably as the traffic-control computer took over the steering. Helene said, "At the Bryce place last night I saw two sculptures by your bankrupt friend."

"Paul Mueller?"

"That's the one. They were very good sculptures. One of them buzzed at me."

"What were you doing at the Bryces?"

"I went to college with Lisa Bryce. She invited me over with Marty."

"I didn't realize you were that old," Munson said.

Helene giggled. "Lisa's a lot younger than her husband, dear. How much does a Paul Mueller sculpture cost?"

"Fifteen, twenty thousand, generally. More for specials."

"And he's broke, even so?"

"Paul has a rare talent for self-destruction," Munson said. "He simply doesn't comprehend money. But it's his artistic salvation, in a way. The more desperately in debt he is, the finer his work becomes. He creates out of his despair, so to speak. Though he seems to have overdone the latest crisis. He's stopped working altogether. It's a sin against humanity when an artist doesn't work."

"You can be so eloquent, Freddy," Helene said softly.

When The Amazing Montini woke Thursday morning, he did not at once realize that anything had changed. His memory, like a good servant, was always there when he needed to call on it, but the array of perfectly fixed facts he carried in his mind remained submerged until required. A librarian might scan shelves and see books missing; Montini could not detect similar vacancies of his synapses. He had been up for half an hour, had stepped under the molecular bath and had punched for his breakfast and had awakened Nadia to tell her to confirm the pod reservations to Vegas, and finally, like a concert pianist running off a few arpeggios to limber his fingers for the day's chores, Montini reached into his memory bank for a little Shakespeare and no Shakespeare came.

He stood quite still, gripping the astrolabe that ornamented his picture window, and peered out at the bridge in sudden bewilderment. It had never been necessary for him to make a conscious effort to recover data. He merely looked and it was there; but where was Shakespeare? Where was the left-hand column of page 136, and the right-hand column of page 654, and the right-hand column of page 806, sixteen lines down? Gone? He drew blanks. The screen of his mind showed him only empty pages.

Easy. This is unusual, but it isn't catastrophic. You must be tense, for some reason, and you're forcing it, that's all. Relax, pull something else out of storage—

The New York *Times*, Wednesday, October 3, 1973. Yes, there it was, the front page, beautifully clear, the story on the baseball game down in the lower right-hand corner, the headline about the jet accident big and black, even the photo credit visible. Fine. Now let's try—

The St. Louis *Post-Dispatch*, Sunday, April 19, 1987. Montini shivered. He saw the top four inches of the page, nothing else. Wiped clean.

He ran through the files of other newspapers he had memorized for his act. Some were there. Some were not. Some, like the *Post-Dispatch*, were obliterated in part.

Color rose to his cheeks. Who had tampered with his memory?

He tried Shakespeare again. Nothing.

He tried the 1997 Chicago data-net directory. It was there.

He tried his third-grade geography textbook. It was there, the big red book with smeary print.

He tried last Friday's five-o'clock xerofax bulletin. Gone.

He stumbled and sank down on a divan he had purchased in Istanbul, he recalled, on the nineteenth of May, 1985, for 4,200 Turkish pounds. "Nadia!" he cried. "Nadia!" His voice was little more than a croak. She came running, her eyes only half frosted, her morning face askew.

"How do I look?" he demanded. "My mouth—is my mouth right? My eyes?"

"Your face is all flushed."

"Aside from that!"

"I don't know," she gasped. "You seem all upset, but—"

"Half my mind is gone," Montini said. "I must have had a stroke. Is there any facial paralysis? That's a symptom. Call my doctor, Nadia! A stroke, a stroke! It's the end for Montini!"

Paul Mueller, awakening at midnight on Wednesday and feeling strangely refreshed, attempted to get his bearings. Why was he fully dressed, and why had he been asleep? A nap, perhaps, that had stretched on too long? He tried to remember what he had been doing earlier in the day, but he was unable to find a clue. He was baffled but not disturbed; mainly he felt a tremendous urge to get to work. The images of five sculptures, fully planned and begging to be constructed, jostled in his mind. Might as well start right now, he thought. Work through till morning. That small twittering silvery one—that's a good one to start with. I'll block out the schematics, maybe even do some of the armature—

"Carole?" he called. "Carole, are you around?"

His voice echoed through the oddly empty apartment.

For the first time Mueller noticed how little furniture there was. A bed—a cot, really, not their double bed—and a table, and a tiny insulator unit for food, and a few dishes. No carpeting. Where were his sculptures, his private collection of his own best work? He walked into his studio and found it bare from wall to wall, all of his tools mysteriously swept away, just a few discarded sketches on the floor. And his wife? "Carole? *Carole?*"

He could not understand any of this. While he dozed, it seemed, someone had cleaned the place out, stolen his furniture, his sculptures, even the carpet. Mueller had heard of such thefts. They came with a van, brazenly, posing as moving men. Perhaps they had given him some sort of drug while they worked. He could not bear the thought that they had taken his sculptures; the rest didn't matter, but he had cherished those dozen pieces dearly. I'd better call the police, he decided, and rushed toward the handset of the data unit, but it wasn't there either. Would burglars take *that* too?

Searching for some answers, he scurried from wall to wall, and saw a note in his own handwriting. *Call Freddy Munson in morning and borrow three bigs. Buy ticket to Caracas. Buy sculpting stuff.*

Caracas? A vacation, maybe? And why buy sculpting stuff? Obviously the tools had been gone before he fell asleep, then. Why? And where was his wife? What was going on? He wondered if he ought to call Freddy right now, instead of waiting until morning. Freddy might know. Freddy was always home by midnight, too. He'd have one of his damned girls with him and wouldn't want to be interrupted, but to hell with that; what good was having friends if you couldn't bother them in a time of crisis?

Heading for the nearest public communicator booth, he rushed out of his apartment and nearly collided with a sleek dunning robot in the hallway. The things show no mercy, Mueller thought. They plague you at all hours. No doubt this one was on its way to bother the deadbeat Nicholson family down the hall.

The robot said, "Mr. Paul Mueller? I am a properly qualified representative of International Fabrication Cartel, Amalgamated. I am here to serve notice that there is an unpaid balance in your account to the extent of $9,150.55, which as of 0900 hours tomorrow morning will accrue compounded penalty interest at the rate of 5 percent per month, since you have not responded to our three previous requests for payment. I must further inform you—"

"You're off your neutrinos," Mueller snapped. "I don't owe a dime to I.F.C.! For once in my life I'm in the black, and don't try to make me believe otherwise."

The robot replied patiently, "Shall I give you a printout of the transactions? On the fifth of January, 2003, you ordered the following metal products from us: three 4-meter tubes of antiqued iridium, six 10-centimeter spheres of—"

"The fifth of January, 2003, happens to be three months from now," Mueller said, "and I don't have time to listen to crazy robots. I've got an important call to make. Can I trust you to patch me into the data net without garbling things?"

"I'm not authorized to permit you to make use of my facilities."

"Emergency override," said Mueller. "Human being in trouble. Go argue with that one!"

The robot's conditioning was sound. It yielded at once to his assertion of an emergency and set up a relay to the main communications net. Mueller supplied Freddy Munson's number. "I can provide audio only," the robot said, putting the call through. Nearly a minute passed. Then Freddy Munson's familiar deep voice snarled from the speaker grille in the robot's chest, "Who is it and what do you want?"

"It's Paul. I'm sorry to bust in on you, Freddy, but I'm in big trouble. I think I'm losing my mind, or else everybody else is."

"Maybe everybody else is. What's the problem?"

"All my furniture's gone. A dunning robot is trying to shake me down for nine bigs. I don't know where Carole is. I can't remember what I was doing earlier today. I've got a note here about getting tickets to Caracas that I wrote myself, and I don't know why. And—"

"Skip the rest," Munson said. "I can't do anything for you. I've got problems of my own."

"Can I come over, at least, and talk?"

"Absolutely not!" In a softer voice Munson said, "Listen, Paul, I didn't mean to yell, but something's come up here, something very distressing—"

"You don't need to pretend. You've got Helene with you and you wish I'd leave you alone. Okay."

"No. Honestly," Munson said. "I've got problems, suddenly. I'm in a totally ungood position to give you any help at all. I need help myself."

"What sort? Anything I can do for you?"

"I'm afraid not. And if you'll excuse me, Paul—"

"Just tell me one thing, at least. Where am I likely to find Carole? Do you have any idea?"

"At her husband's place, I'd say."

"I'm her husband."

There was a long pause. Munson said finally, "Paul, she divorced you last January and married Pete Castine in April."

"No," Mueller said.

"What, no?"

"No, it isn't possible."

"Have you been popping pills, Paul? Sniffing something? Smoking weed? Look, I'm sorry, but I can't take time now to—"

"At least tell me what day today is."

"Wednesday."

"Which Wednesday?"

"Wednesday the eighth of May. Thursday the ninth, actually, by this time of night."

"And the year?"

"For Christ's sake, Paul—"

"The *year?*"

"2003."

Mueller sagged. "Freddy, I've lost half a year somewhere! For me it's last October. 2002. I've got some weird kind of amnesia. It's the only explanation."

"Amnesia," Munson said. The edge of tension left his voice. "Is that what you've got? Amnesia? Can there be such a thing as an epidemic of amnesia? Is it contagious? Maybe you better come over here after all. Because amnesia's my problem too."

Thursday, May 9, promised to be as beautiful as the previous day had been. The sun once again beamed on San Francisco; the sky was clear, the air warm and tender. Commander Braskett awoke early as always, punched for his usual spartan breakfast, studied the morning xerofax news, spent an hour dictating his memoirs, and, about nine, went out for a walk. The streets were strangely crowded, he found, when he got down to the shopping district along Haight Street. People were wandering aimlessly, dazedly, as though they were sleep-walkers. Were they drunk? Drugged? Three times in five minutes Commander Braskett was stopped by young men who wanted to know the date. Not the time, the *date*. He told them, crisply, disdainfully; he tried to be tolerant, but it was difficult for him not to despise people who were so weak that they were unable to refrain from poisoning their minds with stimulants and narcotics and psychedelics and similar trash. At the corner of Haight and Masonic a forlorn-looking pretty girl of about seventeen, with wide blank blue eyes, halted him and said, "Sir, this city is San Francisco, isn't it? I mean, I was supposed to move here from Pittsburgh in May, and if this is May, this is San Francisco, right?" Commander Braskett nodded brusquely and turned away, pained. He was relieved to see an old friend, Lou Sandler, the manager of the Bank of America office across the way. Sandler was standing outside the bank door. Commander Braskett crossed to him and said, "Isn't it a disgrace, Lou, the way this whole street is filled with addicts this morning? What is it, some historical pageant of the 1960's?" And Sandler gave him an empty smile and said, "Is that my name? Lou? You wouldn't happen to know the last name too, would you? Somehow it's slipped my mind." In that moment Commander Braskett realized that something terrible had happened to his city and perhaps to his country, and that the leftist takeover he had long dreaded must now be at hand, and that it was time for him to don his old uniform again and do what he could to strike back at the enemy.

In joy and in confusion, Nate Haldersen awoke that morning realizing that he had been transformed in some strange and wonderful way. His head was throbbing, but not painfully. It seemed to him that a terrible weight had been lifted from his shoulders, that the fierce dead hand about his throat had at last relinquished its grip.

He sprang from bed, full of questions.

Where am I? What kind of place is this? Why am I not at home? Where are my books? Why do I feel so happy?

This seemed to be a hospital room.

There was a veil across his mind. He pierced its filmy folds and realized that he had committed himself to—to Fletcher Memorial—last—August—no, the August before last—suffering with a severe emotional disturbance brought on by—brought on by—

He had never felt happier than at this moment.

He saw a mirror. In it was the reflected upper half of Nathaniel Haldersen, Ph.D. Nate Haldersen smiled at himself. Tall, stringy, long-nosed man, absurdly straw-colored hair, absurd blue eyes, thin lips, smiling. Bony body. He undid his pajama top. Pale, hairless chest; bump of bone like an epaulet on each shoulder. I have been sick a long time, Haldersen thought. Now I must get out of here, back to my classroom. End of leave of absence. Where are my clothes?

"Nurse? Doctor?" He pressed his call button three times. "Hello? Anyone here?"

No one came. Odd; they always came. Shrugging, Haldersen moved out into the hall. He saw three orderlies, heads together, buzzing at the far end. They ignored him. A robot servitor carrying breakfast trays glided past. A moment later one of the younger doctors came running through the hall, and would not stop when Haldersen called to him. Annoyed, he went back into his room and looked about for clothing. He found none, only a little stack of magazines on the closet floor. He thumbed the call button three more times. Finally one of the robots entered the room.

"I am sorry," it said, "but the human hospital personnel is busy at present. May I serve you, Dr. Haldersen?"

"I want a suit of clothing. I'm leaving the hospital."

"I am sorry, but there is no record of your discharge. Without authorization from Dr. Bryce, Dr. Reynolds, or Dr. Kamakura, I am not permitted to allow your departure."

Haldersen sighed. He knew better than to argue with a robot. "Where are those three gentlemen right now?"

"They are occupied, sir. As you may know, there is a medical emergency in the city this morning, and Dr. Bryce and Dr. Kamakura are helping to organize the committee of public safety. Dr. Reynolds did not report for duty today and we are unable to trace him. It is believed that he is a victim of the current difficulty."

"*What* current difficulty?"

"Mass loss of memory on the part of the human population," the robot said.

"An epidemic of amnesia?"

"That is one interpretation of the problem."

"How can such a thing—" Haldersen stopped. He understood now the source of his own joy this morning. Only yesterday afternoon he had discussed with Tim Bryce the application of memory-destroying drugs to his own trauma, and Bryce had said—

Haldersen no longer knew the nature of his own trauma.

"Wait," he said, as the robot began to leave the room. "I need information. Why have I been under treatment here?"

"You have been suffering from social displacements and dysfunctions whose origin, Dr. Bryce feels, lies in a situation of traumatic personal loss."

"Loss of what?"

"Your family, Dr. Haldersen."

"Yes. That's right. I recall, now—I had a wife and two children. Emily. And a little girl—Margaret, Elizabeth, something like that. And a boy named John. What happened to them?"

"They were passengers aboard Intercontinental Airways Flight 103, Copenhagen to San Francisco, September 5, 1991. The plane underwent explosive decompression over the Arctic Ocean and there were no survivors."

Haldersen absorbed the information as calmly as though he were hearing of the assassination of Julius Caesar.

"Where was I when the accident occurred?"

"In Copenhagen," the robot replied. "You had intended to return to San Francisco with your family on Flight 103; however, according to your data file here, you became involved in an emotional relationship with a woman named Marie Rasmussen, whom you had met in Copenhagen, and failed to return to your hotel in time to go to the airport. Your wife, evidently aware of the situation, chose not to wait for you. Her subsequent death, and that of your children, produced a traumatic guilt reaction in which you came to regard yourself as responsible for their terminations."

"I *would* take that attitude, wouldn't I?" Haldersen said. "Sin and retribution. Mea culpa, mea maxima culpa. I always had a harsh view of sin, even when I was sinning. I should have been an Old Testament prophet."

"Shall I provide more information, sir?"

"Is there more?"

"We have in the files Dr. Bryce's report headed, *The Job Complex: A Study in the Paralysis of Guilt.*"

"Spare me that," Haldersen said. "All right, go."

He was alone. The Job Complex, he thought. Not really appropriate, was it? Job was a man without sin, and yet he was punished grievously to satisfy a whim of the Almighty. A little presumptuous, I'd say, to identify myself with him. Cain would have been a better choice. Cain said unto the Lord, My punishment is greater than I can bear. But Cain was a sinner. I was a sinner. I sinned and Emily died for it. When, eleven, eleven-and-a-half years ago? And now I know nothing at all about it except what the machine just told me. Redemption through oblivion, I'd call it. I have expiated my sin and now I'm free. I have no business staying in this hospital any longer. Strait is the gate, and narrow is the way, which leadeth unto life, and few there be that find it. I've got to get out of here. Maybe I can be of some help to others.

He belted his bathrobe, took a drink of water, and went out of the room. No one stopped him. The elevator did not seem to be running, but he found the stairs, and walked down, a little creakily. He had not been this far from his room in more than a year. The lower floors of the hospital were in chaos—doctors, orderlies, robots, patients, all milling around excitedly. The robots were trying to calm people and get them back to their proper places. "Excuse me," Haldersen said serenely. "Excuse me. Excuse me." He left the hospital, unmolested, by the front door. The air outside was as fresh as young wine; he felt like weeping when it hit his nostrils. He was free. Redemption through oblivion. The disaster high above the Arctic no longer dominated his thoughts. He looked upon it precisely as if it had happened to the family of some other man, long ago. Haldersen began to walk briskly down Van Ness, feeling vigor returning to his legs with every stride. A young woman, sobbing wildly, erupted from a building and collided with him. He caught her, steadied her, was surprised at his own strength as he kept her from toppling. She trembled and pressed her head against his chest. "Can I do anything for you?" he asked. "Can I be of any help?"

Panic had begun to enfold Freddy Munson during dinner at Ondine's Wednesday night. He had begun to be annoyed with Helene in the midst of the truffled chicken breasts, and so he had started to think about the details of business; and to his amazement he did not seem to have the details quite right in his mind; and so he felt the early twinges of terror.

The trouble was that Helene was going on and on about the art of sonic sculpture in general and Paul Mueller in particular. Her interest was enough to arouse faint jealousies in Munson. Was she getting ready to leap from his bed to Paul's? Was she thinking of abandoning the wealthy, glamorous, but essentially prosaic stockbroker for the irresponsible, impecunious, fascinatingly gifted sculptor? Of course, Helene kept company with a number of other men, but Munson knew them and discounted them as rivals; they were nonentities, escorts to fill her idle nights when he was too busy for her. Paul Mueller, however, was another case. Munson could not bear the thought that Helene might leave him for Paul. So he shifted his concentration to the day's maneuvers. He had extracted a thousand shares of the $5.87 convertible preferred of Lunar Transit from the Schaeffer account, pledging it as collateral to cover his shortage in the matter of the Comsat debentures, and then, tapping the Howard account for five thousand Southeast Energy Corporation warrants, he had—or had those warrants come out of the Brewster account? Brewster was big on utilities. So was Howard, but that account was heavy on Mid-Atlantic Power, so would it also be loaded with Southeast Energy? In any case, had he put those warrants up against the Zurich uranium futures, or were they riding as his markers in the Antarctic oil-lease thing? He could not remember.

He could not remember.

He could not remember.

Each transaction had been in its own compartment. The partitions were down, suddenly. Numbers were spilling about in his mind as though his brain were in free fall. All of today's deals were tumbling. It frightened him. He began to gobble his food, wanting now to get out of here, to get rid of Helene, to get home and try to reconstruct his activities of the afternoon. Oddly, he could remember quite clearly all that he had done yesterday—the Xerox switch, the straddle on Steel—but today was washing away minute by minute.

"Are you all right?" Helene asked.

"No, I'm not," he said. "I'm coming down with some-thing."

"The Venus Virus. Everybody's getting it."

"Yes, that must be it. The Venus Virus. You'd better keep clear of me tonight."

They skipped dessert and cleared out fast. He dropped Helene off at her flat; she hardly seemed disappointed, which bothered him, but not nearly so much as what was happening to his mind. Alone, finally, he tried to jot down an outline of his day, but even more had left him now. In the restaurant he had known which stocks he had handled, though he wasn't sure what he had done with them. Now he couldn't even recall the specific securities. He was out on the limb for millions of dollars of other people's money, and every detail was in his mind, and his mind was falling apart. By the time Paul Mueller called, a little after midnight, Munson was growing desperate. He was relieved, but not exactly cheered, to learn that whatever strange thing had affected his mind had hit Mueller a lot harder. Mueller had forgotten everything since last Octo-ber.

"You went bankrupt," Munson had to explain to him. "You had this wild scheme for setting up a central clearing house for works of art, a kind of stock ex-change—the sort of thing only an artist would try to start. You wouldn't let me discourage you. Then you began signing notes, and taking on contingent liabilities, and before the project was six weeks old you were hit with half a dozen lawsuits and it all began to go sour."

"When did this happen, precisely?"

"You conceived the idea at the beginning of November. By Christmas you were in severe trouble. You already had a bunch of personal debts that had gone unpaid from before, and your assets melted away, and you hit a terrible bind in your work and couldn't produce a thing. You really don't remember a thing of this, Paul?"

"Nothing."

"After the first of the year the fastest-moving creditors started getting decrees against you. They impounded ev-erything you owned except the furniture, and then they took the furniture. You borrowed from all of your friends, but they couldn't give you nearly enough, because you were borrowing thousands and you owed hundreds of thousands."

"How much did I hit you for?"

"Eleven bigs," Munson said. "But don't worry about that now."

"I'm not. I'm not worrying about a thing. I was in a bind in my work, you say?" Mueller chuckled. "That's all gone. I'm itching to start making things. All I need are the tools—I mean, money to buy the tools."

"What would they cost?"

"Two-and-a-half bigs," Mueller said.

Munson coughed. "All right. I can't transfer the money to your account, because your creditors would lien it right away. I'll get some cash at the bank. You'll have three bigs tomorrow, and welcome to it."

"Bless you, Freddy," Mueller said. "This kind of amnesia is a good thing, eh? I was so worried about money that I couldn't work. Now I'm not worried at all. I guess I'm still in debt, but I'm not fretting. Tell me what happened to my marriage, now."

"Carole got fed up and turned off," said Munson. "She opposed your business venture from the start. When it began to devour you, she did what she could to untangle you from it, but you insisted on trying to patch things together with more loans, and she filed for a decree. When she was free, Pete Castine moved in and grabbed her."

"That's the hardest part to believe. That she'd marry an art dealer, a totally noncreative person, a—a parasite, really—"

"They were always good friends," Munson said. "I won't say they were lovers, because I don't know, but they were close. And Pete's not that horrible. He's got taste, intelligence, everything an artist needs except the gift. I think Carole may have been weary of gifted men, anyway."

"How did I take it?" Mueller asked.

"You hardly seemed to notice, Paul. You were so busy with your financial shenanigans."

Mueller nodded. He sauntered to one of his own works, a three-meter-high arrangement of oscillating rods that ran the whole sound spectrum into the high kilohertzes, and passed two fingers over the activator eye. The sculpture began to murmur. After a few moments Mueller said, "You sounded awfully upset when I called, Freddy. You say you have some kind of amnesia too?"

Trying to be casual about it, Munson said, "I find I

can't remember some important transactions I carried out today. Unfortunately, my only record of them is in my head. But maybe the information will come back to me when I've slept on it."

"There's no way I can help you with that."

"No. There isn't."

"Freddy, where is this amnesia coming from?"

Munson shrugged. "Maybe somebody put a drug in the water supply, or spiked the food, or something. These days, you never can tell. Look, I've got to do some work, Paul. If you'd like to sleep here tonight—"

"I'm wide awake, thanks. I'll drop by again in the morning."

When the sculptor was gone, Munson struggled for a feverish hour to reconstruct his data, and failed. Shortly before two he took a four-hour-sleep pill. When he awakened, he realized in dismay that he had no memories whatever for the period from April 1 to noon yesterday. During those five weeks he had engaged in countless securities transactions, using other people's property as his collateral, and counting on his ability to get each marker in his game back into its proper place before anyone was likely to go looking for it. He had always been able to remember everything. Now he could remember nothing. He reached his office at seven in the morning, as always, and out of habit plugged himself into the data channels to study the Zurich and London quotes, but the prices on the screen were strange to him, and he knew that he was undone.

At the same moment of Thursday morning Dr. Timothy Bryce's house computer triggered an impulse and the alarm voice in his pillow said quietly but firmly, "It's time to wake up, Dr. Bryce." He stirred but lay still. After the prescribed ten-second interval the voice said, a little more sharply, "It's time to wake up, Dr. Bryce." Bryce sat up, just in time; the lifting of his head from the pillow cut off the third, much sterner, repetition, which would have been followed by the opening chords of the *Jupiter* Symphony. The psychiatrist opened his eyes.

He was surprised to find himself sharing his bed with a strikingly attractive girl.

She was a honey blonde, deeply tanned, with light-brown eyes, full pale lips, and a sleek, elegant body. She looked to be fairly young, a good twenty years younger than he was—perhaps twenty-five, twenty-eight. She wore nothing, and she was in a deep sleep, her lower lip sagging in a sort of involuntary pout. Neither her youth nor her beauty nor her nudity surprised him; he was puzzled simply because he had no notion who she was or how she had come to be in bed with him. He felt as though he had never seen her before. Certainly he didn't know her name. Had he picked her up at some party last night? He couldn't seem to remember where he had been last night. Gently he nudged her elbow.

She woke quickly, fluttering her eyelids, shaking her head.

"Oh," she said, as she saw him, and clutched the sheet up to her throat. Then, smiling, she dropped it again. "That's foolish. No need to be modest *now,* I guess."

"I guess. Hello."

"Hello," she said. She looked as confused as he was.

"This is going to sound stupid," he said, "but someone must have slipped me a weird weed last night, because I'm afraid I'm not sure how I happened to bring you home. Or what your name is."

"Lisa." she said. "Lisa—Falk." She stumbled over the second name. "And you're—"

"Tim Bryce."

"You don't remember where we met?"

"No," he said.

"Neither do I."

He got out of bed, feeling a little hesitant about his own nakedness, and fighting the inhibition off. "They must have given us both the same thing to smoke, then. You know"—he grinned shyly—"I can't even remember if we had a good time together last night. I hope we did."

"I think we did," she said. "I can't remember it either. But I feel good inside—the way I usually do after I've—" She paused. "We couldn't have met only just last night, Tim."

"How can you tell?"

"I've got the feeling that I've known you longer than that."

Bryce shrugged. "I don't see how. I mean, without being too coarse about it, obviously we were both high last night, really floating, and we met and came here and—"

"No. I feel at home here. As if I moved in with you weeks and weeks ago."

"A lovely idea. But I'm sure you didn't."

"Why do I feel so much at home here, then?"

"In what way?"

"In every way." She walked to the bedroom closet and let her hand rest on the touchplate. The door slid open; evidently he had keyed the house computer to her finger-prints. Had he done that last night too? She reached in. "My clothing," she said. "Look. All these dresses, coats, shoes. A whole wardrobe. There can't be any doubt. We've been living together and don't remember it!"

A chill swept through him. "What have they done to us? Listen, Lisa, let's get dressed and eat and go down to the hospital together for a checkup. We—"

"Hospital?"

"Fletcher Memorial. I'm in the neurological depart-ment. Whatever they slipped us last night has hit us both with a lacunary retrograde amnesia—a gap in our mem-ories—and it could be serious. If it's caused brain damage, perhaps it's not irreversible yet, but we can't fool around."

She put her hand to her lips in fear. Bryce felt a sudden warm urge to protect this lovely stranger, to guard and comfort her, and he realized he must be in love with her, even though he couldn't remember who she was. He crossed the room to her and seized her in a brief, tight embrace; she responded eagerly, shivering a little. By a quarter to eight they were out of the house and heading for the hospital through unusually light traffic. Bryce led the girl quickly to the staff lounge. Ted Kamakura was there already, in uniform. The little Japanese psychiatrist nodded curtly and said, "Morning, Tim." Then he blinked. "Good morning, Lisa. How come *you're* here?"

"You know her?" Bryce asked.

"What kind of question is that?"

"A deadly serious one."

"Of course I know her," Kamakura said, and his smile of greeting abruptly faded. "Why? Is something wrong about that?"

"You may know her, but I don't," said Bryce.

"Oh, God. Not you too!"

"Tell me who she is, Ted."

"She's your wife, Tim. You married her five years ago."

By half past eleven Thursday morning the Gerards had everything set up and going smoothly for the lunch rush at the Petit Pois. The soup caldron was bubbling, the escargot trays were ready to be popped in the oven, the sauces were taking form. Pierre Gerard was a bit surprised when most of the lunchtime regulars failed to show up. Even Mr. Munson, always punctual at half past eleven, did not arrive. Some of these men had not missed weekday lunch at the Petit Pois in fifteen years. Something terrible must have happened on the stock market, Pierre thought, to have kept all these financial men at their desks, and they were too busy to call him and cancel their usual tables. That must be the answer. It was impossible that any of the regulars would forget to call him. The stock market must be exploding. Pierre made a mental note to call his broker after lunch and find out what was going on.

About two Thursday afternoon, Paul Mueller stopped into Metchnikoff's Art Supplies in North Beach to try to get a welding pen, some raw metal, loudspeaker paint, and the rest of the things he needed for the rebirth of his sculpting career. Metchnikoff greeted him sourly with, "No credit at all, Mr. Mueller, not even a nickel!"

"It's all right. I'm a cash customer this time."

The dealer brightened. "In that case it's all right, maybe. You finished with your troubles?"

"I hope so," Mueller said.

He gave the order. It came to about $2,300; when the time came to pay, he explained that he simply had to run down to Montgomery Street to pick up the cash from his friend Freddy Munson, who was holding three bigs for him. Metchnikoff began to glower again. "Five minutes!" Mueller called. "I'll be back in five minutes!" But when he got to Munson's office, he found the place in confusion, and Munson wasn't there. "Did he leave an envelope for a Mr. Mueller?" he asked a distraught secretary. "I was supposed to pick something important up here this afternoon. Would you please check?" The girl simply ran away from him. So did the next girl. A burly broker told him to get out of the office. "We're closed, fellow," he shouted. Baffled, Mueller left.

Not daring to return to Metchnikoff's with the news that he hadn't been able to raise the cash after all, Mueller simply went home. Three dunning robots were

camped outside his door, and each one began to croak its cry of doom as he approached. "Sorry," Mueller said, "I can't remember a thing about any of this stuff," and he went inside and sat down on the bare floor, angry, thinking of the brilliant pieces he could be turning out if he could only get his hands on the tools of his trade. He made sketches instead. At least the ghouls had left him with pencil and paper. Not as efficient as a computer screen and a light-pen, maybe, but Michelangelo and Benvenuto Cellini had managed to make out all right without computer screens and light-pens.

At four o'clock the doorbell rang.

"Go *away*," Mueller said through the speaker. "See my accountant! I don't want to hear any more dunnings, and the next time I catch one of you idiot robots by my door I'm going to—"

"It's me, Paul," a nonmechanical voice said.

Carole.

He rushed to the door. There were seven robots out there, surrounding her, and they tried to get in; but he pushed them back so she could enter. A robot didn't dare lay a paw on a human being. He slammed the door in their metal faces and locked it.

Carole looked fine. Her hair was longer than he remembered it, and she had gained about eight pounds in all the right places, and she wore an iridescent peekaboo wrap that he had never seen before, and which was really inappropriate for afternoon wear, but which looked splendid on her. She seemed at least five years younger than she really was; evidently a month and a half of marriage to Pete Castine had done more for her than nine years of marriage to Paul Mueller. She glowed. She also looked strained and tense, but that seemed superficial, the product of some distress of the last few hours.

"I seem to have lost my key," she said.

"What are you doing here?"

"I don't understand you, Paul."

"I mean, why'd you come here?"

"I *live* here."

"Do you?" He laughed harshly. "Very funny."

"You always did have a weird sense of humor, Paul." She stepped past him. "Only this isn't any joke. Where *is* everything? The furniture, Paul. My things." Suddenly she was crying. "I must be breaking up. I wake up this morning in a completely strange apartment, all alone, and I spend the whole day wandering in a sort of daze that I don't understand at all, and now I finally come home and I find that you've pawned every damn thing we own, or something and—" She bit her knuckles. "Paul?"

She's got it too, he thought. The amnesia epidemic.

He said quietly, "This is a funny thing to ask, Carole, but will you tell me what today's date is?"

"Why—the fourteenth of September—or is it the fifteenth—"

"2002?"

"What do you think? 1776?"

She's got it worse than I have, Mueller told himself. She's lost a whole extra month. She doesn't remember my business venture. She doesn't remember my losing all the money. *She doesn't remember divorcing me*. She thinks she's still my wife.

"Come in here," he said, and led her to the bedroom. He pointed to the cot that stood where their bed had been. "Sit down, Carole. I'll try to explain. It won't make much sense, but I'll try to explain."

Under the circumstances, the concert by the visiting New York Philharmonic for Thursday evening was cancelled. Nevertheless the orchestra assembled for its rehearsal at half past two in the afternoon. The union required so many rehearsals—with pay—a week; therefore the orchestra rehearsed, regardless of external cataclysms. But there were problems. Maestro Alvarez, who used an electronic baton and proudly conducted without a score, thumbed the button for a downbeat and realized abruptly, with a sensation as of dropping through a trapdoor, that the Brahms Fourth was wholly gone from his mind. The orchestra responded raggedly to his faltering leadership; some of the musicians had no difficulties, but the concertmaster stared in horror at his left hand, wondering how to finger the strings for the notes his violin was supposed to be yielding, and the second oboe could not find the proper keys, and the first bassoon had not yet even managed to remember how to put his instrument together.

By nightfall, Tim Bryce had managed to assemble enough of the story so that he understood what had happened, not only to himself and to Lisa, but to the

entire city. A drug, or drugs, almost certainly distributed through the municipal water supply, had leached away nearly everyone's memory. The trouble with modern life, Bryce thought, is that technology gives us the potential for newer and more intricate disasters every year, but doesn't seem to give us the ability to ward them off. Memory drugs were old stuff, going back thirty, forty years. He had studied several types of them himself. Memory is partly a chemical and partly an electrical process; some drugs went after the electrical end, jamming the synapses over which brain transmissions travel, and some went after the molecular substrata in which long-term memories are locked up. Bryce knew ways of destroying short-term memories by inhibiting synapse transmission, and he knew ways of destroying the deep long-term memories by washing out the complex chains of ribonucleic acid, brain-RNA, by which they are inscribed in the brain. But such drugs were experimental, tricky, unpredictable; he had hesitated to use them on human subjects; he certainly had never imagined that anyone would simply dump them into an aqueduct and give an entire city a simultaneous lobotomy.

His office at Fletcher Memorial had become an improvised center of operations for San Francisco. The mayor was there, pale and shrunken; the chief of police, exhausted and confused, periodically turned his back and popped a pill; a dazed-looking representative of the communications net hovered in a corner, nervously monitoring the hastily rigged system through which the committee of public safety that Bryce had summoned could make its orders known throughout the city.

The mayor was no use at all. He couldn't even remember having run for office. The chief of police was in even worse shape: he had been up all night because he had forgotten, among other things, his home address, and he had been afraid to query a computer about it for fear he'd lose his job for drunkenness. By now the chief of police was aware that he wasn't the only one in the city having memory problems today, and he had looked up his address in the files and even telephoned his wife, but he was close to collapse. Bryce had insisted that both men stay here as symbols of order; he wanted only their faces and their voices, not their fumble-headed official services.

A dozen or so miscellaneous citizens had accumulated

in Bryce's office too. At five in the afternoon he had broadcast an all-media appeal, asking anyone whose memory of recent events was unimpaired to come to Fletcher Memorial. "If you haven't had any city water in the past twenty-four hours, you're probably all right. Come down here. We need you." He had drawn a curious assortment. There was a ramrod-straight old space hero, Taylor Braskett, a pure-foods nut who drank only mountain water. There was a family of French restaurateurs, mother, father, three grown children, who preferred mineral water flown in from their native land. There was a computer salesman named McBurney who had been in Los Angeles on business and hadn't had any of the drugged water. There was a retired cop named Adler who lived in Oakland, where there were no memory problems; he had hurried across the bay as soon as he heard that San Francisco was in trouble. That was before all access to the city had been shut off at Bryce's orders. And there were some others, of doubtful value but of definitely intact memory.

The three screens that the communications man had mounted provided a relay of key points in the city. Right now one was monitoring the Fisherman's Wharf district from a camera atop Ghirardelli Square, one was viewing the financial district from a helicopter over the old Ferry Building Museum, and one was relaying a pickup from a mobile truck in Golden Gate Park. The scenes were similar everywhere: people milling about, asking questions, getting no answers. There wasn't any overt sign of looting yet. There were no fires. The police, those of them able to function, were out in force, and antiriot robots were cruising the bigger streets, just in case they might be needed to squirt their stifling blankets of foam at suddenly panicked mobs.

Bryce said to the mayor, "At half past six I want you to go on all media with an appeal for calm. We'll supply you with everything you have to say."

The mayor moaned.

Bryce said, "Don't worry. I'll feed you the whole speech by bone relay. Just concentrate on speaking clearly and looking straight into the camera. If you come across as a terrified man, it can be the end for all of us. If you look cool, we may be able to pull through."

The mayor put his face in his hands.

Ted Kamakura whispered, "You can't put him on the channels, Tim! He's a wreck, and everyone will see it!"

"The city's mayor has to show himself," Bryce insisted. "Give him a double jolt of bracers. Let him make this one speech and then we can put him to pasture."

"Who'll be the spokesman, then?" Kamakura asked. "You? Me? Police Chief Dennison?"

"I don't know," Bryce muttered. "We need an authority-image to make announcements every half hour or so, and I'm damned if I'll have time. Or you. And Dennison—"

"Gentlemen, may I make a suggestion?" It was the old spaceman, Braskett. "I wish to volunteer as spokesman. You must admit I have a certain look of authority. And I'm accustomed to speaking to the public."

Bryce rejected the idea instantly. That right-wing crackpot, that author of passionate nut letters to every news medium in the state, that latter-day Paul Revere? Him, spokesman for the committee? But in the moment of rejection came acceptance. Nobody really paid attention to far-out political activities like that; probably nine people out of ten in San Francisco thought of Braskett, if at all, simply as the hero of the First Mars Expedition. He was a handsome old horse, too, elegantly upright and lean. Deep voice; unwavering eyes. A man of strength and presence.

Bryce said, "Commander Braskett, if we were to make you chairman of the committee of public safety—"

Ted Kamakura gasped.

"—would I have your assurance that such public announcements as you would make would be confined entirely to statements of the policies arrived at by the entire committee?"

Commander Braskett smiled glacially. "You want me to be a figurehead, is that it?"

"To be our spokesman, with the official title of chairman."

"As I said: to be a figurehead. Very well, I accept. I'll mouth my lies like an obedient puppet, and I won't attempt to inject any of my radical, extremist ideas into my statements. Is that what you wish?"

"I think we understand each other perfectly," Bryce said, and smiled, and got a surprisingly warm smile in return.

He jabbed now at his data board. Someone in the path lab eight stories below his office answered, and Bryce said, "Is there an up-to-date analysis yet?"

"I'll switch you to Dr. Madison."

Madison appeared on the screen. He ran the hospital's radioisotope department, normally: a beefy, red-faced man who looked as though he ought to be a beer salesman. He knew his subject. "It's definitely the water supply, Tim," he said at once. "We tentatively established that an hour and a half ago, of course, but now there's no doubt. I've isolated traces of two different memory-suppressant drugs, and there's the possibility of a third. Whoever it was was taking no chances."

"What are they?" Bryce asked.

"Well, we've got a good jolt of acetylcholine terminase," Madison said, "which will louse up the synapses and interfere with short-term memory fixation. Then there's something else, perhaps a puromycin-derivative protein dissolver, which is going to work on the brain-RNA and smashing up older memories. I suspect also that we've been getting one of the newer experimental amnesifacients, something that I haven't isolated yet, capable of working its way deep and cutting out really basic motor patterns. So they've hit us high, low, and middle."

"That explains a lot. The guys who can't remember what they did yesterday, the guys who've lost a chunk out of their adult memories, and the ones who don't even remember their names—this thing is working on people at all different levels."

"Depending on individual metabolism, age, brain structure, and how much water they had to drink yesterday, yes."

"Is the water supply still tainted?" Bryce asked.

"Tentatively, I'd say no. I've had water samples brought me from the upflow districts, and everything's okay there. The water department has been running its own check; they say the same. Evidently the stuff got into the system early yesterday, came down into the city, and is generally gone by now. Might be some residuals in the pipes; I'd be careful about drinking water even today."

"And what does the pharmacopoeia say about the effectiveness of these drugs?"

Madison shrugged. "Anybody's guess. You'd know that better than I. Do they wear off?"

"Not in the normal sense," said Bryce. "What happens is the brain cuts in a redundancy circuit and gets access to a duplicate set of the affected memories, eventually—shifts to another track, so to speak—provided a duplicate of the sector in question was there in the first place, and provided that the duplicate wasn't blotted out also. Some people are going to get chunks of their memories back, in a few days or a few weeks. Others won't."

"Wonderful," Madison said. "I'll keep you posted, Tim."

Bryce cut off the call and said to the communications man, "You have that bone relay? Get it behind His Honor's ear."

The mayor quivered. The little instrument was fastened in place.

Bryce said, "Mr. Mayor, I'm going to dictate a speech, and you're going to broadcast it on all media, and it's the last thing I'm going to ask of you until you've had a chance to pull yourself together. Okay? Listen carefully to what I'm saying, speak slowly, and pretend that tomorrow is election day and your job depends on how well you come across now. You won't be going on live. There'll be a fifteen-second delay, and we have a wipe circuit so we can correct any stumbles, and there's absolutely no reason to be tense. Are you with me? Will you give it all you've got?"

"My mind is all foggy."

"Simply listen to me and repeat what I say into the camera's eye. Let your political reflexes take over. Here's your chance to make a hero of yourself. We're living history right now, Mr. Mayor. What we do here today will be studied the way the events of the 1906 fire were studied. Let's go, now. Follow me. *People of the wonderful city of San Francisco—*"

The words rolled easily from Bryce's lips, and, wonder of wonders, the mayor caught them and spoke them in a clear, beautifully resonant voice. As he spun out his speech, Bryce felt a surging flow of power going through himself, and he imagined for the moment that he were the elected leader of the city, not merely a self-appointed emergency dictator. It was an interesting, almost ecstatic feeling. Lisa, watching him in action, gave him a loving smile.

He smiled at her. In this moment of glory he was almost able to ignore the ache of knowing that he had lost his entire memory archive of his life with her. Nothing else gone, apparently. But, neatly, with idiot selectivity, the drug in the water supply had sliced away everything pertaining to his five years of marriage. Kamakura had told him, a few hours ago, that it was the happiest marriage of any he knew. Gone. At least Lisa had suffered an identical loss, against all probabilities. Somehow that made it easier to bear; it would have been awful to have one of them remember the good times and the other know nothing. He was almost able to ignore the torment of loss, while he kept busy. Almost.

"The mayor's going to be on in a minute," Nadia said. "Will you listen to him? He'll explain what's been going on."

"I don't care," said The Amazing Montini dully.

"It's some kind of epidemic of amnesia. When I was out before, I heard all about it. *Everyone's* got it. It isn't just you! And you thought it was a stroke, but it wasn't. You're all right."

"My mind is a ruin."

"It's only temporary." Her voice was shrill and unconvincing. "It's something in the air, maybe. Some drug they were testing that drifted in. We're all in this together. I can't remember last week at all."

"What do I care," Montini said. "Most of these people, they have no memories even when they are healthy. But me? Me? I am destroyed. Nadia, I should lie down in my grave now. There is no sense in continuing to walk around."

The voice from the loudspeaker said, "Ladies and gentlemen, His Honor Elliot Chase, the Mayor of San Francisco."

"Let's listen," Nadia said.

The mayor appeared on the wallscreen, wearing his solemn face, his we-face-a-grave-challenge-citizens face. Montini glanced at him, shrugged, looked away.

The mayor said, "People of the wonderful city of San Francisco, we have just come through the most difficult day in nearly a century, since the terrible catastrophe of April, 1906. The earth has not quaked today, nor have we been smitten by fire, yet we have been severely tested by sudden calamity.

"As all of you surely know, the people of San Francisco

have been afflicted since last night by what can best be termed an epidemic of amnesia. There has been mass loss of memory, ranging from mild cases of forgetfulness to near-total obliteration of identity. Scientists working at Fletcher Memorial Hospital have succeeded in determining the cause of this unique and sudden disaster.

"It appears that criminal saboteurs contaminated the municipal water supply with certain restricted drugs that have the ability to dissolve memory structures. *The effect of these drugs is temporary.* There should be no cause for alarm. Even those who are most severely affected will find their memories gradually beginning to return, and there is every reason to expect full recovery in a matter of hours or days."

"He's lying," said Montini.

"The criminals responsible have not yet been apprehended, but we expect arrests momentarily. The San Francisco area is the only affected region, which means the drugs were introduced into the water system just beyond city limits. Everything is normal in Berkeley, in Oakland, in Marin County, and other outlying areas.

"In the name of public safety I have ordered the bridges to San Francisco closed, as well as the Bay Area Rapid Transit and other means of access to the city. We expect to maintain these restrictions at least until tomorrow morning. The purpose of this is to prevent disorder and to avoid a possible influx of undesirable elements into the city while the trouble persists. We San Franciscans are self-sufficient and can look after our own needs without outside interference. However, I have been in contact with the President and with the Governor, and they both have assured me of all possible assistance.

"The water supply is at present free of the drug, and every precaution is being taken to prevent a recurrence of this crime against one million innocent people. However, I am told that some lingering contamination may remain in the pipes for a few hours. I recommend that you keep your consumption of water low until further notice, and that you boil any water you wish to use.

"Lastly. Police Chief Dennison, myself, and your other city officials will be devoting full time to the needs of the city so long as the crisis lasts. Probably we will not have the opportunity to go before the media for further reports. Therefore, I have taken the step of appointing a committee of public safety, consisting of distinguished laymen and scientists of San Francisco, as a coordinating body that will aid in governing the city and reporting to its citizens. The chairman of this committee is the well-known veteran of so many exploits in space, Commander Taylor Braskett. Announcements concerning the developments in the crisis will come from Commander Braskett for the remainder of the evening, and you may consider his words to be those of your city officials. Thank you."

Braskett came on the screen. Montini grunted. "Look at the man they find! A maniac patriot!"

"But the drug will wear off," Nadia said. "Your mind will be all right again."

"I know these drugs. There is no hope. I am destroyed." The Amazing Montini moved toward the door. "I need fresh air. I will go out. Good-bye, Nadia."

She tried to stop him. He pushed her aside. Entering Marina Park, he made his way to the yacht club; the doorman admitted him, and took no further notice. Montini walked out on the pier. The drug, they say, is temporary. It will wear off. My mind will clear. I doubt this very much. Montini peered at the dark, oily water, glistening with light reflected from the bridge. He explored his damaged mind, scanning for gaps. Whole sections of memory were gone. The walls had crumbled, slabs of plaster falling away to expose bare lath. He could not live this way. Carefully, grunting from the exertion, he lowered himself via a metal ladder into the water, and kicked himself away from the pier. The water was terribly cold. His shoes seemed immensely heavy. He floated toward the island of the old prison, but he doubted that he would remain afloat much longer. As he drifted, he ran through an inventory of his memory, seeing what remained to him and finding less than enough. To test whether even his gift had survived, he attempted to play back a recall of the mayor's speech, and found the words shifting and melting. It is just as well, then, he told himself, and drifted on, and went under.

Carole insisted on spending Thursday night with him.

"We aren't man and wife any more," he had to tell her. "You divorced me."

"Since when are you so conventional? We lived together before we were married, and now we can live together after we were married. Maybe we're inventing a new sin, Paul. Post-marital sex."

"That isn't the point. The point is that you came to hate me because of my financial mess, and you left me. If you try to come back to me now, you'll be going against your own rational and deliberate decision of last January."

"For me last January is still four months away," she said. "I don't hate you. I love you. I always have and always will. I can't imagine how I would ever have come to divorce you, but in any case I don't remember divorcing you, and you don't remember being divorced by me, and so why can't we just keep going from the point where our memories leave off?"

"Among other things, because you happen to be Pete Castine's wife now."

"That sounds completely unreal to me. Something you dreamed."

"Freddy Munson told me, though. It's true."

"If I went back to Pete now," Carole said, "I'd feel sinful. Simply because I supposedly married him, you want me to jump into bed with him? I don't want him. I want you. Can't I stay here?"

"If Pete—"

"If Pete, if Pete, if Pete! In my mind I'm Mrs. Paul Mueller, and in your mind I am too, and to hell with Pete, and with whatever Freddy Munson told you, and everything else. This is a silly argument, Paul. Let's quit it. If you want me to get out, tell me so right now in that many words. Otherwise let me stay."

He couldn't tell her to get out.

He had only the one small cot, but they managed to share it. It was uncomfortable, but in an amusing way. He felt twenty years old again for a while. In the morning they took a long shower together, and then Carole went out to buy some things for breakfast, since his service had been cut off and he couldn't punch for food. A dunning robot outside the door told him, as Carole was leaving, "The decree of personal service due has been requested, Mr. Mueller, and is now pending a court hearing."

"I know you not," Mueller said. "Be gone!"

Today, he told himself, he would hunt up Freddy Munson somehow and get that cash from him, and buy the tools he needed, and start working again. Let the world outside go crazy; so long as he was working, all was well. If he couldn't find Freddy, maybe he could swing the purchase on Carole's credit. She was legally divorced from him and none of his credit taint would stain her; as Mrs. Peter Castine she should surely be able to get hold of a couple of bigs to pay Metchnikoff. Possibly the banks were closed on account of the memory crisis today, Mueller considered; but Metchnikoff surely wouldn't demand cash from Carole. He closed his eyes and imagined how good it would feel to be making things once more.

Carole was gone an hour. When she came back, carrying groceries, Pete Castine was with her.

"He followed me," Carole explained. "He wouldn't let me alone."

He was a slim, poised, controlled man, quite athletic, several years older than Mueller—perhaps into his fifties already—but seemingly very young. Calmly he said, "I was sure that Carole had come here. It's perfectly understandable, Paul. She was here all night, I hope?"

"Does it matter?" Mueller asked.

"To some extent. I'd rather have had her spending the night with her former husband than with some third party entirely."

"She was here all night, yes," Mueller said wearily.

"I'd like her to come home with me now. She *is* my wife, after all."

"She has no recollection of that. Neither do I."

"I'm aware of that." Castine nodded amiably. "In my own case, I've forgotten everything that happened to me before the age of twenty-two. I couldn't tell you my father's first name. However, as a matter of objective reality, Carole's my wife, and her parting from you was rather bitter, and I feel she shouldn't stay here any longer."

"Why are you telling all this to me?" Mueller asked. "If you want your wife to go home with you, ask her to go home with you."

"So I did. She says she won't leave unless you direct her to go."

"That's right," Carole said. "I know whose wife I *think* I am. If Paul throws me out I'll go with you. Not otherwise."

Mueller shrugged. "I'd be a fool to throw her out, Pete. I need her and I want her, and whatever breakup she and I had isn't real to us. I know it's tough on you, but I can't help that. I imagine you'll have no trouble getting an annulment once the courts work out some law to cover cases like this."

Castine was silent for a long moment.

At length he said, "How has your work been going, Paul?"

"I gather that I haven't turned out a thing all year."

"That's correct."

"I'm planning to start again. You might say that Carole has inspired me."

"Splendid," said Castine without intonation of any kind. "I trust this little mixup over our—ah—shared wife won't interfere with the harmonious artist-dealer relationship we used to enjoy?"

"Not at all," Mueller said. "You'll still get my whole output. Why the hell should I resent anything you did? Carole was a free agent when you married her. There's only one little trouble."

"Yes?"

"I'm broke. I have no tools, and I can't work without tools, and I have no way of buying tools."

"How much do you need?"

"Two and a half bigs."

Castine said, "Where's your data pickup? I'll make a credit transfer."

"The phone company disconnected it a long time ago."

"Let me give you a check, then. Say, three thousand even? An advance against future sales." Castine fumbled for a while before locating a blank check. "First one of these I've written in five years, maybe. Odd how you get accustomed to spending by telephone. Here you are, and good luck. To both of you." He made a courtly, bitter bow. "I hope you'll be happy together. And call me up when you've finished a few pieces, Paul. I'll send the van. I suppose you'll have a phone again by then." He went out.

"There's a blessing in being able to forget," Nate Haldersen said. "The redemption of oblivion, I call it. What's happened to San Francisco this week isn't necessarily a disaster. For some of us, it's the finest thing in the world."

They were listening to him—at least fifty people, clustering near his feet. He stood on the stage of the bandstand in the park, just across from the De Young Museum. Shadows were gathering. Friday, the second full day of the memory crisis, was ending. Haldersen had slept in the park last night, and he planned to sleep there again tonight; he had realized after his escape from the hospital that his apartment had been shut down long ago and his possessions were in storage. It did not matter. He would live off the land and forage for food. The flame of prophecy was aglow in him.

"Let me tell you how it was with me," he cried. "Three days ago I was in a hospital for mental illness. Some of you are smiling, perhaps, telling me I ought to be back there now, but no! You don't understand. I was incapable of facing the world. Wherever I went, I saw happy families, parents and children, and it made me sick with envy and hatred, so that I couldn't function in society. Why? Why? Because my own wife and children were killed in an air disaster in 1991, that's why, and I missed the plane because I was committing sin that day, and for my sin they died, and I lived thereafter in unending torment! But now all that is flushed from my mind. I have sinned, and I have suffered, and now I am redeemed through merciful oblivion!"

A voice in the crowd called, "If you've forgotten all about it, how come you're telling the story to us?"

"A good question! An excellent question!" Haldersen felt sweat bursting from his pores, adrenalin pumping in his veins. "I know the story only because a machine in the hospital told it to me, yesterday morning. But it came to me from the outside, a secondhand tale. The experience of it within me, the scars, all that has been washed away. The pain of it is gone. Oh, yes, I'm sad that my innocent family perished, but a healthy man learns to control his grief after eleven years, he accepts his loss and goes on. I was sick, sick right *here*, and I couldn't live with my grief, but now I can, I look on it objectively, do you see? And that's why I say there's a blessing in being able to forget. What about you, out there? There must be some of you who suffered painful losses too, and now can no longer remember them, now have been redeemed and released from anguish. Are there any? Are there? Raise your hands. Who's been bathed in holy oblivion? Who out there knows that he's been cleansed, even if he can't remember what it is he's been cleansed from?"

Hands were starting to go up.

They were weeping, now, they were cheering, they were waving at him. Haldersen felt a little like a charlatan. But only a little. He had always had the stuff of a prophet in him, even while he was posing as a harmless academic, a stuffy professor of philosophy. He had had what every prophet needs, a sharp sense of contrast between guilt and purity, an awareness of the existence of sin. It was that awareness that now drove him to celebrate his joy in public, to seek for companions in liberation—no, for disciples—to found the Church of Oblivion here in Golden Gate Park. The hospital could have given him these drugs years ago and spared him from agony. Bryce had refused, Kamakura, Reynolds, all the smooth-talking doctors; they were waiting for more tests, experiments on chimpanzees, God knows what. And God had said, Nathaniel Haldersen has suffered long enough for his sin, and so He had thrust a drug into the water supply of San Francisco, the same drug that the doctors had denied him, and down the pipes from the mountains had come the sweet draught of oblivion.

"Drink with me!" Haldersen shouted. "All you who are in pain, you who live with sorrow! We'll get this drug ourselves! We'll purify our suffering souls! Drink the blessed water, and sing to the glory of God who gives us oblivion!"

Freddy Munson had spent Thursday afternoon, Thursday night, and all of Friday holed up in his apartment with every communications link to the outside turned off. He neither took nor made calls, ignored the telescreens, and had switched on the xerofax only three times in the thirty-six hours.

He knew that he was finished, and he was trying to decide how to react to it.

His memory situation seemed to have stabilized. He was still missing only five weeks of market maneuvers. There wasn't any further decay—not that that mattered; he was in trouble enough—and, despite an optimistic statement last night by Mayor Chase, Munson hadn't seen any evidence that the memory loss was reversing itself. He was unable to reconstruct any of the vanished details.

There was no immediate peril, he knew. Most of the clients whose accounts he'd been juggling were wealthy old bats who wouldn't worry about their stocks until they got next month's account statements. They had given him discretionary powers, which was how he had been able to tap their resources for his own benefit in the first place. Up to now, Munson had always been able to complete each transaction within a single month, so the account balanced for every statement. He had dealt with the problem of the securities withdrawals that the statements ought to show by gimmicking the house computer to delete all such withdrawals provided there was no net effect from month to month; that way he could borrow 10,000 shares of United Spaceways or Comsat or IBM for two weeks, use the stock as collateral for a deal of his own, and get it back into the proper account in time with no one the wiser. Three weeks from now, though, the end-of-the-month statements were going to go out showing all of his accounts peppered by inexplicable withdrawals, and he was going to catch hell.

The trouble might even start earlier, and come from a different direction. Since the San Francisco trouble had begun, the market had gone down sharply, and he would probably be getting margin calls on Monday. The San Francisco exchange was closed, of course; it hadn't been able to open Thursday morning because so many of the brokers had been hit hard by amnesia. But New York's exchanges were open, and they had reacted badly to the news from San Francisco, probably out of fear that a conspiracy was afoot and the whole country might soon be pushed into chaos. When the local exchange opened again on Monday, if it opened, it would most likely open at the last New York prices, or near them, and keep on going down. Munson would be asked to put up cash or additional securities to cover his loans. He certainly didn't have the cash, and the only way he could get additional securities would be to dip into still more of his accounts, compounding his offense; on the other hand, if he didn't meet the margin calls they'd sell him out and he'd never be able to restore the stock to the proper accounts, even if he succeeded in remembering which shares went where.

He was trapped. He could stick around for a few weeks, waiting for the ax to fall, or he could get out right now. He preferred to get out right now.

And go where?

Caracas? Reno? São Paulo? No, debtor sanctuaries

wouldn't do him any good, because he wasn't an ordinary debtor. He was a thief, and the sanctuaries didn't protect criminals, only bankrupts. He had to go farther, all the way to Luna Dome. There wasn't any extradition from the Moon. There'd be no hope of coming back, either.

Munson got on the phone, hoping to reach his travel agent. Two tickets to Luna, please. One for him, one for Helene; if she didn't feel like coming, he'd go alone. No, not round trip. But the agent didn't answer. Munson tried the number several times. Shrugging, he decided to order direct, and called United Spaceways next. He got a busy signal. "Shall we wait-list your call?" the data net asked. "It will be three days, at the present state of the backlog of calls, before we can put it through."

"Forget it," Munson said.

He had just realized that San Francisco was closed off, anyway. Unless he tried to swim for it, he couldn't get out of the city to go to the spaceport, even if he did manage to buy tickets to Luna. He was caught here until they opened the transit routes again. How long would that be? Monday, Tuesday, next Friday? They couldn't keep the city shut forever—could they?

What it came down to, Munson saw, was a contest of probabilities. Would someone discover the discrepancies in his accounts before he found a way of escaping to Luna, or would his escape access become available too late? Put on those terms, it became an interesting gamble instead of a panic situation. He would spend the weekend trying to find a way out of San Francisco, and if he failed, he would try to be a stoic about facing what was to come.

Calm, now, he remembered that he had promised to lend Paul Mueller a few thousand dollars, to help him equip his studio again. Munson was unhappy over having let that slip his mind. He liked to be helpful. And, even now, what were two or three bigs to him? He had plenty of recoverable assets. Might as well let Paul have a little of the money before the lawyers start grabbing it.

One problem. He had less than a hundred in cash on him—who bothered carrying cash?—and he couldn't telephone a transfer of funds to Mueller's account, because Paul didn't have an account with the data net any more, or even a phone. There wasn't any place to get that much cash, either, at this hour of evening, especially with the city paralyzed. And the weekend was coming. Munson had an idea, though. What if he went shopping with Mueller to-morrow, and simply charged whatever the sculptor needed to his own account? Fine. He reached for the phone to arrange the date, remembered that Mueller could not be called, and decided to tell Paul about it in person. Now. He could use some fresh air, anyway.

He half expected to find robot bailiffs outside, waiting to arrest him. But of course no one was after him yet. He walked to the garage. It was a fine night, cool, starry, with perhaps just a hint of fog in the east. Berkeley's lights glittered through the haze, though. The streets were quiet. In time of crisis people stay home, apparently. He drove quickly to Mueller's place. Four robots were in front of it. Munson eyed them edgily, with the wary look of the man who knows that the sheriff will be after him too, in a little while. But Mueller, when he came to the door, took no notice of the dunners.

Munson said, "I'm sorry I missed connections with you. The money I promised to lend you—"

"It's all right, Freddy. Pete Castine was here this morning and I borrowed the three bigs from him. I've already got my studio set up again. Come in and look?"

Munson entered. "Pete Castine?"

"A good investment for him. He makes money if he has work of mine to sell, right? It's in his best interest to help me get started again. Carole and I have been hooking things up all day."

"Carole?" Munson said. Mueller showed him into the studio. The paraphernalia of a sonic sculptor sat on the floor—a welding pen, a vacuum bell, a big texturing vat, some ingots and strands of wire, and such things. Carole was feeding discarded packing cases into the wall disposal unit. Looking up, she smiled uncertainly and ran her hand through her long dark hair.

"Hello, Freddy."

"Everybody good friends again?" he asked, baffled.

"Nobody remembers being enemies," she said. She laughed. "Isn't it wonderful to have your memory blotted out like this?"

"Wonderful," Munson said bleakly.

Commander Braskett said, "Can I offer you people any water?"

Tim Bryce smiled. Lisa Bryce smiled. Ted Kamakura

smiled. Even Mayor Chase, that poor empty husk, smiled. Commander Braskett understood those smiles. Even now, after three days of close contact under pressure, they thought he was nuts.

He had had a week's supply of bottled water brought from his home to the command post here at the hospital. Everybody kept telling him that the municipal water was safe to drink now, that the memory drugs were gone from it; but why couldn't they comprehend that his aversion to public water dated back to an era when memory drugs were unknown? There were plenty of other chemicals in the reservoir, after all.

He hoisted his glass in a jaunty toast and winked at them.

Tim Bryce said, "Commander, we'd like you to address the city again at half past ten this morning. Here's your text."

Braskett scanned the sheet. It dealt mostly with the relaxation of the order to boil water before drinking it. "You want me to go on all media," he said, "and tell the people of San Francisco that it's now safe for them to drink from the taps, eh? That's a bit awkward for me. Even a figurehead spokesman is entitled to some degree of personal integrity."

Bryce looked briefly puzzled. Then he laughed and took the text back. "You're absolutely right, Commander. I can't ask you to make this announcement, in view of— ah—your particular beliefs. Let's change the plan. You open the spot by introducing me, and *I'll* discuss the no-boiling thing. Will that be all right?"

Commander Braskett appreciated the tactful way they deferred to his special obsession. "I'm at your service, Doctor," he said gravely.

Bryce finished speaking and the camera lights left him. He said to Lisa, "What about lunch? Or breakfast, or whatever meal it is we're up to now."

"Everything's ready, Tim. Whenever you are."

They ate together in the holograph room, which had become the kitchen of the command post. Massive cameras and tanks of etching fluid surrounded them. The others thoughtfully left them alone. These brief shared meals were the only fragments of privacy he and Lisa had

had, in the fifty-two hours since he had awakened to find her sleeping beside him.

He stared across the table in wonder at this delectable blond girl who they said was his wife. How beautiful her soft brown eyes were against that backdrop of golden hair! How perfect the line of her lips, the curve of her earlobes! Bryce knew that no one would object if he and Lisa went off and locked themselves into one of the private rooms for a few hours. He wasn't that indispensable; and there was so much he had to begin relearning about his wife. But he was unable to leave his post. He hadn't been out of the hospital or even off this floor for the duration of the crisis; he kept himself going by grabbing the sleep wire for half an hour every six hours. Perhaps it was an illusion born of too little sleep and too much data, but he had come to believe that the survival of the city depended on him. He had spent his career trying to heal individual sick minds; now he had a whole city to tend to.

"Tired?" Lisa asked.

"I'm in that tiredness beyond feeling tired. My mind is so clear that my skull wouldn't cast a shadow. I'm nearing nirvana."

"The worst is over, I think. The city's settling down."

"It's still bad, though. Have you seen the suicide figures?"

"Bad?"

"Hideous. The norm in San Francisco is 220 a year. We've had close to five hundred in the last two and a half days. And that's just the reported cases, the bodies discovered, and so on. Probably we can double the figure. Thirty suicides reported Wednesday night, about two hundred on Thursday, the same on Friday, and about fifty so far this morning. At least it seems as if the wave is past its peak."

"By why, Tim?"

"Some people react poorly to loss. Especially the loss of a segment of their memories. They're indignant—they're crushed—they're scared—and they reach for the exit pill. Suicide's too easy now, anyway. In the old days you reacted to frustration by smashing the crockery; now you go a deadlier route. Of course, there are special cases. A man named Montini they fished out of the bay—a professional mnemonist, who did a trick act in nightclubs, total recall. I can hardly blame him for caving in. And I suppose there were a lot of others who kept their business in their heads—gamblers, stock-market operators, oral poets, musicians—who might decide to end it all rather than try to pick up the pieces."

"But if the effects of the drug wear off—"

"Do they?" Bryce asked.

"You said so yourself."

"I was making optimistic noises for the benefit of the citizens. We don't have any experimental history for these drugs and human subjects. Hell, Lisa, we don't even know the dosage that was administered; by the time we were able to get water samples most of the system had been flushed clean, and the automatic monitoring devices at the city pumping stations were rigged as part of the conspiracy so they didn't show a thing out of the ordinary. I've got no idea at all if there's going to be any measurable memory recovery."

"But there is, Tim. I've already started to get some things back."

"What?"

"Don't scream at me like that! You scared me."

He clung to the edge of the table. "Are you really recovering?"

"Around the edges. I remember a few things already. About us."

"Like what?"

"Applying for the marriage license. I'm standing stark naked inside a diagnostat machine and a voice on the loudspeaker is telling me to look straight into the scanners. And I remember the ceremony, a little. Just a small group of friends, a civil ceremony. Then we took the pod to Acapulco."

He stared grimly. "When did this start to come back?"

"About seven this morning, I guess."

"Is there more?"

"A bit. Our honeymoon. The robot bellhop who came blundering in on our wedding night. You don't—"

"Remember it? No. No. Nothing. Blank."

"That's all I remember, this early stuff."

"Yes, of course," he said. "The older memories are always the first to return in any form of amnesia. The last stuff in is the first to go." His hands were shaking, not entirely from fatigue. A strange desolation crept over him.

Lisa remembered. He did not. Was it a function of her youth, or of the chemistry of her brain, or—?

He could not bear the thought that they no longer shared an oblivion. He didn't want the amnesia to become one-sided for them; it was humiliating not to remember his own marriage when she did. You're being irrational, he told himself. Physician, heal thyself!

"Let's go back inside," he said.

"You haven't finished your—"

"Later."

He went into the command room. Kamakura had phones in both hands and was barking data into a recorder. The screens were alive with morning scenes, Saturday in the city, crowds in Union Square. Kamakura hung up both calls and said, "I've got an interesting report from Dr. Klein at Letterman General. He says they're getting the first traces of memory recovery this morning. Women under thirty, only."

"Lisa says she's beginning to remember too," Bryce said.

"Women under thirty," said Kamakura. "Yes. Also the suicide rate is definitely tapering. We may be starting to come out of it."

"Terrific," Bryce said hollowly.

Haldersen was living in a ten-foot-high bubble that one of his disciples had blown for him in the middle of Golden Gate Park, just west of the Arboretum. Fifteen similar bubbles had gone up around his, giving the region the look of an up-to-date Eskimo village in plastic igloos. The occupants of the camp, aside from Haldersen, were men and women who had so little memory left that they did not know who they were or where they lived. He had acquired a dozen of these lost ones on Friday, and by late afternoon on Saturday he had been joined by some forty more. The news somehow was moving through the city that those without moorings were welcome to take up temporary residence with the group in the park. It had happened that way during the 1906 disaster, too.

The police had been around a few times to check on them. The first time, a portly lieutenant had tried to persuade the whole group to move to Fletcher Memorial. "That's where most of the victims are getting treatment,

you see. The doctors give them something, and then we try
to identify them and find their next of kin—"

"Perhaps it's best for these people to remain away from
their next of kin for a while," Haldersen suggested. "Some
meditation in the park—an exploration of the pleasures of
having forgotten—that's all we're doing here." He would
not go to Fletcher Memorial himself except under duress.
As for the others, he felt he could do more for them in
the park than anyone in the hospital could.

The second time the police came, Saturday afternoon
when his group was much larger, they brought a mobile
communications system. "Dr. Bryce of Fletcher Memorial
wants to talk to you," a different lieutenant said.

Haldersen watched the screen come alive. "Hello, Doctor. Worried about me?"

"I'm worried about everyone, Nate. What the hell are
you doing in the park?"

"Founding a new religion, I think."

"You're a sick man. You ought to come back here."

"No, Doctor. I'm not sick any more. I've had my
therapy and I'm fine. It was a beautiful treatment:
selective obliteration, just as I prayed for. The entire
trauma is gone."

Bryce appeared fascinated by that; his frowning expression of official responsibility vanished a moment, giving
place to a look of professional concern. "Interesting," he
said. "We've got people who've forgotten only nouns, and
people who've forgotten who they married, and people
who've forgotten how to play the violin. But you're the
first one who's forgotten a trauma. You still ought to
come back here, though. You aren't the best judge of your
fitness to face the outside environment."

"Oh, but I am," Haldersen said. "I'm doing fine. And
my people need me."

"Your people?"

"Waifs. Strays. The total wipeouts."

"We want those people in the hospital, Nate. We want
to get them back to their families."

"Is that necessarily a good deed? Maybe some of them
can use a spell of isolation from their families. These
people look happy, Dr. Bryce. I've heard there are a lot of
suicides, but not here. We're practicing mutual supportive
therapy. Looking for the joys to be found in oblivion. It
seems to work."

Bryce stared silently out of the screen for a long moment. Then he said impatiently, "All right, have it your own way for now. But I wish you'd stop coming on like Jesus and Freud combined, and leave the park. You're still a sick man, Nate, and the people with you are in serious trouble. I'll talk to you later."

The contact broke. The police, stymied, left.

Haldersen spoke briefly to his people at five o'clock. Then he sent them out as missionaries to collect other victims. "Save as many as you can," he said. "Find those who are in complete despair and get them into the park before they can take their own lives. Explain that the loss of one's past is not the loss of all things."

The disciples went forth. And came back leading those less fortunate than themselves. The group grew to more than one hundred by nightfall. Someone found the extruder again and blew twenty more bubbles as shelters for the night. Haldersen preached his sermon of joy, looking out at the blank eyes, the slack faces of those whose identities had washed away on Wednesday. "Why give up?" he asked them. "Now is your chance to create new lives for yourself. The slate is clean! Choose the direction you will take, define your new selves through the exercise of free will—you are reborn in holy oblivion, all of you. Rest, now, those who have just come to us. And you others, go forth again, seek out the wanderers, the drifters, the lost ones hiding in the corners of the city—"

As he finished, he saw a knot of people bustling toward him from the direction of the South Drive. Fearing trouble, Haldersen went out to meet them; but as he drew close he saw half a dozen disciples, clutching a scruffy, unshaven, terrified little man. They hurled him at Haldersen's feet. The man quivered like a hare ringed by hounds. His eyes glistened; his wedge of a face, sharp-chinned, sharp of cheekbones, was pale.

"It's the one who poisoned the water supply!" someone called. "We found him in a rooming house on Judah Street. With a stack of drugs in his room, and the plans of the water system, and a bunch of computer programs. He admits it. He admits it!"

Haldersen looked down. "Is this true?" he asked. "Are you the one?"

The man nodded.

"What's your name?"

"Won't say. Want a lawyer."

"Kill him now!" a woman shrieked. "Pull his arms and legs off!"

"Kill him!" came an answering cry from the other side of the group. "Kill him!"

The congregation, Haldersen realized, might easily turn into a mob.

He said, "Tell me your name, and I'll protect you. Otherwise I can't be responsible."

"Skinner," the man muttered miserably.

"Skinner. And you contaminated the water supply."

Another nod.

"Why?"

"To get even."

"With whom?"

"Everyone. Everybody."

Classic paranoid. Haldersen felt pity. Not the others; they were calling out for blood.

A tall man bellowed, "Make the bastard drink his own drug!"

"No, kill him! Squash him!"

The voices became more menacing. The angry faces came closer.

"Listen to me," Haldersen called, and his voice cut through the murmurings. "There'll be no killing here tonight."

"What are you going to do, give him to the police?"

"No," said Haldersen. "We'll hold communion together. We'll teach this pitiful man the blessings of oblivion, and then we'll share new joys ourselves. We are human beings. We have the capacity to forgive even the worst of sinners. Where are the memory drugs? Did someone say you had found the memory drugs? Here. Here. Pass it up here. Yes. Brothers, sisters, let us show this dark and twisted soul the nature of redemption. Yes. Yes. Fetch some water, please. Thank you. Here, Skinner. Stand him up, will you? Hold his arms. Keep him from falling down. Wait a second, until I find the proper dose. Yes. Yes. Here, Skinner. Forgiveness. Sweet oblivion."

It was so good to be working again that Mueller didn't want to stop. By early afternoon on Saturday his studio was ready; he had long since worked out the sketches of the first piece; now it was just a matter of time and effort, and he'd have something to show Pete Castine. He worked on far into the evening, setting up his armature and running a few tests of the sound sequences that he proposed to build into the piece. He had some interesting new ideas about the sonic triggers, the devices that would set off the sound effects when the appreciator came within range. Carole had to tell him, finally, that dinner was ready. "I didn't want to interrupt you," she said, "but it looks like I have to, or you won't ever stop."

"Sorry. The creative ecstasy."

"Save some of that energy. There are other ecstasies. The ecstasy of dinner, first."

She had cooked everything herself. Beautiful. He went back to work again afterward, but at half past one in the morning Carole again interrupted him. He was willing to stop, now. He had done an honest day's work, and he was sweaty with the noble sweat of a job well done. Two minutes under the molecular cleanser and the sweat was gone, but the good ache of virtuous fatigue remained. He hadn't felt this way in years.

He woke to Sunday thoughts of unpaid debts.

"The robots are still there," he said. "They won't go away, will they? Even though the whole city's at a standstill, nobody's told the robots to quit."

"Ignore them," Carole said.

"That's what I've been doing. But I can't ignore the debts. Ultimately there'll be a reckoning."

"You're working again, though! You'll have an income coming in."

"Do you know what I owe?" he asked. "Almost a million. If I produced one piece a week for a year, and sold each piece for twenty bigs, I might pay everything off. But I can't work that fast, and the market can't possibly absorb that many Muellers, and Pete certainly can't buy them all for future sale."

He noticed the way Carole's face darkened at the mention of Pete Castine.

He said, "You know what I'll have to do? Go to Caracas, like I was planning before this memory thing started. I can work there, and ship my stuff to Pete. And maybe in two or three years I'll have paid off my debt, a hundred cents on the dollar, and I can start fresh back here. Do you know if that's possible? I mean, if you jump to a debtor sanctuary, are you blackballed for credit forever, even if you pay off what you owe?"

"I don't know," Carole said distantly.

"I'll find that out later. The important thing is that I'm working again, and I've got to go someplace where I can work without being hounded. And then I'll pay everybody off. You'll come with me to Caracas, won't you?"

"Maybe we won't have to go," Carole said.

"But how—"

"You should be working now, shouldn't you?"

He worked, and while he worked he made lists of creditors in his mind, dreaming of the day when every name on every list was crossed off. When he got hungry he emerged from the studio and found Carole sitting gloomily in the living room. Her eyes were red and puffy-lidded.

"What's wrong?" he asked. "You don't want to go to Caracas?"

"Please, Paul—let's not talk about it—"

"I've really got no alternative. I mean, unless we pick one of the other sanctuaries. São Paulo? Spalato?"

"It isn't that, Paul."

"What, then?"

"I'm starting to remember again."

The air went out of him. "Oh," he said.

"I remember November, December, January. The crazy things you were doing, the loans, the financial juggling. And the quarrels we had. They were terrible quarrels."

"Oh."

"The divorce. I remember, Paul. It started coming back last night, but you were so happy I didn't want to say anything. And this morning it's much clearer. You still don't remember any of it?"

"Not a thing past last October."

"I do," she said, shakily. "You hit me, do you know that? You cut my lip. You slammed me against that wall, right over there, and then you threw the Chinese vase at me and it broke."

"Oh. Oh."

She went on, "I remember how good Pete was to me, too. I think I can almost remember marrying him, being his wife. Paul, I'm scared. I feel everything fitting into place in my mind, and it's as scary as if my mind was breaking into pieces. It was so good, Paul, these last few days. It was like being a newlywed with you again. But now all the sour parts are coming back, the hate, the ugliness, it's all alive for me again. And I feel so bad about Pete. The two of us, Friday, shutting him out. He was a real gentleman about it. But the fact is that he saved me when I was going under, and I owe him something for that."

"What do you plan to do?" he asked quietly.

"I think I ought to go back to him. I'm his wife. I've got no right to stay here."

"But I'm not the same man you came to hate," Mueller protested. "I'm the old Paul, the one from last year and before. The man you loved. All the hateful stuff is gone from me."

"Not from me, though. Not now."

They were both silent.

"I think I should go back, Paul."

"Whatever you say."

"I think I should. I wish you all kinds of luck, but I can't stay here. Will it hurt your work if I leave again?"

"I won't know until you do."

She told him three or four more times that she felt she ought to go back to Castine, and then, politely, he suggested that she should go back right now, if that was how she felt, and she did. He spent half an hour wandering around the apartment, which seemed so awfully empty again. He nearly invited one of the dunning robots in for company. Instead, he went back to work. To his surprise, he worked quite well, and in an hour he had ceased thinking about Carole entirely.

Sunday afternoon, Freddy Munson set up a credit transfer and managed to get most of his liquid assets fed into an old account he kept at the Bank of Luna. Toward evening, he went down to the wharf and boarded a three-man hovercraft owned by a fisherman willing to take his chances with the law. They slipped out into the bay without running lights and crossed the bay on a big diagonal, landing some time later a few miles north of Berkeley. Munson found a cab to take him to the Oakland airport, and caught the midnight shuttle to L.A., where, after a lot of fancy talking, he was able to buy his way aboard the next Luna-bound rocket, lifting off at ten o'clock Monday morning. He spent the night in the spaceport terminal. He had taken with him nothing except the clothes he wore; his fine possessions, his paintings, his suits, his Mueller sculptures, and all the rest remained in his apartment, and ultimately would be sold to satisfy the judgments against him. Too bad. He knew that he wouldn't be coming back to Earth again, either, not with a larceny warrant or worse awaiting him. Also too bad. It had been so nice for so long, here, and who needed a memory drug in the water supply? Munson had only one consolation. It was an article of his philosophy that sooner or later, no matter how neatly you organized your life, fate opened a trapdoor underneath your feet and catapulted you into something unknown and unpleasant. Now he knew that it was true, even for him.

Too, too bad. He wondered what his chances were of starting over up there. Did they need stockbrokers on the Moon?

Addressing the citizenry on Monday night, Commander Braskett said, "The committee of public safety is pleased to report that we have come through the worst part of the crisis. As many of you have already discovered, memories are beginning to return. The process of recovery will be more swift for some than others, but great progress has been made. Effective at six A.M. tomorrow, access routes to and from San Francisco will reopen. There will be normal mail service and many businesses will return to normal. Fellow citizens, we have demonstrated once again the real fiber of the American spirit. The Founding Fathers must be smiling down upon us today! How superbly we avoided chaos, and how beautifully we pulled together to help one another in what could have been an hour of turmoil and despair!

"Dr. Bryce requests me to remind you that anyone still suffering severe impairment of memory—especially those experiencing loss of identity, confusion of vital functions, or other disability—should report to the emergency ward at Fletcher Memorial Hospital. Treatment is available there, and computer analysis is at the service of those unable to find their homes and loved ones. I repeat—"

Tim Bryce wished that the good commander hadn't slipped in that plug for the real fiber of the American spirit, especially in view of the necessity to invite the remaining victims to the hospital with his next words. But it would be uncharitable to object. The old spaceman had done a beautiful job all weekend as the Voice of the Crisis, and some patriotic embellishments now were harmless.

The crisis, of course, was nowhere near as close to

being over as Commander Braskett's speech had suggested, but public confidence had to be buoyed.

Bryce had the latest figures. Suicides now totaled 900
since the start of trouble on Wednesday; Sunday had been
an unexpectedly bad day. At least 40,000 people were still
unaccounted for, although they were tracing 1,000 an
hour and getting them back to their families or else into
an intensive-care section. Probably 750,000 more continued to have memory difficulties. Most children had fully
recovered, and many of the women were mending; but
older people, and men in general, had experienced
scarcely any memory recapture. Even those who were
nearly healed had no recall of events of Tuesday and
Wednesday, and probably never would; for large numbers
of people, though, big blocks of the past would have to be
learned from the outside, like history lessons.

Lisa was teaching him their marriage that way.

The trips they had taken—the good times, the bad—the
parties, the friends, the shared dreams—she described
everything, as vividly as she could, and he fastened on
each anecdote, trying to make it a part of himself again.
He knew it was hopeless, really. He'd know the outlines,
never the substance. Yet it was probably the best he could
hope for.

He was so horribly tired, suddenly.

He said to Kamakura, "Is there anything new from the
park yet? That rumor that Haldersen's actually got a
supply of the drug?"

"Seems to be true, Tim. The word is that he and his
friends caught the character who spiked the water supply,
and relieved him of a roomful of various amnesifacients."

"We've got to seize them," Bryce said.

Kamakura shook his head. "Not just yet. Police are
afraid of any actions in the park. They say it's a volatile
situation."

"But if those drugs are loose—"

"Let me worry about it, Tim. Look, why don't you and
Lisa go home for a while? You've been here without a
break since Thursday."

"So have—"

"No. Everybody else has had a breather. Go on, now.
We're over the worst. Relax, get some real sleep, make
some love. Get to know that gorgeous wife of yours again
a little."

Bryce reddened. "I'd rather stay here until I feel I can afford to leave."

Scowling, Kamakura walked away from him to confer with Commander Braskett. Bryce scanned the screens, trying to figure out what was going on in the park. A moment later, Braskett walked over to him.

"Dr. Bryce?"

"What?"

"You're relieved of duty until sundown Tuesday."

"Wait a second—"

"That's an order, Doctor. I'm chairman of the committee of public safety, and I'm telling you to get yourself out of this hospital. You aren't going to disobey an order, are you?"

"Listen, Commander—"

"Out. No mutiny, Bryce. Out! Orders."

Bryce tried to protest, but he was too weary to put up much of a fight. By noon, he was on his way home, soupy-headed with fatigue. Lisa drove. He sat quite still, struggling to remember details of his marriage. Nothing came.

She put him to bed. He wasn't sure how long he slept; but then he felt her against him, warm, satin-smooth.

"Hello," she said. "Remember me?"

"Yes," he lied gratefully. "Oh, yes, yes, yes!"

Working right through the night, Mueller finished his armature by dawn on Monday. He slept a while, and in early afternoon began to paint the inner strips of loud-speakers on: a thousand speakers to the inch, no more than a few molecules thick, from which the sounds of his sculpture would issue in resonant fullness. When that was done, he paused to contemplate the needs of his sculpture's superstructure, and by seven that night was ready to move to the next phase. The demons of creativity possessed him; he saw no reason to eat and scarcely any to sleep.

At eight, just as he was getting up momentum for the long night's work, he heard a knock at the door. Carole's signal. He had disconnected the doorbell, and robots didn't have the sense to knock. Uneasily, he went to the door. She was there.

"So?" he said.

"So I came back. So it starts all over."

"What's going on?"

"Can I come in?" she asked.

"I suppose. I'm working, but come in."

She said, "I talked it all over with Pete. We both decided I ought to go back to you."

'You aren't much for consistency, are you?" he asked.

"I have to take things as they happen. When I lost my memory, I came to you. When I remembered things again, I felt I ought to leave. I didn't *want* to leave. I felt I *ought* to leave. There's a difference."

"Really," he said.

"Really. I went to Pete, but I didn't want to be with him. I wanted to be here."

"I hit you and made your lip bleed. I threw the Ming vase at you."

"It wasn't Ming, it was K'ang-hsi."

"Pardon me. My memory still isn't so good. Anyway, I did terrible things to you, and you hated me enough to want a divorce. So why come back?"

"You were right, yesterday. You aren't the man I came to hate. You're the old Paul."

"And if my memory of the past nine months returns?"

"Even so," she said. "People change. You've been through hell and come out the other side. You're working again. You aren't sullen and nasty and confused. We'll go to Caracas, or wherever you want, and you'll do your work and pay your debts, just as you said yesterday."

"And Pete?"

"He'll arrange an annulment. He's being swell about it."

"Good old Pete," Mueller said. He shook his head. "How long will the neat happy ending last, Carole? If you think there's a chance you'll be bouncing back in the other direction by Wednesday, say so now. I'd rather not get involved again, in that case."

"No chance. None."

"Unless I throw the Ch'ien-lung vase at you."

"K'ang-hsi," she said.

"Yes. K'ang-hsi." He managed to grin. Suddenly he felt the accumulated fatigue of these days register all at once. "I've been working too hard," he said. "An orgy of creativity to make up for lost time. Let's go for a walk."

"Fine," she said.

They went out, just as a dunning robot was arriving. "Top of the evening to you, sir," Mueller said.

"Mr. Mueller, I represent the accounts receivable department of the Acme Brass and—"

"See my attorney," he said.

Fog was rolling in off the sea now. There were no stars. The downtown lights were invisible. He and Carole walked west, toward the park. He felt strangely light-headed, not entirely from lack of sleep. Reality and dream had merged; these were unusual days. They entered the park from the Panhandle and strolled toward the museum area, arm in arm, saying nothing much to one another. As they passed the conservatory Mueller became aware of a crowd up ahead, thousands of people staring in the direction of the music shell. "What do you think is going on?" Carole asked. Mueller shrugged. They edged through the crowd.

Ten minutes later they were close enough to see the stage. A tall, thin, wild-looking man with unruly yellow hair was on the stage. Beside him was a small, scrawny man in ragged clothing, and there were a dozen others flanking them, carrying ceramic bowls.

"What's happening?" Mueller asked someone in the crowd.

"Religious ceremony."

"Eh?"

"New religion. Church of Oblivion. That's the head prophet up there. You haven't heard about it yet?"

"Not a thing."

"Started around Friday. You see that ratty-looking character next to the prophet?"

"Yes."

"He's the one that put the stuff in the water supply. He confessed and they made him drink his own drug. Now he doesn't remember a thing, and he's the assistant prophet. Craziest damn stuff!"

"And what are they doing up there?"

"They've got the drug in those bowls. They drink and forget some more. They drink and forget some more."

The gathering fog absorbed the sounds of those on the stage. Mueller strained to listen. He saw the bright eyes of fanaticism; the alleged contaminator of the water looked positively radiant. Words drifted out into the night.

"Brothers and sisters ... the joy, the sweetness of forgetting ... come up here with us, take communion with us ... oblivion ... redemption ... even for the most wicked ... forget ... forget ..."

They were passing the bowls around on stage, drinking, smiling. People were going up to receive the communion, taking a bowl, sipping, nodding happily. Toward the rear of the stage the bowls were being refilled by three sober-looking functionaries.

Mueller felt a chill. He suspected that what had been born in this park during this week would endure, somehow, long after the crisis of San Francisco had become part of history; and it seemed to him that something new and frightening had been loosed upon the land.

"Take . . . drink . . . forget . . ." the prophet cried.

And the worshipers cried, *"Take . . . drink . . . forget . . ."*

The bowls were passed.

"What's it all *about?*" Carole whispered.

"Take . . . drink . . . forget . . ."

"Take . . . drink . . . forget . . ."

"Blessed is sweet oblivion."

"Blessed is sweet oblivion."

"Sweet it is to lay down the burden of one's soul."

"Sweet it is to lay down the burden of one's soul."

"Joyous it is to begin anew."

"Joyous it is to begin anew."

The fog was deepening. Mueller could barely see the aquarium building just across the way. He clasped his hand tightly around Carole's and began to think about getting out of the park.

He had to admit, though, that these people might have hit on something true. Was he not better off for having taken a chemical into his bloodstream, and thereby shedding a portion of his past? Yes, of course. And yet—to mutilate one's mind this way, deliberately, happily, to drink deep of oblivion—

"Blessed are those who are able to forget," the prophet said.

"Blessed are those who are able to forget," the crowd roared in responese.

"Blessed are those who are able to forget," Mueller heard his own voice cry. And he began to tremble. And he felt sudden fear: He sensed the power of this strange new movement, the gathering strength of the prophet's appeal to unreason. It was time for a new religion, maybe, a cult that offered emancipation from all inner burdens. They would synthesize this drug and turn it out by the ton,

Mueller thought, and repeatedly dose cities with it, so that everyone could be converted, so that everyone might taste the joys of oblivion. No one will be able to stop them. After a while, no one will *want* to stop them. And so we'll go on, drinking deep, until we're washed clean of all pain and all sorrow, of all sad recollection, we'll sip a cup of kindness and part with auld lang syne, we'll give up the griefs we carry around, and we'll give up everything else, identity, soul, self, mind. We will drink sweet oblivion. Mueller shivered. Turning suddenly, tugging roughly at Carole's arm, he pushed through the joyful worshiping crowd, and hunted somberly in the fogwrapped night, trying to find some way out of the park.

To the Dark Star

We came to the dark star, the microcephalon and the adapted girl, and I, and our struggle began. A poorly assorted lot we were, to begin with. The microcephalon hailed from Quendar IV, where they grow their people with greasy gray skins, looming shoulders, and virtually no heads at all. He—it—was wholly alien, at least. The girl was not, and so I hated her.

She came from a world in the Procyon system, where the air was more or less Earth-type, but the gravity was double ours. There were other differences, too. She was thick through the shoulders, thick through the waist, a block of flesh. The genetic surgeons had begun with human raw material, but they had transformed it into something nearly as alien as the microcephalon. Nearly.

We were a scientific team, so they said. Sent out to observe the last moments of a dying star. A great interstellar effort. Pick three specialists at random, put them in a ship, hurl them halfway across the universe to observe what man had never observed before. A fine idea. Noble. Inspiring. We knew our subject well. We were ideal.

But we felt no urge to cooperate, because we hated one another.

The adapted girl—Miranda—was at the controls the day that the dark star actually came into sight. She spent hours studying it before she deigned to let us know that we were at our destination. Then she buzzed us out of our quarters.

I entered the scanning room. Miranda's muscular bulk overflowed the glossy chair before the main screen. The microcephalon stood beside her, a squat figure on a tripod-like arrangement of bony legs, the great shoulders

128

hunched and virtually concealing the tiny cupola of the head. There was no real reason why an organism's brain *had* to be in its skull, and not safely tucked away in the thorax; but I had never grown accustomed to the sight of the creature. I fear I have little tolerance for aliens.

"Look," Miranda said, and the screen glowed.

The dark star hung in dead center, at a distance of perhaps eight light-days—as close as we dared to come. It was not quite dead, and not quite dark. I stared in awe. It was a huge thing, some four solar masses, the imposing remnant of a gigantic star. On the screen there glowed what looked like an enormous lava field. Islands of ash and slag the size of worlds drifted in a sea of molten and glowing magma. A dull red illumination burnished the screen. Black against crimson, the ruined star still throbbed with ancient power. In the depths of that monstrous slag-heap compressed nuclei groaned and gasped. Once the radiance of this star had lit a solar system; but I did not dare think of the billions of years that had passed since then, nor of the possible civilizations that had hailed the source of all light and warmth before the catastrophe.

Miranda said, "I've picked up the thermals already. The surface temperature averages about nine hundred degrees. There's no chance of the landing."

I scowled at her. "What good is the *average* temperature? Get a specific. One of those islands—"

"The ash masses are radiating at two hundred and fifty degrees. The interstices go from one thousand degrees on up. Everything works out to a mean of nine hundred degrees, and you'd melt in an instant if you went down there. You're welcome to go, brother. With my blessing."

"I didn't say—"

"You implied that there'd be a safe place to land on that fireball," Miranda snapped. Her voice was a basso boom; there was plenty of resonance space in that vast chest of hers. "You snidely cast doubt on my ability to—"

"We will use the crawler to make our inspection," said the microcephalon in its reasonable way. "There never was any plan to make a physical landing on the star."

Miranda subsided. I stared in awe at the sight that filled our screen.

A star takes a long time to die, and the relict I viewed impressed me with its colossal age. It had blazed for billions of years, until the hydrogen that was its fuel had at last been exhausted, and its thermonuclear furnace started to sputter and go out. A star has defenses against growing cold; as its fuel supply dwindles, it begins to contract, raising its density and converting gravitational potential energy into thermal energy. It takes on new life; now a white dwarf, with a density of tons per cubic inch, it burns in a stable way until at last it grows dark.

We have studied white dwarfs for centuries, and we know their secrets—so we think. A cup of matter from a white dwarf now orbits the observatory on Pluto for our further illumination.

But the star of our screen was different.

It had once been a large star—greater than the Chandrasekhar limit, 1.2 solar masses. Thus it was not content to shrink step by step to the status of a white dwarf. The stellar core grew so dense that catastrophe came before stability; when it had converted all its hydrogen to iron-56, it fell into catastrophic collapse and went supernova. A shock wave ran through the core, converting the kinetic energy of collapse into heat. Neutrinos spewed outward; the envelope of the star reached temperatures upwards of 200 billion degrees; thermal energy became intense radiation, streaming away from the agonized star and shedding the luminosity of a galaxy for a brief, fitful moment.

What we beheld now was the core left behind by the supernova explosion. Even after that awesome fury, what was intact was of great mass. The shattered hulk had been cooling for eons, cooling toward the final death. For a small star, that death would be the simple death of coldness: the ultimate burnout, the black dwarf drifting through the void like a hideous mound of ash, lightless, without warmth. But this, our stellar core, was still beyond the Chandrasekhar limit. A special death was reserved for it, a weird and improbable death.

And that was why we had come to watch it perish, the microcephalon and the adapted girl and I.

I parked our small vessel in an orbit that gave the dark star plenty of room. Miranda busied herself with her measurements and computations. The microcephalon had more abstruse things to do. The work was well divided; we each had our chores. The expense of sending a ship so great a distance had necessarily limited the size of the expedition. Three of us: a representative of the basic human stock, a representative of the adapted colonists, a representative of the race of microcephalons, the Quendar people, the only other intelligent beings in the known universe.

Three dedicated scientists. And therefore three who would live in serene harmony during the course of the work, since as everyone knows scientists have no emotions and think only of their professional mysteries. As everyone knows. When did that myth start to circulate, anyway?

I said to Miranda, "Where are the figures for radial oscillation?"

She replied, "See my report. It'll be published early next year in—"

"Damn you, are you doing that deliberately? I need those figures now!"

"Give me your totals on the mass-density curve, then."

"They aren't ready. All I've got is raw data."

"That's a lie! The computer's been running for days! I've seen it," she boomed at me.

I was ready to leap at her throat. It would have been a mighty battle; her 300-pound body was not trained for personal combat as mine was, but she had all the advantages of strength and size. Could I club her in some vital place before she broke me in half? I weighed my options.

Then the microcephalon appeared and made peace once more, with a few feather-soft words.

Only the alien among us seemed to conform at all to the stereotype of that emotionless abstraction, "the scientist." It was not true, of course; for all we could tell, the microcephalon seethed with jealousies and lusts and angers, but we had no clue to their outward manifestation. Its voice was as flat as a vocoder transmission. The creature moved peacefully among us, the mediator between Miranda and me. I despised it for its mask of tranquility. I suspected, too, that the microcephalon loathed the two of us for our willingness to vent our emotions, and took a sadistic pleasure from asserting superiority by calming us.

We returned to our research. We still had some time before the last collapse of the dark star.

It had cooled nearly to death. Now there was still some thermonuclear activity within that bizarre core, enough to keep the star too warm for an actual landing. It was radiating primarily in the optical band of the spectrum, and by stellar standards its temperature was nil, but for us it would be like prowling the heart of a live volcano.

Finding the star had been a chore. Its luminosity was so low that it could not be detected optically at a greater distance than a light-month or so; it had been spotted by a satellite-borne X-ray telescope that had detected the emanations of the degenerate neutron gas of the core. Now we gathered round and performed our functions of measurement. We recorded things like neutron drip and electron capture. We computed the time remaining before the final collapse. Where necessary, we collaborated; most of the time we went our separate ways. The tension aboard ship was nasty. Miranda went out of her way to provoke me. And, though I like to think that I was beyond and above her beastliness, I have to confess that I matched her, obstruction for obstruction. Our alien companion never made any overt attempt to annoy us; but indirect aggression can be maddening in close quarters, and the microcephalon's benign indifference to us was as potent a force for dissonance as Miranda's outright shrewishness or my own deliberately mulish responses.

The star hung in our viewscreen, bubbling with vitality that belied its dying state. The islands of slag, thousands of miles in diameter, broke free and drifted at random on the sea of inner flame. Now and then spouting eruptions of stripped particles came heaving up out of the core. Our figures showed that the final collapse was drawing near, and that meant that an awkward choice was upon us. Someone was going to have to monitor the last moments of the dark star. The risks were high. It could be fatal.

None of us mentioned that ultimate responsibility.

We moved toward the climax of our work. Miranda continued to annoy me in every way, sheerly for the devilishness of it. How I hated her! We had begun this voyage coolly, with nothing dividing us but professional jealousy. But the months of proximity had turned our quarrel into a personal feud. The mere sight of her maddened me, and I'm sure she reacted the same way. She devoted her energies to an immature attempt to trouble me. Lately she took to walking around the ship in the nude, I suspect trying to stir some spark of sexual feeling in me that she could douse with a blunt, mocking refusal. The trouble was that I could feel no desire whatever for a grotesque adapted creature like Miranda, a mound of muscle and bone twice my size. The sight of her massive udders and monumental buttocks stirred nothing in me but disgust.

The witch! Was it desire she was trying to kindle by exposing herself that way, or loathing? Either way, she had me. She must have known that.

In our third month in orbit around the dark star, the microcephalon announced, "The coordinates show an approach to the Schwarzschild radius. It is time to send our vehicle to the surface of the star."

"Which one of us rides monitor?" I asked.

Miranda's beefy hand shot out at me. "You do."

"I think you're better equipped to make the observations," I told her sweetly.

"Thank you, no."

"We must draw lots," said the microcephalon.

"Unfair," said Miranda. She glared at me. "He'll do something to rig the odds. I couldn't trust him."

"How else can we choose?" the alien asked.

"We can vote," I suggested. "I nominate Miranda."

"I nominate him," she snapped.

The microcephalon put his ropy tentacles across the tiny nodule of skull between his shoulders. "Since I do not choose to nominate myself," he said mildly, "it falls to me to make a deciding choice between the two of you. I refuse the responsibility. Another method must be found."

We let the matter drop for the moment. We still had a few more days before the critical time was at hand.

With all my heart I wished Miranda into the monitor capsule. It would mean at best her death, at worst a sober muting of her abrasive personality, if she were the one who sat in vicariously on the throes of the dark star. I was willing to stop at nothing to give her that remarkable and demolishing experience.

What was going to happen to our star may sound strange to a layman; but the theory had been outlined by Einstein and Schwarzschild a thousand years ago, and had been confirmed many times, though never until our expedition had it been observed at close range. When matter reaches a sufficiently high density, it can force the local curvature of space to close around itself, forming a pocket isolated from the rest of the universe. A collapsing supernova core creates just such a Schwarzschild singularity. After it has cooled to near-zero temperature, a core of the proper Chandrasekhar mass undergoes a violent collapse to zero volume, simultaneously attaining an infinite density.

In a way, it swallows itself and vanishes from this universe—for how could the fabric of the continuum tolerate a point of infinite density and zero volume?

Such collapses are rare. Most stars come to a state of cold equilibrium and remain there. We were on the threshold of a singularity, and we were in a position to put an observer vehicle right on the surface of the cold star, sending back an exact description of the events up until the final moment when the collapsing core broke through the walls of the universe and disappeared.

Someone had to ride gain on the equipment, though. Which mean, in effect, vicariously participating in the death of the star. We had learned in other cases that it becomes difficult for the monitor to distinguish between reality and effect; he accepts the sensory percepts from the distant pickup as his own experience. A kind of psychic backlash results; often, an unwary brain is burned out entirely.

What impact would the direct experience of being crushed out of existence in a singularity have on a monitoring observer?

I was eager to find out. But not with myself as the sacrificial victim.

I cast about for some way to get Miranda into that capsule. She, of course, was doing the same for me. It was she who made her move first by attempting to drug me into compliance.

What drug she used, I have no idea. Her people are fond of the nonaddictive hallucinogens, which help them break the monotony of their stark, oversized world. Somehow Miranda interfered with the programming of my food supply and introduced one of her pet alkaloids. I began to feel the effects an hour after I had eaten. I walked to the screen to study the surging mass of the dark star—much changed from its appearance of only a few months before—and as I looked, the image in the screen began to swirl and melt, and tongues of flame did an eerie dance along the horizons of the star.

I clung to the rail. Sweat broke from my pores. Was the ship liquefying? The floor heaved and bucked beneath me. I looked at the back of my hand and saw continents of ash set in a grouting of fiery magma.

Miranda stood behind me. "Come with me to the capsule," she murmured. "The monitor's ready for launching now. You'll find it wonderful to see the last moments."

Lurching after her, I padded through the strangely altered ship. Miranda's adapted form was even more alien than usual; her musculature rippled and flowed, her golden hair held all the colors of the spectrum, her flesh was oddly puckered and cratered, with wiry filaments emerging from the skin. I felt quite calm about entering the capsule. She slid back the hatch, revealing the gleaming console of the panel within, and I began to enter, and then suddenly the hallucination deepened and I saw in the darkness of the capsule a devil beyond all imagination.

I dropped to the floor and lay there twitching.

Miranda seized me. To her I was no more than a doll. She lifted me, began to thrust me into the capsule. Perspiration soaked me. Reality returned. I slipped from her grasp and wriggled away, rolling toward the bulkhead. Like a beast of primordial forests she came ponderously after me.

"No," I said. "I won't go."

She halted. Her face twisted in anger, and she turned away from me in defeat. I lay panting and quivering until my mind was purged of phantoms. It had been close.

It was my turn a short while later. Fight force with force, I told myself. I could not risk more of Miranda's treachery. Time was running short.

From our surgical kit I took a hypnoprobe used for anesthesia, and rigged it in series with one of Miranda's telescope antennae. Programming it for induction of docility, I left it to go to work on her. When she made her observations, the hypnoprobe would purr its siren song of sinister coaxing, and—perhaps—Miranda would bend to my wishes.

It did not work.

I watched her going to her telescopes. I saw her

broad-beamed form settling in place. In my mind I heard the hypnoprobe's gentle whisper, as I knew it must sound to Miranda. It was telling her to relax, to obey. "The capsule ... get into the capsule ... you will monitor the crawler ... you ... you ... you will do it. ..."

I waited for her to arise and move like a sleepwalker to the waiting capsule. Her tawny body was motionless. Muscles rippled beneath that obscenely bare flesh. The probe had her! Yes! It was getting to her!

No.

She clawed at the telescope as though it were a steel-tipped wasp drilling for her brain. The barrel recoiled, and she pushed herself away from it, whirling around. Her eyes glowed with rage. Her enormous body reared up before me. She seemed half berserk. The probe had had some effect on her; I could see her dizzied strides, and knew that she was awry. But it had not been potent enough. Something within that adapted brain of hers gave her the strength to fight off the murky shroud of hypnotism.

"You did that!" she roared. "You gimmicked the telescope, didn't you?"

"I don't know what you mean, Miranda."

"Liar! Fraud! Sneak!"

"Calm down. You're rocking us out of orbit."

"I'll rock all I want! What was that thing that had its fingers in my brain? You put it there! What was it, the hypnoprobe you used?"

"Yes," I admitted coolly. "And what was it you put into my food? Which hallucinogen?"

"It didn't work."

"Neither did my hypnoprobe. Miranda, someone's got to get into that capsule. In a few hours we'll be at the critical point. We don't dare come back without the essential observations. Make the sacrifice."

"For *you?*"

"For science," I said, appealing to that noble abstraction.

I got the horselaugh I deserved. Then Miranda strode toward me. She had recovered her coordination in full, now, and it seemed as though she were planning to thrust me into the capsule by main force. Her ponderous arms enfolded me. The stink of her thickened hide made me retch. I felt ribs creaking within me. I hammered at her body, searching for the pressure points that would drop her in a felled heap. We punished each other cruelly, grunting back and forth across the cabin. It was a fierce contest of skill against mass. She would not fall, and I would not crush.

The toneless buzz of the microcephalon said, "Release each other. The collapsing star is nearing its Schwarzschild radius. We must act now."

Miranda's arms slipped away from me. I stepped back, glowering at her, to suck breath into my battered body. Livid bruises were appearing on her skin. We had come to a mutual awareness of mutual strength; but the capsule still was empty. Hatred hovered like a globe of ball lightning between us. The gray, greasy alien creature stood to one side.

I would not care to guess which of us had the idea first, Miranda or I. But we moved swiftly. The microcephalon scarcely murmured a word of protest as we hustled it down the passage and into the room that held the capsule. Miranda was smiling. I felt relief. She held the alien tight while I opened the hatch, and then she thrust it through. We dogged the hatch together.

"Launch the crawler," she said.

I nodded and went to the controls. Like a dart from a blowgun the crawler housing was expelled from our ship and journeyed under high acceleration to the surface of the dark star. It contained a compact vehicle with sturdy jointed legs, controlled by remote pickup from the observation capsule aboard ship. As the observer moved arms and feet within the control harnesses, servo relays actuated the hydraulic pistons in the crawler, eight light-days away. It moved in parallel response, clambering over the slag-heaps of a solar surface that no organic life could endure.

The microcephalon operated the crawler with skill. We watched through the shielded video pickups, getting a close-range view of that inferno. Even a cold sun is more terrifyingly hot than any planet of man.

The signals coming from the star altered with each moment, as the full force of the red-shift gripped the fading light. Something unutterably strange was taking place down there; and the mind of our microcephalon was rooted to the scene. Tidal gravitational forces lashed the star. The crawler was lifted, heaved, compressed, subjected to strains that slowly ripped it apart. The alien witnessed it all, and dictated an account of what he saw, slowly, methodically, without a flicker of fear.

The singularity approached The tidal forces aspired toward infinity. The microcephalon sounded bewildered at last as it attempted to describe the topological phenomena that no eye had seen before. Infinite density, zero volume—how did the mind comprehend it? The crawler was contorted into an inconceivable shape; and yet its sensors obstinately continued to relay data, filtered through the mind of the microcephalon and into our computer banks.

Then came silence. Our screens went dead. The unthinkable had at last occurred, and the dark star had passed within the radius of singularity. It had collapsed into oblivion, taking with it the crawler. To the alien in the observation capsule aboard our ship, it was as though he too had vanished into that pocket of hyperspace that passed all understanding.

I looked toward the heavens. The dark star was gone. Our detectors picked up the outpouring of energy that marked its annihilation. We were buffeted briefly on the wave of force that ripped outward from the place where the star had been, and then all was calm.

Miranda and I exchanged glances.

"Let the microcephalon out," I said.

She opened the hatch. The alien sat quite calmly at the control console. It did not speak. Miranda assisted it from the capsule. Its eyes were expressionless; but they had never shown anything, anyway.

We are on our way back to the worlds of our galaxy, now. The mission has been accomplished. We have relayed priceless and unique data.

The microcephalon has not spoken since we removed it from the capsule. I do not believe it will speak again.

Miranda and I perform our chores in harmony. The hostility between us is gone. We are partners in crime, now edgy with guilt that we do not admit to one another. We tend our shipmate with loving care.

Someone had to make the observations, after all. There were no volunteers. The situation called for force, or the deadlock would never have been broken.

But Miranda and I hated each other, you say? Why, then, should we cooperate?

We both are humans, Miranda and I. The microcephalon is not. In the end, that made the difference. In the last analysis, Miranda and I decided that we humans must stick together. There are ties that bind.

We speed onward toward civilization.

She smiles at me. I do not find her hateful now. The microcephalon is silent.

The Fangs of the Trees

From the plantation house atop the gray, needle-sharp spire of Dolan's Hill, Zen Holbrook could see everything that mattered: the groves of juice-trees in the broad valley, the quick rushing stream where his niece Naomi liked to bathe, the wide, sluggish lake beyond. He could also see the zone of suspected infection in Sector C at the north end of the valley, where—or was it just his imagination?—the lustrous blue leaves of the juice-trees already seemed flecked with the orange of the rust disease.

If his world started to end, that was where the end would start.

He stood by the clear curved window of the info center at the top of the house. It was early morning; two pale moons still hung in a dawn-streaked sky, but the sun was coming up out of the hill country. Naomi was already up and out, cavorting in the stream. Before Holbrook left the house each morning, he ran a check on the whole plantation. Scanners and sensors offered him remote pickups from every key point out there. Hunching forward, Holbrook ran thick-fingered hands over the command nodes and made the relay screens flanking the window light up. He owned forty thousand acres of juice-trees—a fortune in juice, though his own equity was small and the notes he had given were immense. His kingdom. His empire. He scanned Sector C, his favorite. Yes. The screen showed long rows of trees, fifty feet high, shifting their ropy limbs restlessly. This was the endangered zone, the threatened sector. Holbrook peered intently at the leaves of the trees. Going rusty yet? The lab reports would come in a little later. He studied the trees, saw the gleam of their eyes, the sheen of their fangs. Some good trees in that sector. Alert, keen, good producers.

His pet trees. He liked to play a little game with himself, pretending the trees had personalities, names, identities. It didn't take much pretending.

Holbrook turned on the audio. "Morning, Caesar," he said. "Alcibiades. Hector. Good morning, Plato."

The trees knew their names. In response to his greeting their limbs swayed as though a gale were sweeping through the grove. Holbrook saw the fruit, almost ripe, long and swollen and heavy with the hallucinogenic juice. The eyes of the trees—glittering scaly plates embedded in crisscrossing rows on their trunks—flickered and turned, searching for him. "I'm not in the grove, Plato." Holbrook said. "I'm still in the plantation house. I'll be down soon. It's a gorgeous morning, isn't it?"

Out of the musty darkness at ground level came the long, raw pink snout of a juice-stealer, jutting uncertainly from a heap of cast-off leaves. In distaste Holbrook watched the audacious little rodent cross the floor of the grove in four quick bounds and leap onto Caesar's massive trunk, clambering cleverly upward between the big tree's eyes. Caesar's limbs fluttered angrily, but he could not locate the little pest. The juice-stealer vanished in the leaves and reappeared thirty feet higher, moving now in the level where Caesar carried his fruit. The beast's snout twitched. The juice-stealer reared back on its four hind limbs and got ready to suck eight dollars' worth of dreams from a nearly ripe fruit.

From Alcibiades' crown emerged the thin, sinuous serpentine form of a grasping tendril. Whiplash-fast it crossed the interval between Alcibiades and Caesar and snapped into place around the juice-stealer. The animal had time only to whimper in the first realization that it had been caught before the tendril choked the life from it. On a high arc the tendril returned to Alcibiades' crown; the gaping mouth of the tree came clearly into view as the leaves parted; the fangs parted; the tendril uncoiled; and the body of the juice-stealer dropped into the tree's maw. Alicibiades gave a wriggle of pleasure: a mincing, camping quiver of his leaves, arch and coy, self-congratulations for his quick reflexes, which had brought him so tasty a morsel. He was a clever tree, and a handsome one, and very pleased with himself. Forgivable vanity, Holbrook thought. You're a good tree, Alcibiades. All the trees in Sector C are good trees. What if you have the rust,

Alcibiades? What becomes of your shining leaves and sleek limbs if I have to burn you out of the grove?

"Nice going," he said. "I like to see you wide awake like that."

Alcibiades went on wriggling. Socrates, four trees diagonally down the row, pulled his limbs tightly together in what Holbrook knew was a gesture of displeasure, a grumpy harrumph. Not all the trees cared for Alcibiades' vanity, his preening, his quickness.

Suddenly Holbrook could not bear to watch Sector C any longer. He jammed down on the command nodes and switched to Sector K, the new grove, down at the southern end of the valley. The trees here had no names and would not get any. Holbrook had decided long ago that it was a silly affectation to regard the trees as though they were friends or pets. They were income-producing property. It was a mistake to get this involved with them—as he realized more clearly now that some of his oldest friends were threatened by the rust that was sweeping from world to world to blight the juice-tree plantations.

With more detachment he scanned Sector K.

Think of them as trees, he told himself. Not animals. Not people. *Trees.* Long tap roots, going sixty feet down into the chalky soil, pulling up nutrients. They cannot move from place to place. They photosynthesize. They blossom and are pollinated and produce bulging phallic fruit loaded with weird alkaloids that cast interesting shadows in the minds of men. Trees. Trees. Trees.

But they have eyes and teeth and mouths. They have prehensile limbs. They can think. They can react. They have souls. When pushed to it, they can cry out. They are adapted for preying on small animals. They digest meat. Some of them prefer lamb to beef. Some are thoughtful and solemn; some volatile and jumpy; some placid, almost bovine. Though each tree is bisexual, some are plainly male by personality, some female, some ambivalent. Souls. Personalities.

Trees.

The nameless trees of Sector K tempted him to commit the sin of involvement. That fat one could be Buddha, and there's Abe Lincoln, and you, you're William the Conqueror, and—

Trees.

He had made the effort and succeeded. Coolly he surveyed the grove, making sure there had been no damage during the night from prowling beasts, checking on the ripening fruit, reading the info that came from the sap sensors, the monitors that watched sugar levels, fermentation stages, manganese intake, all the intricately balanced life processes on which the output of the plantation depended. Holbrook handled practically everything himself. He had a staff of three human overseers and three dozen robots; the rest was done by telemetry, and usually all went smoothly. Usually. Properly guarded, coddled, and nourished, the trees produced their fruit three seasons a year; Holbrook marketed the goods at the pickup station near the coastal spaceport, where the juice was processed and shipped to Earth. Holbrook had no part in that; he was simply a fruit producer. He had been here ten years and had no plans for doing anything else. It was a quiet life, a lonely life, but it was the life he had chosen.

He swung the scanners from sector to sector, until he had assured himself that all was well throughout the plantation. On his final swing he cut to the stream and caught Naomi just as she was coming out from her swim. She scrambled to a rocky ledge overhanging the swirling water and shook out her long, straight, silken golden hair. Her back was to the scanner. With pleasure Holbrook watched the rippling of her slender muscles. Her spine was clearly outlined by shadow; sunlight danced across the narrowness of her waist, the sudden flare of her hips, the taut mounds of her buttocks. She was fifteen; she was spending a month of her summer vacation with Uncle Zen; she was having the time of her life among the juice-trees. Her father was Holbrook's older brother. Holbrook had seen Naomi only twice before, once when she was a baby, once when she was about six. He had been a little uneasy about having her come here, since he knew nothing about children and in any case had no great hunger for company. But he had not refused his brother's request. Nor was she a child. She turned, now, and his screens gave him apple-round breasts and flat belly and deep-socketed navel and strong, sleek thighs. Fifteen. No child. A woman. She was unselfconscious about her nudity, swimming like this every morning; she knew there were scanners. Holbrook was not easy about watching her.

Should I look? Not really proper. The sight of her roiled him suspiciously. What the hell: I'm her uncle. A muscle twitched in his cheek. He told himself that the only emotions he felt when he saw her this way were pleasure and pride that his brother had created something so lovely. Only admiration; that was all he let himself feel. She was tanned, honey-colored, with islands of pink and gold. She seemed to give off a radiance more brilliant than that of the early sun. Holbrook clenched the command node. I've lived too long alone. My niece. My niece. Just a kid. Fifteen. Lovely. He closed his eyes, opened them slit-wide, chewed his lip. Come on, Naoimi, cover yourself up!

When she put her shorts and halter on, it was like a solar eclipse. Holbrook cut off the info center and went down through the plantation house, grabbing a couple of breakfast capsules on his way. A gleaming little bug rolled from the garage; he jumped into it and rode out to give her her morning hello.

She was still near the stream, playing with a kitten-sized many-legged furry thing that was twined around an angular little shrub. "Look at this, Zen! she called to him. "Is it a cat or a caterpillar?"

"Get away from it!" he yelled with such vehemence that she jumped back in shock. His needler was already out, and his finger on the firing stud. The small animal, unconcerned, continued to twist legs about branches.

Close against him, Naomi gripped his arm and said huskily, "Don't kill it, Zen. Is it dangerous?"

"I don't know."

"Please don't kill it."

"Rule of thumb on this planet," he said. "Anything with a backbone and more than a dozen legs is probably deadly."

"*Probably!*" Mockingly.

"We still don't know every animal here. That's one I've never seen before, Naomi."

"It's too cute to be deadly. Won't you put the needler away?"

He holstered it and went close to the beast. No claws, small teeth, weak body. Bad signs: a critter like that had no visible means of support, so the odds were good that it hid a venomous sting in its furry little tail. Most of the various many-leggers here did. Holbrook snatched up a yard-long twig and tentatively poked it toward the animal's midsection.

Fast response. A hiss and a snarl and the rear end coming around, *wham!* and a wicked-looking stinger slamming into the bark of the twig. When the tail pulled back, a few drops of a reddish fluid trickled down the twig. Holbrook stepped away; the animal eyed him warily and seemed to be begging him to come within striking range.

"Cuddly," Holbrook said. "Cute. Naomi, don't you want to live to be sweet sixteen?"

She was standing there looking pale, shaken, almost stunned by the ferocity of the little beast's attack. "It seemed so gentle," she said. "Almost tame."

He turned the needler aperture to fine and gave the animal a quick burn through the head. It dropped from the shrub and curled up and did not move again. Naomi stood with her head averted. Holbrook let his arm slide about her shoulders.

"I'm sorry, honey," he said. "I didn't want to kill your little friend. But another minute and he'd have killed you. Count the legs when you play with wildlife here. I told you that. Count the legs."

She nodded. It would be a useful lesson for her in not trusting to appearances. Cuddly is as cuddly does. Holbrook scuffed at the coppery-green turf and thought for a moment about what it was like to be fifteen and awakening to the dirty truths of the universe. Very gently he said, "Let's go visit Plato, eh?"

Naomi brightened at once. The other side of being fifteen: you have resilience.

They parked the bug just outside the Sector C grove and went in on foot. The trees didn't like motorized vehicles moving among them; they were connected only a few inches below the loam of the grove floor by a carpet of mazy filaments that had some neurological function for them, and though the weight of a human didn't register on them, a bug riding down a grove would wrench a chorus of screams from the trees. Naomi went barefoot. Holbrook, beside her, wore knee boots. He felt impossibly big and lumpy when he was with her; he was hulking enough as it was, but her litheness made it worse by contrast.

She played his game with the trees. He had introduced her to all of them, and now she skipped along, giving her morning greeting to Alcibiades and Hector, to Seneca, to

Henry the Eighth and Thomas Jefferson and King Tut.
Naomi knew all the trees as well as he did, perhaps better;
and they knew her. As she moved among them they rippled
and twittered and groomed themselves, every one of them
holding itself tall and arraying its limbs and branches in
comely fashion; even dour old Socrates, lopsided and
stumpy, seemed to be trying to show off. Naomi went to
the big gray storage box in midgrove where the robots left
chunks of meat each night, and hauled out some snacks
for her pets. Cubes of red, raw flesh; she filled her arms
with the bloody gobbets and danced gaily around the
grove, tossing them to her favorites. Nymph in thy
orisons, Holbrook thought. She flung the meat high, hard,
vigorously. As it sailed through the air tendrils whipped
out from one tree or another to seize it in midflight and
stuff it down the waiting gullet. The trees did not *need*
meat, but they liked it, and it was common lore among
the growers that well-fed trees produced the most juice.
Holbrook gave his trees meat three times a week, except
for Sector D, which rated a daily ration.

"Don't skip anyone," Holbrook called to her.

"You know I won't."

No piece fell uncaught to the floor of the grove. Sometimes two trees at once went for the same chunk and a
little battle resulted. The trees weren't necessarily friendly
to one another; there was bad blood between Caesar and
Henry the Eighth, and Cato clearly despised both Socrates
and Alcibiades, though for different reasons. Now and
then Holbrook or his staff found lopped-off limbs lying on
the ground in the morning. Usually, though, even trees of
conflicting personalities managed to tolerate one another.
They had to, condemned as they were to eternal proximity. Holbrook had once tried to separate two Sector F
trees that were carrying on a vicious feud; but it was
impossible to dig up a full-grown tree without killing it
and deranging the nervous systems of its thirty closest
neighbors, as he had learned the hard way.

While Naomi fed the trees and talked to them and
caressed their scaly flanks, petting them the way one might
pet a tame rhino, Holbrook quietly unfolded a telescoping
ladder and gave the leaves a new checkout for rust. There
wasn't much point to it, really. Rust didn't become visible
on the leaves until it had already penetrated the root
structure of the tree, and the orange spots he thought he

saw were probably figments of a jumpy imagination. He'd have the lab report in an hour or two, and that would tell him all he'd need to know, one way or the other. Still, he was unable to keep from looking. He cut a bundle of leaves from one of Plato's lower branches, apologizing, and turned them over in his hands, rubbing their glossy undersurfaces. What's this here, these minute colonies of reddish particles? His mind tried to reject the possibility of rust. A plague striding across the worlds, striking him so intimately, wiping him out? He had built this plantation on leverage: a little of his money, a lot from the bank. Leverage worked the other way too. Let rust strike the plantation and kill enough trees to sink his equity below the level considered decent for collateral, and the bank would take over. They might hire him to stay on as manager. He had heard of such things happening.

Plato rustled uneasily.

"What is it, old fellow?" Holbrook murmured. "You've got it, don't you? There's something funny swimming in your guts, eh? I know. I know. I feel it in my guts too. We have to be philosophers, now. Both of us." He tossed the leaf sample to the ground and moved the ladder up the row to Alcibiades. "Now, my beauty, now. Let me look. I won't cut any leaves off you." He could picture the proud tree snorting, stamping in irritation. "A little bit speckled under there, no? You have it too. Right?" The tree's outer branches clamped tight, as though Alcibiades were huddling into himself in anguish. Holbrook rolled onward, down the row. The rust spots were far more pronounced than the day before. No imagination, then. Sector C had it. He did not need to wait for the lab report. He felt oddly calm at this confirmation, even though it announced his own ruin.

"Zen?"

He looked down. Naomi stood at the foot of the ladder, holding a nearly ripened fruit in her hand. There was something grotesque about that; the fruits were botany's joke, explicitly phallic, so that a tree in ripeness with a hundred or more jutting fruits looked like some archetype of the ultimate male, and all visitors found it hugely amusing. But the sight of a fifteen-year-old girl's hand so thoroughly filled with such an object was obscene, not funny. Naomi had never remarked on the shape of the fruits, nor did she show any embarrassment now. At first he had ascribed it to innocence or shyness, but as he came to know her better, he began to suspect that she was deliberately pretending to ignore that wildly comic biological coincidence to spare *his* feelings. Since he clearly thought of her as a child, she was tactfully behaving in a childlike way, he supposed; and the fascinating complexity of his interpretation of her attitudes had kept him occupied for days.

"Where did you find that?" he asked.

"Right here. Alcibiades dropped it."

The dirty-minded joker, Holbrook thought. He said, "What of it?"

"It's ripe. It's time to harvest this grove now, isn't it?" She squeezed the fruit; Holbrook felt his face flaring. "Take a look," she said, and tossed it up to him.

She was right: harvest time was about to begin in Sector C, five days early. He took no joy of it; it was a sign of the disease that he now knew infested these trees.

"What's wrong?" she asked.

He jumped down beside her and held out the bundle of leaves he had cut from Plato. "You see these spots? It's rust. A blight that strikes juice-trees."

"No!"

"It's been going through one system after another for the past fifty years. And now it's here despite all quarantines."

"What happens to the trees?"

"A metabolic speedup," Holbrook said. "That's why the fruit is starting to drop. They accelerate their cycles until they're going through a year in a couple of weeks. They become sterile. They defoliate. Six months after the onset, they're dead." Holbrook's shoulders sagged. "I've suspected it for two or three days. Now I know."

She looked interested but not really concerned. "What causes it, Zen?"

"Ultimately, a virus. Which passes through so many hosts that I can't tell you the sequence. It's an interchange-vector deal, where the virus occupies plants and gets into their seeds, is eaten by rodents, gets into their blood, gets picked up by stinging insects, passed along to a mammal, then—oh, hell, what do the details matter? It took eighty years just to trace the whole sequence. You can't quarantine your world against everything, either. The rust is bound to slip in, piggybacking on some kind of living thing. And here it is."

"I guess you'll be spraying the plantation, then."

"No."

"To kill the rust? What's the treatment?"

"There isn't any," Holbrook said.

"But—"

"Look, I've got to go back to the plantation house. You can keep yourself busy without me, can't you?"

"Sure." She pointed out to the meat. "I haven't even finished feeding them yet. And they're especially hungry this morning."

He started to tell her that there was no point in feeding them now, that all the trees in this sector would be dead by nightfall. But an instinct warned him that it would be too complicated to start explaining that to her now. He flashed a quick, sunless smile and trotted to the bug. When he looked back at her, she was hurling a huge slab of meat toward Henry the Eighth, who seized it expertly and stuffed it in his mouth.

The lab report came sliding from the wall output around two hours later, and it confirmed what Holbrook already knew: rust. At least half the planet had heard the news by then, and Holbrook had had a dozen visitors so far. On a planet with a human population of slightly under four hundred, that was plenty. The district governor, Fred Leitfried, showed up first, and so did the local agricultural commissioner, who also happened to be Fred Leitfried. A two-man delegation from the Juice-Growers' Guild arrived next. Then came Mortensen, the rubbery-faced little man who ran the processing plant, and Heemskerck of the export line, and somebody from the bank, along with a representative of the insurance company. A couple of neighboring growers dropped over a little later; they offered sympathetic smiles and comradely graspings of the shoulder, but not very far beneath their commiserations lay potential hostility. They wouldn't come right out and say it, but Holbrook didn't need to be a telepath to know what they were thinking: *Get rid of those rusty trees before they infect the whole damned planet.*

In their position he'd think the same. Even though the rust vectors had reached this world, the thing wasn't all that contagious. It could be confined; neighboring plantations could be saved, and even the unharmed groves of his own place—if he moved swiftly enough. If the man next door had rust on his trees, Holbrook would be as itchy as these fellows were about getting it taken care of quickly.

Fred Leitfried, who was tall and bland-faced and blue-eyed and depressingly somber even on a cheerful occasion, looked about ready to burst into tears now. He said, "Zen, I've ordered a planetwide rust alert. The biologicals will be out within thirty minutes to break the carrier chain. We'll begin on your property and work in a widening radius until we've isolated this entire quadrant. After that we'll trust to luck."

"Which vector are you going after?" Mortensen asked, tugging tensely at his lower lip.

"Hoppers," said Leitfried. "They're biggest and easiest to knock off, and we know that they're potential rust carriers. If the virus hasn't been transmitted to them yet, we can interrupt the sequence there and maybe we'll get out of this intact."

Holbrook said hollowly, "You know that you're talking about exterminating maybe a million animals."

"I know, Zen."

"You think you can do it?"

"We have to do it. Besides," Leitfried added, "the contingency plans were drawn a long time ago, and everything's ready to go. We'll have a fine mist of hopper-lethals covering half the continent before nightfall."

"A damned shame," muttered the man from the bank. "They're such peaceful animals."

"But now they're threats," said one of the growers. "They've got to go."

Holbrook scowled. He liked hoppers himself; they were big rabbitty things, almost the size of bears, that grazed on worthless scrub and did no harm to humans. But they had been identified as susceptible to infection by the rust virus, and it had been shown on other worlds that by knocking out one basic stage in the transmission sequence the spread of the rust could be halted, since the viruses would die if they were unable to find an adequate host for the next stage in their life cycle. Naomi is fond of the hoppers, he thought. She'll think we're bastards for wiping them out. But we have our trees to save. And if we were real bastards, we'd have wiped them out before the rust ever got here, just to make things a little safer for ourselves.

Leitfried turned to him. "You know what you have to do now, Zen?"

"Yes."

"Do you want help?"

"I'd rather do it myself."

"We can get you ten men."

"It's just one sector, isn't it?" he asked. "I can do it. I *ought* to do it. They're my trees."

"How soon will you start?" asked Borden, the grower whose plantation adjoined Holbrook's on the east. There was fifty miles of brush country between Holbrook's land and Borden's, but it wasn't hard to see why the man would be impatient about getting the protective measures under way.

Holbrook said, "Within an hour, I guess. I've got to calculate a little, first. Fred, suppose you come upstairs with me and help me check the infected area on the screens?"

"Right."

The insurance man stepped forward. "Before you go, Mr. Holbrook—"

"Eh?"

"I just want you to know, we're in complete approval. We'll back you all the way."

Damn nice of you, Holbrook thought sourly. What was insurance for, if not to back you all the way? But he managed an amiable grin and a quick murmur of thanks.

The man from the bank said nothing. Holbrook was grateful for that. There was time later to talk about refurbishing the collateral, renegotiation of notes, things like that. First it was necessary to see how much of the plantation would be left after Holbrook had taken the required protective measures.

In the info center, he and Leitfried got all the screens going at once. Holbrook indicated Sector C and tapped out a grove simulation on the computer. He fed in the data from the lab report. "These are the infected trees," he said, using a light-pen to circle them on the output screen. "Maybe fifty of them altogether." He drew a larger circle. "This is the zone of possible incubation. Another eighty or a hundred trees. What do you say, Fred?"

The district governor took the light-pen from Holbrook

and touched the stylus tip to the screen. He drew a wider circle that reached almost to the periphery of the sector.

"These are the ones to go, Zen."

"That's four hundred trees."

"How many do you have altogether?"

Holbrook shrugged. "Maybe seven, eight thousand."

"You want to lose them all?"

"Okay," Holbrook said. "You want a protective moat around the infection zone, then. A sterile area."

"Yes."

"What's the use? If the virus can come down out of the sky, why bother to——"

"Don't talk that way," Leitfried said. His face grew longer and longer, the embodiment of all the sadness and frustration and despair in the universe. He looked the way Holbrook felt. But his tone was incisive as he said, "Zen, you've got just two choices here. You can get out into the groves and start burning, or you can give up and let the rust grab everything. If you do the first, you've got a chance to save most of what you own. If you give up, we'll burn you out anyway, for our own protection. And we won't stop just with four hundred trees."

"I'm going," Holbrook said. "Don't worry about me."

"I wasn't worried. Not really."

Leitfried slid behind the command nodes to monitor the entire plantation while Holbrook gave his orders to the robots and requisitioned the equipment he would need. Within ten minutes he was organized and ready to go.

"There's a girl in the infected sector," Leitfried said. "That niece of yours, huh?"

"Naomi. Yes."

"Beautiful. What is she, eighteen, nineteen?"

"Fifteen."

"Quite a figure on her, Zen."

"What's she doing now?" Holbrook asked. "Still feeding the trees?"

"No, she's sprawled out underneath one of them. I think she's talking to them. Telling them a story, maybe? Should I cut in the audio?"

"Don't bother. She likes to play games with the trees. You know, give them names and imagine that they have personalities. Kid stuff."

"Sure," said Leitfried. Their eyes met briefly and evasively. Holbrook looked down. The trees *did* have personalities, and every man in the juice business knew it, and probably there weren't many growers who didn't have a much closer relationship to their groves than they'd ever admit to another man. Kid stuff. It was something you didn't talk about.

Poor Naomi, he thought.

He left Leitfried in the info center and went out the back way. The robots had set everything up just as he had programmed: the spray truck with the fusion gun mounted in place of the chemical tank. Two or three of the gleaming little mechanicals hovered around, waiting to be asked to hop aboard, but he shook them off and slipped behind the steering panel. He activated the data output and the small dashboard screen lit up; from the info center above, Leitfried greeted him and threw him the simulated pattern of the infection zone, with the three concentric circles glowing to indicate the trees with rust, those that might be incubating, and the safety-margin belt that Leitfried had insisted on his creating around the entire sector.

The truck rolled off toward the groves.

It was midday, now, of what seemed to be the longest day he had ever known. The sun, bigger and a little more deeply tinged with orange than the sun under which he had been born, lolled lazily overhead, not quite ready to begin its tumble into the distant plains. The day was hot, but as soon as he entered the groves, where the tight canopy of the adjoining trees shielded the ground from the worst of the sun's radiation, he felt a welcome coolness seeping into the cab of the truck. His lips were dry. There was an ugly throbbing just back of his left eyeball. He guided the truck manually, taking it on the access track around Sectors A, D, and G. The trees, seeing him, flapped their limbs a little. They were eager to have him get out and walk among them, slap their trunks, tell them what good fellows they were. He had no time for that now.

In fifteen minutes he was at the north end of his property, at the edge of Sector C. He parked the spray truck on the approach lip overlooking the grove; from here he could reach any tree in the area with the fusion gun. Not quite yet, though.

He walked into the doomed grove.

Naomi was nowhere in sight. He would have to find her

before he could begin firing. And even before that, he had some farewells to make. Holbrook trotted down the main avenue of the sector. How cool it was here, even at noon! How sweet the loamy air smelled! The floor of the grove was littered with fruit; dozens had come down in the past couple of hours. He picked one up. Ripe: he split it with an expert snap of his wrist and touched the pulpy interior to his lips. The juice, rich and sweet, trickled into his mouth. He tasted just enough of it to know that the product was first-class. His intake was far from a hallucinogenic dose, but it would give him a mild euphoria, sufficient to see him through the ugliness ahead.

He looked up at the trees. They were tightly drawn in, suspicious, uneasy.

"We have troubles, fellows," Holbrook said. "You, Hector, you know it. There's a sickness here. You can feel it inside you. There's no way to save you. All I can hope to do is save the other trees, the ones that don't have the rust yet. Okay? Do you understand? Plato? Caesar? I've got to do this. It'll cost you only a few weeks of life, but it may save thousands of other trees."

An angry rustling in the branches. Alcibiades had pulled his limbs away disdainfully. Hector, straight and true, was ready to take his medicine. Socrates, lumpy and malformed, seemed prepared also. Hemlock or fire, what did it matter? Crito, I owe a cock to Asclepius. Caesar seemed enraged; Plato was actually cringing. They understood, all of them. He moved among them, patting them, comforting them. He had begun his plantation with this grove. He had expected these trees to outlive him.

He said, "I won't make a long speech. All I can say is good-by. You've been good fellows, you've lived useful lives, and now your time is up, and I'm sorry as hell about it. That's all. I wish this wasn't necessary." He cast his glance up and down the grove. "End of speech. So long."

Turning away, he walked slowly back to the spray truck. He punched for contact with the info center and said to Leitfried, "Do you know where the girl is?"

"One sector over from you to the south. She's feeding the trees," He flashed the picture on Holbrook's screen.

"Give me an audio line, will you?"

Through his speakers Holbrook said, "Naomi? It's me, Zen."

She looked around, halting just as she was about to toss

a chunk of meat. "Wait a second," she said. "Catherine the Great is hungry, and she won't let me forget it." The meat soared upward, was snared, disappeared into the mouth of a tree. "Okay," Naomi said. "What is it, now?"

"I think you'd better go back to the plantation house."

"I've still got lots of trees to feed."

"Do it this afternoon."

"Zen, what's going on?"

"I've got some work to do, and I'd rather not have you in the groves when I'm doing it."

"Where are you now?"

"C."

"Maybe I can help you, Zen. I'm only in the next sector down the line. I'll come right over."

"*No*. Go back to the house." The words came out as a cold order. He had never spoken to her like that before. She looked shaken and startled; but she got obediently into her bug and drove off. Holbrook followed her on his screen until she was out of sight.

"Where is she now?" he asked Leitfried.

"She's coming back. I can see her on the access track."

"Okay," Holbrook said. "Keep her busy until this is over. I'm going to get started."

He swung the fusion gun around, aiming its stubby barrel into the heart of the grove. In the squat core of the gun a tiny pinch of sun-stuff was hanging suspended in a magnetic pinch, available infinitely for an energy tap more than ample for his power needs today. The gun had no sight, for it was not intended as a weapon; he thought he could manage things, though. He was shooting at big targets. Sighting by eye, he picked out Socrates at the edge of the grove, fiddled with the gun mounting for a couple of moments of deliberate hesitation, considered the best way of doing this thing that awaited him, and put his hand to the firing control. The tree's neural nexus was in its crown, back of the mouth. One quick blast there—

Yes.

An arc of white flame hissed through the air. Socrates' misshapen crown was bathed for an instant in brilliance. A quick death, a clean death, better than rotting with rust. Now Holbrook drew his line of fire down from the top of the dead tree, along the trunk. The wood was sturdy stuff; he fired again and again, and limbs and branches and leaves shriveled and dropped away, while the trunk itself remained intact, and great oily gouts of smoke rose above the grove. Against the brightness of the fusion beam Holbrook saw the darkness of the naked trunk outlined, and it surprised him how straight the old philosopher's trunk had been, under the branches. Now the trunk was nothing more than a pillar of ash; and now it collapsed and was gone.

From the other trees of the grove came a terrible low moaning.

They knew that death was among them; and they felt the pain of Socrates' absence through the network of root-nerves in the ground. They were crying out in fear and anguish and rage.

Doggedly Holbrook turned the fusion gun on Hector.

Hector was a big tree, impassive, stoic, neither a complainer nor a preener. Holbrook wanted to give him the good death he deserved, but his aim went awry; the first bolt struck at least eight feet below the tree's brain center, and the echoing shriek that went up from the surrounding trees revealed what Hector must be feeling. Holbrook saw the limbs waving frantically, the mouth opening and closing in a horrifying rictus of torment. The second bolt put an end to Hector's agony. Almost calmly, now, Holbrook finished the job of extirpating that noble tree.

He was nearly done before he became aware that a bug had pulled up beside his truck and that Naomi had erupted from it, flushed, wide-eyed, close to hysteria. "Stop!" she cried. "Stop it, Uncle Zen! Don't burn them!"

As she leaped into the cab of the spray truck she caught his wrists with surprising strength and pulled herself up against him. She was gasping, panicky, her breasts heaving, her nostrils wide.

"I told you to go to the plantation house," he snapped.

"I did. But then I saw the flames."

"Will you get out of here?"

"Why are you burning the trees?"

"Because they're infected with rust," he said. "They've got to be burned out before it spreads to the others."

"That's *murder*."

"Naomi, look, will you get back to—"

"You killed Socrates!" she muttered, looking into the grove. "And—and Caesar? No. Hector. Hector's gone too. You burned them right out!"

"They aren't people. They're trees. Sick trees that are going to die soon anyway. I want to save the others."

"But why kill them? There's got to be some kind of drug you can use, Zen. Some kind of spray. There's a drug to cure everything now."

"Not this."

"There has to be."

"Only the fire," Holbrook said. Sweat rolled coldly down his chest, and he felt a quiver in a thigh muscle. It was hard enough doing this without her around. He said as calmly as he could manage it, "Naomi, this is something that must be done, and fast. There's no choice about it. I love these trees as much as you do, but I've got to burn them out. It's like the little leggy thing with the sting in its tail: I couldn't afford to be sentimental about it, simply because it looked cute. It was a menace. And right now Plato and Caesar and the others are menaces to everything I own. They're plague-bearers. Go back to the house and lock yourself up somewhere until it's over."

"I won't let you kill them!" Tearfully. Defiantly.

Exasperated, he grabbed her shoulders, shook her two or three times, pushed her from the truck cab. She tumbled backward but landed lithely. Jumping down beside her, Holbrook said, "Dammit, don't make me hit you, Naomi. This is none of your business. I've got to burn out those trees, and if you don't stop interfering—"

"There's got to be some other way. You let those other men panic you, didn't you, Zen? They're afraid the infection will spread, so they told you to burn the trees fast, and you aren't even stopping to think, to get other opinions, you're just coming in here with your gun and killing intelligent, sensitive, lovable—"

"Trees," he said. "This is incredible, Naomi. For the last time—"

Her reply was to leap up on the truck and press herself to the snout of the fusion gun, breasts close against the metal. "If you fire, you'll have to shoot through me!"

Nothing he could say would make her come down. She was lost in some romantic fantasy, Joan of Arc of the juice-trees, defending the grove against his barbaric assault. Once more he tried to reason with her; once more she denied the need to extirpate the trees. He explained with all the force he could summon the total impossibility of saving these trees; she replied with the power of sheer

irrationality that there must be some way. He cursed. He
called her a stupid hysterical adolescent. He begged. He
wheedled. He commanded. She clung to the gun.

"I can't waste any more time," he said finally. "This has
to be done in a matter of hours or the whole plantation
will go." Drawing his needler from its holster, he
dislodged the safety and gestured at her with the weapon.
"Get down from there," he said icily.

She laughed. "You expect me to think you'd shoot me?"

Of course, she was right. He stood there sputtering
impotently, red-faced, baffled. The lunacy was spreading:
his threat had been completely empty, as she had seen at
once. Holbrook vaulted up beside her on the truck, seized
her, tried to pull her down.

She was strong, and his perch was precarious. He
succeeded in pulling her away from the gun but had
surprisingly little luck in getting her off the truck itself. He
didn't want to hurt her, and in his solicitousness he found
himself getting second best in the struggle. A kind of
hysterical strength was at her command; she was all
elbows, knees, clawing fingers. He got a grip on her at one
point, found with horror that he was clutching her breasts,
and let go in embarrassment and confusion. She hopped
away from him. He came after her, seized her again, and
this time was able to push her to the edge of the truck.
She leaped off, landed easily, turned, ran into the grove.

So she was still outthinking him. He followed her in; it
took him a moment to discover where she was. He found
her hugging Caesar's base and staring in shock at the
charred places where Socrates and Hector had been.

"Go on," she said. "Burn up the whole grove! But you'll
burn me with it!"

Holbrook lunged at her. She stepped to one side and
began to dart past him, across to Alcibiades. He pivoted
and tried to grab her, lost his balance, and went sprawling,
clutching at the air for purchase. He started to fall.

Something wiry and tough and long slammed around his
shoulders.

"Zen!" Naomi yelled. "The tree—Alcibiades—"

He was off the ground now. Alcibiades had snared him
with a grasping tendril and was lifting him toward his
crown. The tree was struggling with the burden; but then
a second tendril gripped him too and Alcibiades had an

easier time. Holbrook thrashed about a dozen feet off the ground.

Cases of trees attacking humans were rare. It had happened perhaps five times altogether, in the generations that men had been cultivating juice-trees here. In each instance the victim had been doing something that the grove regarded as hostile—such as removing a diseased tree.

A man was a big mouthful for a juice-tree. But not beyond its appetite.

Naomi screamed, and Alcibiades continued to lift. Holbrook could hear the clashing of fangs above; the tree's mouth was getting ready to receive him. Alcibiades the vain, Alcibiades the mercurial, Alcibiades the unpredictable—well named, indeed. But was it treachery to act in self-defense? Alcibiades had a strong will to survive. He had seen the fates of Hector and Socrates. Holbrook looked up at the ever closer fangs. So this is how it happens, he thought. Eaten by one of my own trees. My friends. My pets. Serves me right for sentimentalizing them. They're carnivores. Tigers with roots.

Alcibiades screamed.

In the same instant one of the tendrils wrapped about Holbrook's body lost its grip. He dropped about twenty feet in a single dizzying plunge before the remaining tendril steadied itself, leaving him dangling a few yards above the floor of the grove. When he could breathe again, Holbrook looked down and saw what had happened. Naomi had picked up the needler that he had dropped when he had been seized by the tree, and had burned away one tendril. She was taking aim again. There was another scream from Alcibiades; Holbrook was aware of a great commotion in the branches above him; he tumbled the rest of the way to the ground and landed hard in a pile of mulched leaves. After a moment he rolled over and sat up. Nothing broken. Naomi stood above him, arms dangling, the needler still in her hand.

"Are you all right?" she asked soberly.

"Shaken up a little, is all." He started to get up. "I owe you a lot," he said. "Another minute and I'd have been in Alcibiades' mouth."

"I almost let him eat you, Zen. He was just defending himself. But I couldn't. So I shot off the tendrils."

"Yes. Yes. I owe you a lot." He stood up and took a

couple of faltering steps toward her. "Here," he said. "You better give me that needler before you burn a hole in your foot." He stretched out his hand.

"Wait a second," she said, glacially calm. She stepped back as he neared her.

"What?"

"A deal, Zen. I rescued you, right? I didn't have to. Now you leave those trees alone. At least check up on whether there's a spray, okay? A deal."

"But—"

"You owe me a lot, you said. So pay me. What I want from you is a promise, Zen. If I hadn't cut you down, you'd be dead now. Let the trees live too."

He wondered if she would use the needler on him.

He was silent a long moment, weighing his options. Then he said, "All right, Naomi. You saved me, and I can't refuse you what you want. I won't touch the trees. I'll find out if something can be sprayed on them to kill the rust."

"You mean that, Zen?"

"I promise. By all that's holy. Will you give me that needler, now?"

"Here," she cried, tears running down her reddened face. "Here! Take it! Oh God, Zen, how awful all this is!"

He took the weapon from her and holstered it. She seemed to go limp, all resolve spent, once she surrendered it. She stumbled into his arms, and he held her tight, feeling her tremble against him. He trembled too, pulling her close to him, aware of the ripe cones of her young breasts jutting into his chest. A powerful wave of what he recognized bluntly as desire surged through him. Filthy, he thought. He winced as this morning's images danced in his brain, Naomi nude and radiant from her swim, apple-round breasts, firm thighs. My niece. Fifteen. God help me. Comforting her, he ran his hands across her shoulders, down to the small of her back. Her clothes were light; her body was all too present within them.

He threw her roughly to the ground.

She landed in a heap, rolled over, put her hand to her mouth as he fell upon her. Her screams rose, shrill and piercing, as his body pressed down on her. Her terrified eyes plainly told that she feared he would rape her, but he had other perfidies in mind. Quickly he flung her on her face, catching her right hand and jerking her arm up behind her back. Then he lifted her to a sitting position.

"Stand up," he said. He gave her arm a twist by way of persuasion. She stood up.

"Now walk. Out of the grove, back to the truck. I'll break your arm if I have to."

"What are you doing?" she asked in a barely audible whisper.

"Back to the truck," he said. He levered her arm up another notch. She hissed in pain. But she walked.

At the truck, he maintained his grip on her and reached in to call Leitfried at his info center.

"What was that all about, Zen? We tracked most of it, and—"

"It's too complicated to explain. The girl's very attached to the trees, is all. Send some robots out here to get her right away, okay?"

"You *promised*," Naomi said.

The robots arrived quickly. Steely-fingered, efficient, they kept Naomi pinioned as they hustled her into a bug and took her to the plantation house. When she was gone, Holbrook sat down for a moment beside the spray truck, to rest and clean his mind. Then he climbed into the truck cab again.

He aimed the fusion gun first at Alcibiades.

It took a little over three hours. When he was finished, Sector C was a field of ashes, and a broad belt of emptiness stretched from the outer limit of the devastation to the nearest grove of healthy trees. He wouldn't know for a while whether he had succeeded in saving the plantation. But he had done his best.

As he rode back to the plantation house, his mind was less on the work of execution he had just done than on the feel of Naomi's body against his own, and on the things he had thought in that moment when he hurled her to the ground. A woman's body, yes. But a child. A child still, in love with her pets. Unable yet to see how in the real world one weighs the need against the bond, and does one's best. What had she learned in Sector C today? That the universe often offers only brutal choices? Or merely that the uncle she worshiped was capable of treachery and murder?

They had given her sedation, but she was awake in her

room, and when he came in she drew the covers up to conceal her pajamas. Her eyes were cold and sullen.

"You promised," she said bitterly. "And then you tricked me."

"I had to save the other trees. You'll understand, Naomi."

"I understand that you lied to me, Zen."

"I'm sorry. Forgive me?"

"You can go to hell," she said, and those adult words coming from her not-yet-adult face were chilling.

He could not stay longer with her. He went out, upstairs, to Fred Leitfried in the info center. "It's all over," he said softly.

"You did it like a man, Zen."

"Yeah. Yeah."

In the screen he scanned the sector of ashes. He felt the warmth of Naomi against him. He saw her sullen eyes. Night would come, the moons would do their dance across the sky, the constellations to which he had never grown accustomed would blaze forth. He would talk to her again, maybe. Try to make her understand. And then he would send her away, until she was finished becoming a woman.

"Starting to rain," Leitfried said. "That'll help the ripening along, eh?"

"Most likely."

"You feel like a killer, Zen?"

"What do you think?"

"I know. I know."

Holbrook began to shut off the scanners. He had done all he meant to do today. He said quietly, "Fred, they were trees. Only trees. Trees, Fred, *trees*."

Hidden Talent

The spaceport on Mondarran IV was a small one, as might be expected on the sort of fifth-rate backwater world it was. Rygor Davison picked up his lone suitcase at the baggage depot and struck out into the dry windy heat of mid-afternoon. The sun—G-type, hot—was high overhead, and a dusty brown dirt road ran crookedly away from the rudimentary spaceport toward a small grey village about a thousand meters away.

There was no one on hand to greet him. Not an impressive welcome, he thought, and began to walk down the dirt road toward the village which would be his home for the next five years—if he survived.

After he had gone half a dozen steps, he heard someone behind him, turned and saw a small boy heavily tanned, come trotting down the road. He was about eleven, and clad in a pair of golden swim trunks and nothing else. He seemed to be in a hurry.

"Whoa, youngster!" Davison called.

The boy looked up questioningly, slowed, and stopped, panting slightly. "Just get here? I saw the ship come down!"

Davison grinned. "Just got here. What's the hurry?"

"Witch," the boy gasped. "They're giving him the business this afternoon. I don't want to miss it. Come on—hurry along."

Davison stiffened. "What's going to happen, boy?"

"They're roasting a witch," the boy said, speaking very clearly, as one would to an idiot or an extremely young child. "Hurry along, if you want to get there on time—but don't make me miss it."

Davison hefted his suitcase and began to stride rapidly

163

alongside the boy, who urged him impatiently on. Clouds of dust rose from the road and swirled around them.

A witch-burning, eh? He shuddered despite himself, and wondered if the Esper Guild had sent him to his death.

The Guild of Espers operated quietly but efficiently. They had found Davison, had trained him, had developed his enormous potential of telekinetic power. And they had sent him to the outworlds to learn how *not* to use it.

It had been Lloyd Kechnie, Davison's guide, who explained it to him. Kechnie was a wiry, bright-eyed man with a hawk's nose and a gorilla's eyebrows. He had worked with Davison for eight years.

"You're a damned fine telekinetic," Kechnie told him. "The guild can't do anything more for you. And in just a few years, you'll be ready for a full discharge."

"Few *years?* But I thought—"

"You're the best tk I've seen," said Kechnie. "You're so good that by now it's second nature for you to use your power. You don't know *how* to hide it. Someday you'll regret that. You haven't learned restraint." Kechnie leaned forward over his desk. "Ry, we've decided to let you sink or swim—and you're not the first we've done this to. We're going to send you to a psiless world—one where the powers haven't been developed. You'll be *forced* to hide your psi, or else be stoned for witchcraft or some such thing."

"Can't I stay on Earth and learn?" Davison asked hopefully.

"Uh-uh. It's too easy to get by here. In the outworlds, you'll face an all-or-nothing situation. That's where you're going."

Davison had gone on the next ship. And now, on Mondarran IV, he was going to learn—or else.

"Where you come from?" the boy asked after a few minutes of silence. "You going to be a colonist here?"

"For a while," Davison said. "I'm from Dariak III." He didn't want to give any hint of his Earth background. Dariak III was a known psiless world. It might mean his life if they suspected he was an esper.

"Dariak III?" the boy said. "Nice world?"

"Not very," Davison said. "Rains a lot."

Suddenly a flash of brilliant fire burst out over the village ahead, illuminating the afternoon sky like a bolt of low-mounting lightning.

"Oh, damn," the boy said disgustedly. "There's the flare. I missed the show after all. I guess I should have started out earlier."

"Too late, eh?" Davison felt more than a little relieved. He licked dry lips. "Guess we missed all the fun."

"It's real exciting," the boy said enthusiastically. "Especially when they're good witches, and play tricks before we can burn 'em. You should see some of the things they do, once we've got 'em pinned to the stake."

I can imagine, Davison thought grimly. He said nothing.

They continued walking, moving at a slower pace now, and the village grew closer. He could pick out the nearer buildings fairly clearly, and was able to discern people moving around in the streets. Overhead, the sun shone down hard.

A shambling, ragged figure appeared and came toward them as they headed down the final twist in the road. "Hello, Dumb Joe," the boy said cheerily, as the figure approached.

The newcomer grunted a monosyllable and kept moving. He was tall and gaunt-looking, with a grubby growth of beard, open-seamed moccasins, and a battered leather shirt. He paused as he passed Davison, looked closely into his face, and smiled, revealing yellow-stained teeth.

"Got a spare copper, friend?" Dumb Joe asked in a deep, rumbling voice. "Somethin' for a poor man?"

Davison fumbled in his pocket and pulled out a small coin. The boy glared at him disapprovingly, but he dropped the coin into the waiting palm of the panhandler.

"Best of luck, mister," the beggar said, and shuffled away. After a few steps he turned and said, "Too bad you missed the roasting, mister. It was real good."

They proceeded on into the town. Davison saw that it consisted of a sprawling group of two-storey shacks, prefabs, apparently, strung loosely around a central plaza—in the heart of which, Davison noticed, was a sturdy steel post with something unpleasant smouldering at its base. He shuddered, and looked away.

"What's the matter, mister?" the boy asked derisively. "Don't they roast witches on Dariak III?"

"Not very often," Davison said. He found that his fingers were trembling, and he struggled to regain control over them.

He thought of Kechnie, comfortably back on Earth. While he was out here, on a fly-plagued dust hole of a world, doomed to spend the next five years in a pokey village twiddling his thumbs. It was like a prison sentence.

No—worse. In prison, you don't have any worries. You just go through your daily rock-crumbling, and they give you three meals and a place, of sorts, to sleep. No agonies.

Here it was different. Davison barely repressed a curse. He'd have to be on constant lookout, suppressing his psi, hiding his power—or he'd wind up shackled to that steel gibbet in the central plaza, providing a morning's entertainment for the villagers before he went up in flames.

Then he grinned. *Kechnie knows what he's doing,* he admitted despite himself. *If I survive this, I'll be fit for anything they can throw at me.*

He squared his shoulders, fixed a broad grin on his face, and headed forward into the town.

A tall man with a weather-creased face the colour of curdled turpentine came toward him, loping amiably.

"Hello, stranger. My name's Domarke—I'm the Mayor. You new down here?"

Davison nodded. "Just put down from Dariak III. Thought I'd try my luck here."

"Glad to have you, friend," Domarke said pleasantly. "Too bad you missed our little show. You probably saw the flare from the spaceport."

"Sorry I missed it too," Davison forced himself to say. "You have much trouble with witches down here?"

Domarke's face darkened. "A little," he said. "Not much. Every once in a while, there's a guy who pulls off some kind of fancy stunt. We've been pretty quick to send them to their Master the second we spot them. We don't want none of that kind here, brother."

"I don't blame you," Davison said. "Men aren't supposed to do things the way those guys do."

"Nossir," the Mayor said. "But we fix 'em when they do. There was a fellow down from Lanargon Seven last year, took a job here as a beekeeper. Nice boy—young, with a good head on his shoulders. Saw a lot of my daughter. We all liked him. We never suspected he was a wronger."

"Witch, eh?"

"Sure was," Domarke said. "Swarm of his bees got loose and broke up. They come after him, and started stinging away. Next thing we know, he's looking at them kinda funny and fire starts shootin' from his fingertips." Domarke shook his head retrospectively. "Burned all those bees to tatters. He didn't even try to stop us when we strung him up."

"Strung him up? How come you didn't burn him?" Davison asked, morbidly curious.

Domarke shrugged. "Wasn't any point to it. Those guys in league with fire, you don't get anywhere trying to burn 'em. We hang them on the spot."

One of Kechnie's boys, probably, Davison thought. *A pyrotic sent out here to learn how to control his power. He didn't learn fast enough.*

He chewed at his lower lip for a second and said, "Guess it's about time I got to my point. Who can I see about getting a room in this town?"

They found him a room with a family named Rinehart, on a small farm about ten minutes' walk from the heart of the village. They had posted a sign advertising for a hired hand.

He moved in that afternoon, unpacked his meagre belongings, and hung up his jacket in the tiny closet they provided. Then he went downstairs to meet his hosts.

It was a family of five. Rinehart was a balding man of fifty-five or so, dark skinned from long hours of toil in the blazing sun, heavy-jowled and jovial. His wife—Ma—was a formidable woman in an amazingly archaic-looking apron. Her voice was a mellow masculine boom, and she radiated an atmosphere of simple, traditional folksiness. It was, thought Davison, a frame of mind long since extinct on so sophisticated a planet as Earth.

They had three children—Janey, a long-legged, full-bodied girl of eighteen or so; Bo, a sullen-faced muscular seventeen-year-old; and Buster, a chubby eleven-year-old. It seemed to be a happy familial setup, thought Davison.

He left his room—painstakingly opening and closing the door by hand—and ambled down the stairs. He slipped on the fourth from the bottom, started to slide, and teeked against the landing to hold himself upright. He caught his balance, straightened up, and then, as he realized what he had done, he paused and felt cold droplets of sweat starting out on his forehead.

No one had seen. No one *this* time.

But how many more slips would there be?

He let the shock filter out of his nervous system, waited a moment while the blood returned to his cheeks, and then finished descending the stairs and entered the living-room. The Rineharts were already gathered.

Janey appeared in the doorway and glanced indolently at Davison. "Supper's on," she said.

Davison sat down. Rinehart, at the head of the table, uttered a brief but devout blessing, finishing up with a word of prayer for the new hired hand who had come among them. Then Janey appeared from the back with a tray of steaming soup.

"Hot stuff," she said, and Bo and Buster moved apart to let her serve it. She brought the tray down—and then it happened. Davison saw it starting, and bit his lip in anguish.

One of the scalding bowls of soup began to slide off the end of the tray. He watched, almost in slow motion, as it curled over the lip of the tray, dipped, and poured its steaming contents on his bare right arm.

Tears of pain came to his eyes—and he didn't know which hurt more, the pain of the soup on his arm or the real shock he had received when he had forced himself to keep from teeking the falling soup halfway across the room.

He bit hard into his lip, and sat there, shivering from the mental effort the restraint had cost him.

Janey put down the tray and fussed embarrassedly over him. "Gee, Ry, I didn't mean that! Gosh, did I burn you?"

"I'll live," he said. "Don't trouble yourself about it."

He mopped the soup away from his corner of the table, feeling the pain slowly subside.

Kechnie, Kechnie, you didn't send me on any picnic!

Rinehart gave him a job, working in the fields.

The staple crop of Mondarran IV was something called Long Beans, a leguminous vegetable that everyone ate in great quantities, pounded down into wheat, and used for a dozen other purposes. It was a tough, almost indestructible plant that yielded three crops a year in the constant warmth of Mondarran IV.

Rinehart had a small farm, ten acres or so, spreading out over a rolling hill that overlooked a muddy swimming-hole. It was almost time for the year's second crop, and that meant a laborious process of stripping the stalks of the twisted pods that contained beans.

"You bend down like this and rip," Rinehart said, demonstrating for Davison. "Then you swivel around and drop the pod in the basket behind you."

Rinehart strapped the harness around Davison's shoulders, then donned his own, and together they started through the field. Overhead, the sun was high. It always seems to be noon on this planet, Davison thought, as he began to sweat.

Purple-winged flies buzzed noisily around the thick stalks of the bean-plants. Dragging the basket behind him, Davison advanced through the field, struggling to keep up with Rinehart. The older man was already ten feet ahead of him in the next furrow, ducking, bobbing, yanking, and depositing the pod in the basket all in a smooth series of motions.

It was hard work. Davison felt his hands beginning to redden from the contact with the rough sandpaper surfaces of the plants' leaves, and his back started to ache from the constant repetition of the unaccustomed pattern of motion. Down, up, reach around. Down, up, reach around.

He ground his teeth together and forced himself to keep going. His arm was throbbing from the exertion of using muscles that had lain unbothered for years. Sweat rolled down his forehead, crept into his collar, fell beadily into his eyebrows. His clothes seemed to be soaked through and through.

He reached the end of the furrow at last, and looked up. Rinehart was waiting there for him, arms akimbo looking almost as cool and fresh as he had when they had begun. He was grinning.

"Tough sled, eh, Ry?"

Too winded to say anything, Davison simply nodded.

"Don't let it get you. A couple of weeks out here, and it'll toughen you up. I know how you city fellows are at the start."

Davison mopped his forehead. "You wouldn't think just pulling pods off a plant could be so rough," he said.

"It's tough work, and I'm not denying it," Rinehart said. He pounded Davison affectionately on the back. "You'll get used to it. Come on back to the house, and I'll get you some beer."

Davison started in as a full-time picker the next day. It was, like all the other days promised to be, hot.

The whole family was out with him—the two elder Rineharts, Janey, Bo, and Buster. Each had his own harness strapped on, with the basket behind for dropping in the pods.

"We'll start down at the east end," Rinehart said, and without further discussion the entire crew followed him down. Each took a furrow. Davison found himself with Janey on his left, Bo Rinehart on his right. Further down the field, he could see Dirk Rinehart already fearsomely making his way through the close-packed rows of plants, a two-legged picking machine and nothing more. He watched the older man's effortless motions for a moment, and then, conscious that Janey and Bo were already a few steps ahead of him, he set to work.

The morning sun was still climbing in the sky, and the day had not yet reached its peak of heat, but Davison began to perspire after only a few moments of bending and yanking. He stopped to rub his sleeve over his forehead and heard light, derisive laughter come from up ahead.

Flushing hotly, he glanced up and saw Janey pausing in her furrow, hands on her hips, grinning back at him. It was much the same pose her father had taken the day before, and it irritated him. Without saying anything, he bent his head and returned to the job of picking.

A muscle at the base of his right arm began to complain. It was the business of reaching back and thrusting the picked pod into the basket that was doing it, straining the armsocket muscles in a way they had never been used before.

Kechnie's mocking words drifted back to him. *"You don't want your muscles to atrophy, son."* They had been words spoken lightly, in jest—but, Davison now realized, they carried with themselves a certain measure of truth.

He had relied on his psi for the ordinary tasks of life, had gloried in his mastery of the power to relieve himself of a portion of everyday drudgery. Little things—things like opening doors, pulling up hassocks, moving furniture. It was simpler to teek an object than to drag it, Davison had always felt. Why not use a power, if you have it to perfection?

The answer was that he didn't have it to perfection—yet. Perfection implied something more than utter control of objects; it meant, also, learning moderation, knowing when to use the psi and when not to.

On Earth, where it didn't matter, he had used his power almost promiscuously. Here he didn't dare to—and his aching muscles were paying the price of his earlier indulgence. Kechnie had known what he was doing, all right.

They reached the end of the furrow finally. Davison and Buster Rinehart came in in a dead heat for last place, and Buster didn't even seem winded. Davison thought he caught a shred of disapproval on Rinehart's face, as if he were disappointed at his hired hand's performance, but he wasn't sure. There was a definite expression of scorn on Janey's face; her eyes under their heavy lids, sparkled at him almost insultingly.

He glanced away, over to Rinehart, who was emptying his basket into the truck that stood in the middle of the field. "Let's dump here before we start the next row," he said.

The field seemed to stretch out endlessly. Davison lifted his basket with nerveless fingers and watched the grey-green pods tumble into the back of the truck. He replaced it in his harness, feeling oddly light now that the dragging weight no longer pulled down on him.

He had a fleeting thought as they moved on to the next batch of furrows: *How simple it would be to teek the pods into the baskets! No more bending, no swivelling, no arms that felt like they were ready to fall off.*

Simple. Sure, simple—but if Janey or Bo or any of the others should happen to turn around and see the beanpods floating mysteriously into Davison's basket, he'd be roasting by nightfall.

Damn Kechnie, he thought savagely, and wiped a glistening bead of sweat from his face.

What had seemed like a wry joke half an hour before now hung temptingly before Davison's eyes as a very real possibility.

He was almost an entire furrow behind the rest of them. He was disgracing himself. And his poor, unused, unathletic body was aching mercilessly.

He had the power and he wasn't using it. He was penning it up within himself, and it hurt. It was the scalding soup all over again; he didn't know if it hurt more to keep bending and dragging his numb arm back up again in the blistering heat, or to pen the psi up within him until it seemed almost to be brimming out over the edges of his mind.

Davison forced himself to concentrate on what he was doing, forced himself to forget the power. *This is the learning process,* he told himself grimly. *This is growing up. Kechnie knows what he's doing.*

They reached the end of the furrow, and through a dim haze of fatigue he heard Rinehart say, "Okay, let's knock off for a while. It's getting too hot to work, anyway."

He shucked off his harness and dropped it where he was, and began to walk back toward the farmhouse. With an unvoiced sigh of relief, Davison wriggled out of the leather straps and stood up straight.

He made his way across the field, noticing Janey fall in at his side. "You look pretty bushed, Ry," she said.

"I am. Takes a while to get used to this sort of work, I guess."

"Guess so," the girl said. She reached out and kicked a clump of dirt. "You'll toughen up," she said. "Either that or you'll fall apart. Last hired man we had fell apart. But you look like better stuff."

"Hope you're right," he said, wondering who the last hired man was and what power it was that he had cooped up within himself. For some, it wouldn't be so bad. A precog wouldn't need a training session like this—but precogs were one in a quadrillion. Telepaths might not, either, since anyone who had tp already had such a high-voltage mind that this sort of kindergarten toilet-training was unnecessary.

It was only the garden-variety espers who needed trips to the psiless worlds, Davison thought. Telekinetics and pyrotics, and others whose simple, unspecialized powers lulled them into false security.

A new thought was entering Davison's mind as he crossed the field, with Janey's distracting legs flashing at his side. A normal man needed some sort of sexual release; long-enforced continence required a special kind of mind, and most men simply folded from the sustained tension.

How about a normal esper? Could he keep his power

bottled up like this for five years? He was feeling the strain already, and it was just a couple of days.

Just a couple of days, Davison thought. He'd been hiding his psi only that long. Then he stopped to think how many days there were in five years, and he began to perspire afresh.

Two more days in the field toughened him to the point where each picking-session was no longer a nightmare. His body was a healthy one, and his muscles adapted without too much protest to their new regime. He could hold his own in the field now, and he felt a gratifying broadening of muscle and increase of vigor, a development of mere physical power which somehow pleased him mightily.

"Look at him eat," Ma Rinehart commented one night at supper. "He puts it away like it's the last meal he's ever going to see."

Davison grinned and shovelled down another mouthful of food. It was true; he was eating as he had never eaten before. His entire life on Earth seemed peculiarly pale and cloistered, next to this ground-hugging job on Mondarran IV. He was rounding into fine shape, physically.

But what was happening to his mind was starting to worry him.

He had the tk well under control, he thought, despite the fairly constant temptation to use it. It hurt, but he went right on living without making use of his paranormal powers. But there was a drawback developing.

Early on the fifth morning of his stay on Mondarran IV, he came awake in an instant, sitting up in bed and staring around. His brain seemed to be on fire; he blinked, driving the spots away, and climbed out of bed.

He stood there uneasily for a moment or two, wondering what had happened to him, listening to the pounding of his heart. Then he reached out, found the trousers draped over a chair, and slipped into them. He walked to the window and looked out.

It was still long before dawn. The sun was not yet gleaming on the horizon, and high above, the twin moons moved in stately procession through the sky. They cast a glittering, icy light on the fields. Outside, it was terribly quiet.

Davison knew what had happened. It was the reaction of his tortured, repressed mind, jolting him out of sleep to scream its protest at the treatment it was receiving. You couldn't just stop teeking, just like that. You had to taper off. That was it, thought Davison. Taper off.

He made his way down the stairs, sucking in his breath in fear every time they creaked, and left the farmhouse by the side door. He trotted lightly over the ground to the small barn that stood at the edge of the field brimming over with picked bean pods.

Quickly, in the pre-dawn silence, he hoisted himself up the ladder and into the barn. The warm, slightly musty odor of masses of pods drifted up at him. He dropped from the ladder, landed hip-deep in pods.

Then, cautiously, he brought his tk into use. A flood of relief came over him as he teeked. He reached out, lifted a solitary pod, flipped it a few feet in the air, and let it fall back. Then another; then, two at a time. It continued for almost fifteen minutes. He revelled in the use of his power, throwing the pods merrily about.

One thing alarmed him, though. He didn't seem to have his old facility. There was a definite effort involved in the telekinesis now, and he sensed a faint fatigue after a few moments of activity. This had never happened to him before.

The ominous thought struck him: suppose abstinence hurt his ability? Suppose five solid years of abstinence—assuming he could hold out that long—were to rob him of his power forever?

It didn't seem likely. After all, others had gone on these five-year exiles and returned with their powers unimpaired. They had abstained—or had they? Had they been forced into some expedient such as this, forced to rise in the small hours and go behind someone's barn to teek or to set fires?

Davison had no answers. Grimly, he teeked a few more pods into the air, and then, feeling refreshed, he climbed back out the window and down the long ladder.

Buster Rinehart was standing on the ground, looking up curiously at him.

He caught his breath sharply and continued descending.

"Hey there," Buster said. "What you doin' in there, Ry? Why ain't you asleep?"

"I could ask you the same thing," Davison said, determined to bluff it out. His hands were shaking. What if

Buster had spied on him, watched him using his power? Would they take a small boy's word on so serious a charge? Probably they would, on a psiless, witch-hysterical world like this. "What are you doing out of bed, Buster? Your mother would whale you if she knew you were up and around at this hour."

"She don't mind," the boy said. He held out a bucket that slopped over with greasy-looking pale worms. "I was out gettin' fishbait. It's the only time you can dig it, in the middle of the night with the moons shining." He grinned confidentially up at Davison. "Now what's your story?"

"I couldn't sleep. I just went for a walk," Davison said nervously, hating the necessity of defending himself in front of this boy. "That's all."

"That's what I thought. Having sleepin' troubles, eh?" Buster asked. "I know what's the matter with you, Ry. You're out mooning after my sister. She's got you so crazy for her you can't sleep. Right?"

Davison nodded immediately. "But don't tell her, will you?" He reached in a pocket and drew out a small coin, and slipped it into the boy's palm. Instantly the stubby fingers closed around it, and the coin vanished. "I don't want her to know anything about the way I feel till I've been here a while longer," Davison said.

"I'll keep shut," said the boy. His eyes sparkled in the light of the twin moons. He grasped the can of worms more tightly. He was in possession of a precious secret now, and it excited him.

Davison turned and headed back to the farmhouse, grinning wryly. The net was getting tighter, he thought. He was at the point where he had to invent imaginary romances with long-legged farm-girls in order to save his skin.

It had worked, this once. But he couldn't risk getting out there a second time. His private teeking in the barn would have to stop. He'd need to find an outlet somewhere else.

When morning finally came, Davison went downstairs and confronted old Rinehart.

"Can you spare me for today, sir? I'd like to have some free time, if it's all right with you."

The farmer frowned and scratched the back of one ear. "Free time? At harvest? Is it really necessary, boy? We'd like to get everything picked before season's out. It's going to be planting-time again soon enough, you know."

"I know," Davison said. "But I'd still like to have the morning free. I need to think some things out."

"Okay, Ry. I'm no slave-driver. Take the morning off, if you want. You can make up the time on Sunday."

The heat was just beginning as he trudged away from the Rinehart farm and down to the muddy swimming-hole at the far end of their land. He skirted it and headed on into the thick forest that separated their land from that of wealthy Lord Gabrielson.

He struck out into the forest, which was delightfully cool. Thick-boled, redleaved trees stood arrayed in a closely-packed stand of what looked like virgin timber; the soil was dark and fertile looking, and a profusion of wild vegetation spread heavily over the ground. Above, there was the chittering of colorful birds, and occasionally a curious bat-winged creature fluttered from branch to branch of the giant trees.

He knew why he was on Mondarran IV: to learn moderation. To learn to handle his power? That much was clear. But how was he going to survive?

The religious set-up here was one of jealous orthodoxy, it seemed, and the moral code made no allowance for any deviatory abilities. Psi meant witchcraft—a common equation apparently, on these backwater psiless worlds. The farmers here had little contact with the more sophisticated planets from which they had sprung, ten or twenty centuries before, and somehow they had reached a point of cultural equilibrium that left no room for psi.

That meant that Davison would have to suppress his power. Only—he *couldn't* suppress it. Five days of watchful self-control and he was half out of his mind from the strain. And what if he ran into a position where he *had* to use his psi or be killed? Suppose that tree over there were to fall directly on him; he could push it away, but what would that avail if someone were watching—someone who would cry "Witch!"

Yet men had come to Mondarran IV and returned, and survived. That meant they had found the way. Davison threaded further on into the forest, trying to arrange his thoughts coherently.

He glanced up ahead. A winding river trickled softly through the trees. And, it seemed to him, up ahead a blue curl of smoke rose up over the bushes. Was someone using a fire there?

Cautiously, he tiptoed forward cursing every time his foot cracked a twig. After a few tense moments, he rounded a bend in the path and discovered where the fire was coming from.

Squatting at the edge of the river, holding a pan in one hand, was Dumb Joe—the beggar he had encountered on the road from the spaceport. The beggar was still clad in his tattered leather outfit, and he seemed to be roasting a couple of fish over a small fire.

Grinning in relief, Davison came closer. And then the grin vanished, and he stood in open-jawed astonishment.

Dumb Joe was roasting fish all right. But there wasn't any fire—except for the radiation that seemed to be streaming from his fingertips.

Dumb Joe was a pyrotic.

Davison hung in midstride, frozen in amazement. Dumb Joe, a filthy, ignorant half-imbecile of a beggar, was casually squatting in the seclusion of the forest, psionically cooking a couple of fish for breakfast. A little further up the bank, Davison saw a rudely-constructed shack which was evidently Dumb Joe's home.

The answer to the whole thing flooded through his mind instantly. It made perfect sense.

It was impossible to live in Mondarran society with a psi power and survive the full five years. It was too hard to keep from unintentional uses of power, and the strains attendant on the whole enterprise were too great for most men to stand.

But one could live *alongside* society—as a wandering hobo, perhaps, frying fish in the forest—and no one would notice, no one would be on hand to see your occasional practice of psi. No one would suspect a flea-ridden tramp of being a witch. Of course not!

Davison took another step forward, and started to say something to Dumb Joe. But Dumb Joe looked up at the sound of the footstep. He spotted Davison standing some twenty feet away, glared angrily at him, and let the pan of fish drop to the ground. Reaching down to his hip, he whipped out a mirror-surfaced hunting knife, and without the slightest hesitation sent it whistling straight at Davison.

In the brief flashing instant after the knife left Dumb Joe's hand, a thought tore through Davison's mind. Dumb Joe would have to be an Earthman like himself, serving his five-year stay out on Mondarran. And therefore it wasn't necessary to hide his own psi power from him, wasn't necessary to let the blade strike—

Davison whisked the knife aside and let it plant itself to the hilt in the soft earth near his foot. He stooped, picked it up, and glanced at Dumb Joe.

"You—teeked it away," the beggar said, almost incredulously. "You're not a spy!"

Davison smiled. "No, I'm a tk. And you're a pyrotic!"

A slow grin crept over Dumb Joe's stubblebearded face. He crossed the ground to where Davison was standing, and seized his hand. "You're an Earthman. A real Earthman," he said exultantly, in a half whisper.

Davison nodded. "You too?"

"Yes," Dumb Joe said. "I've been here three years, and you're the first I've dared speak to. All the others I've seen have been burned."

"*All* of them?" Davison asked.

"I didn't mean that," Dumb Joe said. "Actually hardly any get burned. The Guild doesn't lose as many men as you might think. But the ones I've known about got roasted. I didn't dare approach those I wasn't sure about. You're the first—and you saw me first. I shouldn't have been so careless, but no one ever comes out this way but me."

"Or another crazy Earthman," Davison said.

He didn't dare to spend much time with Dumb Joe—whose real name, he discovered was Joseph Flanagan, formerly of Earth.

In their hurried conversation in the forest, Flanagan explained the whole thing to him. It was a perfectly logical development. Apparently a great many of the Earthmen sent to such planets adopted the guise of a tramp, and moved with shambling gait and rolling eyes from one village to another, never staying anywhere too long, never tipping their hands as to the power they possessed.

They could always slip off to the forest and use their power privately, to relieve the strain of abstinence. It didn't matter. No one was watching them; no one expected them to be witches. It was perfect camouflage.

"We'd better go," Flanagan said. "It isn't safe, even this way. And I want to last out my remaining two years. Lord, it'll be good to take baths again regularly!"

Davison grinned. "You've really got it figured," he said.

"It's the simplest way," said Flanagan. "You can't bat your head against the wall forever. I tried living in the village, the way you're doing. I almost cracked inside a month, maybe less. You can't come down to their level and hope to survive; you've got to get *below* their level, where they don't expect to find witches. Then they'll leave you alone."

Davison nodded in agreement. "That makes sense."

"I'll have to go now," said Flanagan. He allowed his muscles to relax, adopted the crooked gait and the character of Dumb Joe again, and without saying goodbye began to straggle off further into the forest. Davison stood there for a while, watching him go, and then turned and started back the way he came.

He had an answer now, he thought.

But by the time he had emerged from the forest and felt the noonday sun beating down, he wasn't so sure. Kechnie had once told him, *"Don't run away."* He hadn't explained—but now Davison knew what he meant.

Dumb Joe Flanagan would last out his five years with a minimum of effort, and when he returned he would get his release and become a member of the Guild. But had he really accomplished his goal to the fullest? Not really, Davison told himself. It wouldn't be possible for him to hide as a beggar forever; sometime, somewhere, it would be necessary for him to function as a member of society, and then Flanagan's five years of shambling would do him little good.

There had to be some other way, Davison thought fiercely. Some way to stick out the five years without burying his head like an ostrich. Some way that would leave him fit to return to society, or to live in some psiless society, and still have his psi power under firm control.

He strode through the hot fields. Off in the distance, he could see the Rinehart family finishing up a furrow. It was noon, and they would be knocking off now. As he looked, he saw sturdy Dirk Rinehart finish his furrow and empty his pods into the waiting truck, and before he had come within shouting distance the rest of them had done so too, and were standing around relaxing after a hard morning's work.

"Well, look who's back!" Janey exclaimed, as Davison drew near. "Have a nice morning's relaxation?"

"I did some heavy thinking, Janey," Davison said mildly. "And I'll be making up my time on Sunday, while you're resting. It balances out."

Old Rinehart came over, smiling. "All thought out, youngster? I hope so, because there's a rough afternoon's work waiting for us."

"I'll be with you," Davison said. He clamped his lips together, not listening to what they were saying, wondering only where the way out might lie.

"Hey, look at me," called a piping voice from behind him.

"Put those down!" Dirk Rinehart ordered sternly. "Get down from there before you break your neck!"

Davison turned and saw Buster Rinehart, standing upon the cab of the truck. He had some bean pods in his hands and he was energetically juggling them through the air. "Look at me!" he yelled again, evidently proud of his own acrobatic skill. "I'm juggling!"

A moment later he lost control of the pods. They fell and scattered all over the ground. A moment later, the boy was yowling in pain as his father's palm administered punishment vigorously.

Davison chuckled. Then he laughed louder, as he realized what had happened.

He had his answer at last.

Davison gave notice at the end of the week, after working particularly hard in the field. He felt a little guilty about quitting just before planting time, and he had grown to like the Rineharts more than a little. But it was necessary to pull out and move on.

He told Dirk Rinehart he would go after another week had elapsed, and though the farmer had obviously not been pleased by the news, he made no protest. When his week was up, Davison left, gathering his goods together in his suitcase and departing by foot.

He needed to cover quite a distance—far enough from the village so that no one would trace him. He hired one of the nearby farmers' sons to drive him to the next town, giving him one of his remaining coins to do so. Folded in his hip pocket was the crumpled wad of bills that was his salary for his stay at Rinehart's above room and board. He didn't want to touch that money at all.

The boy drove him through the flat, monotonous Mondarran countryside to another town only slightly larger than the first, and otherwise almost identical.

"Thanks," Davison said simply, got out and started to walk. He entered the town—it too, had its witch-pole—and started looking around for a place to live. He had many preparations to tend to before he would be ready.

Six months later, the signs started to appear all over the local countryside. They were gaudy, printed in three colors, bright and eye-catching. They said, simply,

THE PRESTIDIGITATOR IS COMING!

It caused a stir. As Davison drove his gilded, ornate chariot into the first town on his itinerary, the rambling village on the far side of Lord Gabrielson's domain, a crowd gathered before him and preceded him down the main street, shouting and whooping. It wasn't every day of the year that a traveling magician came to town.

He drove solemnly behind them down the wide street, turned the chariot around, and parked it almost in front of the steel witch-pole. He set the handbrakes, lowered the little platform on which he was going to perform, and stepped out, resplendent in his red-and-gold costume with billowing cloak, in full view of the crowd. He saw a little ripple of anticipation run through them at his appearance.

A tall yokel in the front called out, "Are you the presti—prestig—the whatever you are?"

"I am Marius the Prestidigitator, indeed," Davison said in a sepulchral voice. He was enjoying it.

"Well, just what do you do, Mr. Marius?" the yokel replied.

Davison grinned. This was better than having a shill or a trained stooge in the crowd. "Young man, I perform feats that stagger the imagination, that astound the mind, that topple reality." He waved his arms over his head in a wild, grandiose gesture. "I can call spirits from the vasty deep!" he thundered. "I hold the secrets of life and death!"

"That's what all you magicians say," someone drawled boredly from the back of the crowd. "Let's see you do something, before we have to pay!"

"Very well, unbeliever!" Davison roared. He reached

behind himself, drew forth a pair of wax candles, struck a match, and lit the candles. "Observe the way I handle these tapers," he said sonorously. "Notice that I handle the fiery flames without experiencing the slightest harm."

He hefted the candles, tossed them aloft, and began to rotate them telekinetically so that whenever they came down, it was the unlit end he grasped. He juggled the two candles for a moment or two, then reached back, drew forth a third, and inserted it into the rotation. He remained that way for a moment, and the crowd grew silent as Davison tottered around under the candles, pretending to be having all sorts of difficulties. Finally, when the wax became too pliable to handle easily, he teeked the candles down and caught them. He waved them aloft. The crowd responded with a tinkle of coins.

"Thank you, thank you," he said. He pulled out a box full of colored globes, and began to juggle them without prologue. Within a few seconds he had five of them going at once—actually manipulated by tk, while he waved his hands impressively but meaninglessly beneath them. He sent up a sixth, then a seventh.

He smiled pleasantly to himself as he juggled. Quite possibly these people had encountered telekinetics before, and had burned them for witches. But those were *real* telekinetics; he was only a sleight-of-hand artist, a man of exceptional coordination, a wandering charlatan—a fake. Everyone knew magicians were phonies, and that it was by tricky fingerwork that he kept all those globes aloft.

When the shower of coins had stopped, he caught the balls and restored them to their box. He began a new trick—one which involved a rapid line of patter while he set up an elaborate balancing stunt. Piling chairs on top of thin planks and adding odd pieces of furniture from the back of his chariot to make the edifice even more precarious, he assembled a balanced heap some twelve feet high. He ran round it rapidly ostensibly guiding it with his hands, actually keeping the woodpile under a firm tk control.

Finally he was satisfied with the balance. He began to climb slowly. When he reached the uppermost chair—balanced crazily on one of its legs alone—he climbed up, bracing himself, and by teeking against the ground, lifted himself and balanced for a long moment by one hand.

Then he swung down, leaped lightly to the ground, and waved one hand in triumph. A clatter of coins resulted.

This was the way, he thought, as the crowd roared its approval. They'd never suspect he was using a sort of *real* magic. He could practice control of his psi in ordinary life, and this charlatanry would give him the needed outlet as well. When he returned to Earth, he'd be adjusted, more so than the ones like Dumb Joe. Davison was remaining in society. He wasn't running away.

A small boy in the first row stood up. "Aw, I know how you did that," he shouted derisively. "It was just a trick. You had it all—"

"Don't give the show away, sonny," Davison interrupted in a loud stage whisper. "Let's just keep these things secret—between us magicians, huh?"

The Song
the Zombie Sang *

From the fourth balcony of the Los Angeles Music Center the stage was little more than a brilliant blur of constantly changing chromatics—stabs of bright green, looping whorls of crimson. But Rhoda preferred to sit up there. She had no use for the Golden Horseshoe seats, buoyed on their grab-grav plates, bobbling loosely just beyond the fluted lip of the stage. Down there the sound flew off, flew up and away, carried by the remarkable acoustics of the Center's Takamuri dome. The colors were important, but it was the sound that really mattered, the patterns of resonance bursting from the hundred quivering outputs of the ultracembalo.

And if you sat below, you had the vibrations of the people down there—

She was hardly naive enough to think that the poverty that sent students up to the top was more ennobling than the wealth that permitted access to a Horseshoe; yet even though she had never actually sat through an entire concert down there, she could not deny that music heard from the fourth balcony was purer, more affecting, lasted longer in the memory. Perhaps it *was* the vibrations of the rich.

Arms folded on the railing of the balcony, she stared down at the rippling play of colors that washed the sprawling proscenium. Dimly she was aware that the man at her side was saying something. Somehow responding didn't seem important. Finally he nudged her, and she turned to him. A faint, mechanical smile crossed her face. "What is it, Laddy?"

Ladislas Jirasek mournfully extended a chocolate bar.

* In collaboration with Harlan Ellison

Its end was ragged from having been nibbled. "Man cannot live by Bekh alone," he said.

"No, thanks, Laddy." She touched his hand lightly.

"What do you see down there?"

"Colors. That's all."

"No music of the spheres? No insight into the truths of your art?"

"You promised not to make fun of me."

He slumped back in his seat. "I'm sorry. I forget sometimes."

"Please, Laddy. If it's the liaison thing that's bothering you, I—"

"I didn't say a word about liaison, did I?"

"It was in your tone. You were starting to feel sorry for yourself. Please don't. You know I hate it when you start dumping guilts on me."

He had sought an official liaison with her for months, almost since the day they had met in Contrapuntal 301. He had been fascinated by her, amused by her, and finally had fallen quite hopelessly in love with her. Still she kept just beyond his reach. He had had her, but had never possessed her. Because he did feel sorry for himself, and she knew it, and the knowledge put him, for her, forever in the category of men who were simply not for long-term liaison.

She stared down past the railing. Waiting. Taut. A slim girl, honey-colored hair, eyes the lightest gray, almost the shade of aluminum. Her fingers lightly curved as if about to pounce on a keyboard. Music uncoiling eternally in her head.

"They say Bekh was brilliant in Stuttgart last week," Jirasek said hopefully.

"He did the Kreutzer?"

"And Timijian's Sixth and *The Knife* and some Scarlatti."

"Which?"

"I don't know. I don't remember what they said. But he got a ten-minute standing ovation, and *Der Musikant* said they hadn't heard such precise ornamentation since—"

The houselights dimmed.

"He's coming," Rhoda said, leaning forward. Jirasek slumped back and gnawed the chocolate bar down to its wrapper.

Coming out of it was always gray. The color of aluminum. He knew the charging was over, knew he'd been unpacked, knew when he opened his eyes that he would be at stage right, and there would be a grip ready to roll the ultracembalo's input console onstage, and the filament gloves would be in his right-hand jacket pocket. And the taste of sand on his tongue, and the gray fog of resurrection in his mind.

Nils Bekh put off opening his eyes.

Stuttgart had been a disaster. Only he knew how much of a disaster. Timi would have known, he thought. He would have come up out of the audience during the scherzo, and he would have ripped the gloves off my hands, and he would have cursed me for killing his vision. And later they would have gone to drink the dark, nutty beer together. But Timijian was dead. Died in '20, Bekh told himself. Five years before me.

I'll keep my eyes closed, I'll dampen the breathing. Will the lungs to suck more shallowly, the bellows to vibrate rather than howl with winds. And they'll think I'm malfunctioning, that the zombianic response wasn't triggered this time. That I'm still dead, really dead, not—

"Mr. Bekh."

He opened his eyes.

The stage manager was a thug. He recognized the type. Stippling of unshaved beard. Crumpled cuffs. Latent homosexuality. Tyrant to everyone backstage except, perhaps, the chorus boys in the revivals of Romberg and Friml confections.

"I've known men to develop diabetes just catching a matinee," Bekh said.

"What's that? I don't understand."

Bekh waved it away. "Nothing. Forget it. How's the house?"

"Very nice, Mr. Bekh. The houselights are down. We're ready."

Bekh reached into his right-hand jacket pocket and removed the thin electronic gloves, sparkling with their rows of minisensors and pressors. He pulled the right glove tight, smoothing all wrinkles. The material clung like a second skin. "If you please," he said. The grip rolled the console onstage, positioned it, locked it down with the dogging pedals, and hurried offstage left through the curtains.

Now Bekh strolled slowly out. Moving with great care: tubes of glittering fluids ran through his calves and thighs, and if he walked too fast the hydrostatic balance was disturbed and the nutrients didn't get to his brain. The fragility of the perambulating dead was a nuisance, one among many. When he reached the grab-grav plate he signalled the stage manager. The thug gave the sign to the panel-man, who passed his fingers over the color-coded keys, and the grab-grav plate rose slowly, majestically. Up through the floor of the stage went Nils Bekh. As he emerged, the chromatics keyed sympathetic vibrations in the audience, and they began to applaud.

He stood silently, head slightly bowed, accepting their greeting. A bubble of gas ran painfully through his back and burst near his spine. His lower lip twitched slightly. He suppressed the movement. Then he stepped off the plate, walked to the console, and began pulling on the other glove.

He was a tall, elegant man, very pale, with harsh brooding cheekbones and a craggy, massive nose that dominated the flower-gentle eyes, the thin mouth. He looked properly romantic. An important artistic asset, they told him when he was starting out, a million years ago.

As he pulled and smoothed the other glove, he heard the whispering. When one has died, one's hearing becomes terribly acute. It made listening to one's own performances that much more painful. But he knew what the whispers were all about. Out there someone was saying to his wife:

"Of course he doesn't *look* like a zombie. They kept him in cold till they had the techniques. *Then* they wired him and juiced him and brought him back."

And the wife would say, "How does it work, how does he keep coming back to life, what is it?"

And the husband would lean far over on the arm of his chair, resting his elbow, placing the palm of his hand in front of his mouth and looking warily around to be certain that no one would overhear the blurred inaccuracies he was about to utter. And he would try to tell his wife about the residual electric charge of the brain cells, the persistence of the motor responses after death, the lingering mechanical vitality on which they had seized. In vague and rambling terms he would speak of the built-in life-support system that keeps the brain flushed with necessary fluids. The surrogate hormones, the chemicals that take the place of blood. "You know how they stick an electric wire up a frog's leg, when they cut it off. Okay. Well, when the leg jerks, they call that a galvanic response. Now if you can get a whole *man* to jerk when you put a current through him—not really jerking, I mean that he walks around, he can play his instrument—"

"Can he think too?"

"I suppose. I don't know. The brain's intact. They don't let it decay. What they do, they use every part of the body for its mechanical function—the heart's a pump, the lungs are bellows—and they wire in a bunch of contacts and leads and then there's a kind of twitch, an artificial burst of life—of course, they can keep it going only five, six hours, then the fatigue-poisons start to pile up and clog the lines—but that's long enough for a concert, anyway—"

"So what they're really doing is they take a man's brain, and they keep it alive by using his own body as the life-support machine," the wife says brightly. "Is that it? Instead of putting him into some kind of box, they keep him in his own skull, and do all the machinery inside his body—"

"That's it. That's it exactly, more or less. More or less."

Bekh ignored the whispers. He had heard them all hundreds of times before. In New York and Beirut, in Hanoi and Knossos, in Kenyatta and Paris. How fascinated they were. Did they come for the music, or to see the dead man walk around?

He sat down on the player's ledge in front of the console, and laid his hands along the metal fibers. A deep breath: old habit, superfluous, inescapable. The fingers already twitching. The pressors seeking the keys. Under the close-cropped gray hair, the synapses clicking like relays. Here, now. Timijian's Ninth Sonata. Let it soar. Bekh closed his eyes and put his shoulders into his work, and from the ring of outputs overhead came the proper roaring tones. There. It has begun. Easily, lightly, Bekh rang in the harmonics, got the sympathetic pipes vibrating, built up the texture of sound. He had not played the Ninth for two years. Vienna. How long is two years? It seemed hours ago. He still heard the reverberations. And duplicated them exactly; this performance differed from the last one no more than one playing of a recording differs from another. An image sprang into his mind: a glistening sonic cube sitting at the console in place of a man. Why do they need me, when they could put a cube in the slot and have the same thing at less expense? And I could rest. And I could rest. There. Keying in the subsonics. This wonderful instrument! What if Bach had known it? Beethoven? To hold a whole world in your fingertips. The entire spectrum of sound, and the colors, too, and more: hitting the audience in a dozen senses at once. Of course, the music is what matters. The frozen, unchanging music. The pattern of sounds emerging now as always, now as he had played it at the premier in '19. Timijian's last work. Decibel by decibel, a reconstruction of my own performance. And look at them out there. Awed. Loving. Bekh felt tremors in his elbows; too tense, the nerves betraying him. He made the necessary compensations. Hearing the thunder reverberating from the fourth balcony. What is this music all about? Do I in fact understand any of it? Does the sonic cube comprehend the B Minor Mass that is recorded within itself? Does the amplifier understand the symphony it amplifies? Bekh smiled. Closed his eyes. The shoulders surging, the wrists supple. Two hours to go. Then they let me sleep again. Is it fifteen years, now? Awaken, perform, sleep. And the adoring public cooing at me. The women who would love to give themselves to me. Necrophiliacs? How could they even want to touch me? The dryness of the tomb on my skin. Once there were women, yes, Lord, yes! Once. Once there was life, too. Bekh leaned back and swept forward. The old virtuoso swoop; brings down the house. The chill in their spines. Now the sound builds toward the end of the first movement. Yes, yes, so. Bekh opened the topmost bank of outputs and heard the audience respond, everyone sitting up suddenly as the new smash of sound cracked across the air. Good old Timi: a wonderful sense of the theatrical. Up. Up. Knock them back in their seats. He smiled with satisfaction at his own effects. And then the sense of emptiness. Sound for its own sake. Is this what music means? Is this a masterpiece? I know nothing any more. How tired I am of playing for them. Will they applaud? Yes, and stamp their feet and congratulate one another on having been lucky enough to hear me tonight. And what do they know? What do I know. I am dead. I am nothing. I am nothing. With a demonic two-handed plunge he hammered out the final fugal screams of the first movement.

Weatherex had programmed mist, and somehow it fit Rhoda's mood. They stood on the glass landscape that swept down from the Music Center, and Jirasek offered her the pipe. She shook her head absently, thinking of other things. "I have a pastille," she said.

"What do you say we look up Inez and Treat, see if they want to get something to eat?"

She didn't answer.

"Rhoda?"

"Will you excuse me, Laddy? I think I want to be all by myself for a while."

He slipped the pipe into his pocket and turned to her. She was looking through him as if he were no less glass than the scene surrounding them. Taking her hands in his own, he said, "Rhoda, I just don't understand. You won't even give me time to find the words."

"Laddy—"

"No. This time I'll have my say. Don't pull away. Don't retreat into that little world of yours, with your half-smiles and your faraway looks."

"I want to think about the music."

"There's more to life than music, Rhoda. There has to be. I've spent as many years as you working inside my head, working to create something. You're better than I am, you're maybe better than anyone I've ever heard, maybe even better than Bekh some day. Fine: you're a great artist. But is that all? There's something more. It's idiocy to make your art your religion, your whole existence."

"Why are you doing this to me?"

"Because I love you."

"That's an explanation, not an excuse. Let me go, Laddy. Please."

"Rhoda, art doesn't mean a damn thing if it's just craft, if it's just rote and technique and formulas. It doesn't mean anything if there isn't love behind it and caring, and commitment to life. You deny all that. You split yourself and smother the part that fires the art. . . ."

He stopped abruptly. It was not the sort of speech a man could deliver without realizing, quickly, crushingly, how sententious and treacly it sounded. He dropped her hands. "I'll be at Treat's, if you want to see me later." He turned and walked away into the shivering reflective night.

Rhoda watched him go. She suspected there were things

she should have said. But she hadn't said them. He disappeared. Turning, she stared up at the overwhelming bulk of the Music Center, and began slowly to walk toward it.

"Maestro, you were exquisite tonight," the pekinese woman said in the Green Room. "Golden," added the bullfrog sycophant. "A joy. I cried, really cried," trilled the birds. Nutrients bubbled in his chest. He could feel valves flapping. He dipped his head, moved his hands, whispered thankyous. Staleness settled grittily behind his forehead. "Superb." "Unforgettable." "Incredible." Then they went away and he was left, as always, with the keepers. The man from the corporation that owned him, the stage manager, the packers, the electrician. "Perhaps it's time," said the corporation man, smoothing his mustache lightly. He had learned to be delicate with the zombie.

Bekh sighed and nodded. They turned him off.

"Want to get something to eat first?" the electrician said. He yawned. It had been a long tour, late nights, meals in jetports, steep angles of ascent and rapid re-entries.

The corporation man nodded. "All right. We can leave him here for a while. I'll put him on standby." He touched a switch.

The lights went off in banks, one by one. Only the nightlights remained for the corporation man and the electrician, for their return, for their final packing.

The Music Center shut down.

In the bowels of the self-contained system the dust-eaters and a dozen other species of cleanup machines began stirring, humming softly.

In the fourth balcony, a shadow moved. Rhoda worked her way toward the downslide, emerging in the center aisle of the orchestra, in the horseshoe, around the pit, and onto the stage. She went to the console and let her hands rest an inch above the keys. Closing her eyes, catching her breath. I will begin my concert with the Timijian Ninth Sonata for Unaccompanied Ultracembalo. A light patter of applause, gathering force, now tempestuous. Waiting. The fingers descending. The world alive with her music. Fire and tears, joy, radiance. All of them caught in the spell. How miraculous. How wonderfully she plays. Looking out into the darkness, hearing in her tingling mind the terrible echoes of the silence. Thank you. Thank you all so much. Her eyes moist. Moving away from the console. The flow of fantasy ebbing.

She went on into the dressing room and stood just within the doorway, staring across the room at the corpse of Nils Bekh in the sustaining chamber, his eyes closed, his chest still, his hands relaxed at his sides. She could see the faintest bulge in his right jacket pocket where the thin gloves lay, fingers folded together.

Then she moved close to him, looked down into his face, and touched his cheek. His beard never grew. His skin was cool and satiny, a strangely feminine texture. Strangely, through the silence, she remembered the sinuous melody of the Liebestod, that greatest of all laments, and rather than the great sadness the passage always brought to her, she felt herself taken by anger. Gripped by frustration and disappointment, choked by betrayal, caught in a seizure of violence. She wanted to rake the pudding-smooth skin of his face with her nails. She wanted to pummel him. Deafen him with screams. Destroy him. For the lie. For the lies, the many lies, the unending flow of lying notes, the lies of his life after death.

Her trembling hand hovered by the side of the chamber. Is this the switch?

She turned him on.

He came out of it. Eyes closed. Rising through a universe the color of aluminum. Again, then. Again. He thought he would stand there a moment with eyes closed, collecting himself, before going onstage. It got harder and harder. The last time had been so bad. In Los Angeles, in that vast building, balcony upon balcony, thousands of blank faces, the ultracembalo such a masterpiece of construction. He had opened the concert with Timi's Ninth. So dreadful. A sluggish performance, note-perfect, the tempi flawless, and yet sluggish, empty, shallow. And tonight it would happen again. Shamble out on stage, don the gloves, go through the dreary routine of recreating the greatness of Nils Bekh.

His audience, his adoring followers. How he hated them! How he longed to turn on them and denounce them for what they had done to him. Schnabel rested. Horowitz rested. Joachim rested. But for Bekh there was no rest. They had not allowed him to go. Oh, he could have refused to let them sustain him. But he had never been that strong. He had had strength for the loveless, lightless years of living with his music, yes. For that there had never been enough time. Strong was what he had had to be. To come from where he had been, to learn what had to be learned, to keep his skills once they were his. Yes. But in dealing with people, in speaking out, in asserting himself ... in short, having courage ... no, there had been very little of that. He had lost Dorothea, he had acceded to Wizmer's plans, he had borne the insults Lisbeth and Neil and Cosh—ah, gee, Cosh, was he still alive?—the insults they had used to keep him tied to them, for better or worse, always worse. So he had gone with them, done their bidding, never availed himself of his strength—if in fact there was strength of that sort buried somewhere in him—and in the end even Sharon had despised him.

So how could he go to the edge of the stage, stand there in the full glare of the lights and tell them what they were? Ghouls. Selfish ghouls. As dead as he was, but in a different way. Unfeeling, hollow.

But if he could! If he could just once outwit the corporation man, he would throw himself forward and he would shout—

Pain. A stinging pain in his cheek. His head jolted back; the tiny pipes in his neck protested. The sound of flesh on flesh echoed in his mind. Startled, he opened his eyes. A girl before him. The color of aluminum, her eyes. A young face. Fierce. Thin lips tightly clamped. Nostrils flaring. Why is she so angry? She was raising her hand to slap him again. He threw his hands up, wrists crossed, palms forward, to protect his eyes. The second blow landed more heavily than the first. Were delicate things shattering within his reconstructed body?

The look on her face! She hated him.

She slapped him a third time. He peered out between his fingers, astonished by the vehemence of her eyes. And felt the flooding pain, and felt the hate, and felt a terribly wonderful sense of life for just that one moment. Then he remembered too much, and he stopped her.

He could see as he grabbed her swinging hand that she

found his strength improbable. Fifteen years a zombie, moving and living for only seven hundred four days of that time. Still, he was fully operable, fully conditioned, fully muscled.

The girl winced. He released her and shoved her away. She was rubbing her wrists and staring at him silently, sullenly.

"If you don't like me," he asked, "why did you turn me on?"

"So I could tell you I know what a fraud you are. These others, the ones who applaud and grovel and suck up to you, they don't know, they have no idea, but I know. How can you do it? How can you have made such a disgusting spectacle of yourself?" She was shaking. "I heard you when I was a child," she said. "You changed my whole life. I'll never forget it. But I've heard you lately. Slick formulas, no real insight. Like a machine sitting at the console. A player piano. You know what player pianos were, Bekh. That's what you are."

He shrugged. Walking past her, he sat down and glanced in the dressing-room mirror. He looked old and weary, the changeless face changing now. There was a flatness to his eyes. They were without sheen, without depths. An empty sky.

"Who are you?" he asked quietly. "How did you get in here?"

"Report me, go ahead. I don't care if I'm arrested. Someone had to say it. You're shameful! Walking around, pretending to make music—don't you see how awful it is? A performer is an interpretative artist, not just a machine for playing the notes. I shouldn't have to tell you that. An interpretative artist. Artist. Where's your art now? Do you see beyond the score? Do you grow from performance to performance?"

Suddenly he liked her very much. Despite her plainness, despite her hatred, despite himself. "You're a musician."

She let that pass.

"What do you play?" Then he smiled. "The ultracembalo, of course. And you must be very good."

"Better than you. Clearer, cleaner, deeper. Oh, God, what am I doing here? You *disgust* me."

"How can I keep on growing?" Bekh asked gently. "The dead don't grow."

Her tirade swept on, as if she hadn't heard. Telling him

over and over how despicable he was, what a counterfeit of greatness. And then she halted in midsentence. Blinking, reddening, putting hands to lips. "Oh," she murmured, abashed, starting to weep. "Oh. *Oh!*"

She went silent.

It lasted a long time. She looked away, studied the walls, the mirror, her hands, her shoes. He watched her. Then, finally, she said, "What an arrogant little snot I am. What a cruel foolish bitch. I never stopped to think that you—that maybe—I just didn't think—" He thought she would run from him. "And you won't forgive me, will you? Why should you? I break in, I turn you on, I scream a lot of cruel nonsense at you—"

"It wasn't nonsense. It was all quite true, you know. Absolutely true." Then, softly, he said, "Break the machinery."

"Don't worry. I won't cause any more trouble for you. I'll go, now. I can't tell you how foolish I feel, haranguing you like that. A dumb little puritan puffed up with pride in her own art. Telling *you* that you don't measure up to my ideals. When I—"

"You didn't hear me. I asked you to break the machinery."

She looked at him in a new way, slightly out of focus. "What are you talking about?"

"To stop me. I want to be gone. Is that so hard to understand? You, of all people, should understand that. What you say is true, very very true. Can you put yourself where I am? A thing, not alive, not dead, just a thing, a tool, an implement that unfortunately thinks and remembers and wishes for release. Yes, a player piano. My life stopped and my art stopped, and I have nothing to belong to now, not even the art. For it's always the same. Always the same tones, the same reaches, the same heights. Pretending to make music, as you say. Pretending."

"But I can't—"

"Of course you can. Come, sit down, we'll discuss it. And you'll play for me."

"Play for you?"

He reached out his hand and she started to take it, then drew her hand back. "You'll have to play for me," he said quietly. "I can't let just anyone end me. That's a big, important thing, you see. Not just anyone. So you'll play for me." He got heavily to his feet. Thinking of Lisbeth,

Sharon, Dorothea. Gone, all gone now. Only he, Bekh, left behind, some of him left behind, old bones, dried meat. Breath as stale as Egypt. Blood the color of pumice. Sounds devoid of tears and laughter. Just sounds.

He led the way, and she followed him, out onto the stage, where the console still stood uncrated. He gave her his gloves, saying, "I know they aren't yours. I'll take that into account. Do the best you can." She drew them on slowly, smoothing them.

She sat down at the console. He saw the fear in her face, and the ecstasy, also. Her fingers hovering over the keys. Pouncing. God, Timi's Ninth! The tones swelling and rising, and the fear going from her face. Yes. Yes. He would not have played it that way, but yes, just so. Timi's notes filtered through *her* soul. A striking interpretation. Perhaps she falters a little, but why not? The wrong gloves, no preparation, strange circumstances. And how beautifully she plays. The hall fills with sound. He ceases to listen as a critic might; he becomes part of the music. His own fingers moving, his muscles quivering, reaching for pedals and stops, activating the pressors. As if he plays through her. She goes on, soaring higher, losing the last of her nervousness. In full command. Not yet a finished artist, but so good, so wonderfully good! Making the mighty instrument sing. Draining its full resources. Underscoring this, making that more lean. Oh, yes! He is in the music. It engulfs him. Can he cry? Do the tearducts still function? He can hardly bear it, it is so beautiful. He has forgotten, in all these years. He has not heard anyone else play for so long. Seven hundred four days. Out of the tomb. Bound up in his own meaningless performances. And now this. The rebirth of music. It was once like this all the time, the union of composer and instrument and performer, soulwrenching, all-encompassing. For him. No longer. Eyes closed, he plays the movement through to its close by way of her body, her hands, her soul. When the sound dies away, he feels the good exhaustion that comes from total submission to the art.

"That's fine," he said, when the last silence was gone. "That was very lovely." A catch in his voice. His hands were still trembling; he was afraid to applaud.

He reached for her, and this time she took his hand. For a moment he held her cool fingers. Then he tugged gently, and she followed him back into the dressing room, and he laid down on the sofa, and he told her which mechanisms to break, after she turned him off, so he would feel no pain. Then he closed his eyes and waited.

"You'll just—go?" she asked.

"Quickly. Peacefully."

"I'm afraid. It's like murder."

"I'm dead," he said. "But not dead enough. You won't be killing anything. Do you remember how my playing sounded to you? Do you remember why I came here? Is there life in me?"

"I'm still afraid."

"I've earned my rest," he said. He opened his eyes and smiled. "It's all right. I like you." And, as she moved toward him, he said, "Thank you."

Then he closed his eyes again.

She turned him off.

Then she did as he had instructed her. Picking her way past the wreckage of the sustaining chamber, she left the dressing room. She found her way out of the Music Center—out onto the glass landscape, under the singing stars, and she was crying for him.

Laddy. She wanted very much to find Laddy now. To talk to him. To tell him he was almost right about what he'd told her. Not entirely, but more than she had believed ... before. She went away from there. Smoothly, with songs yet to be sung.

And behind her, a great peace had settled. Unfinished, at last the symphony had wrung its last measure of strength and sorrow.

It did not matter what Weatherex said was the proper time for mist or rain or fog. Night, the stars, the songs were forever.

Flies

Here is Cassiday:
transfixed on a table.

There wasn't much left of him. A brain-box; a few ropes
of nerves; a limb. The sudden implosion had taken care of
the rest. There was enough, though. The golden ones
didn't need much to go by. They had found him in the
wreckage of the drifting ship as it passed through their
zone, back of Iapetus. He was alive. He could be repaired.
The others on the ship were beyond hope.

Repair him? Of course. Did one need to be human in
order to be humanitarian? Repair, yes. By all means. And
change. The golden ones were creative.

What was left of Cassiday lay in drydock on a somewhere table in a golden sphere of force. There was no
change of season here; only the sheen of the walls, the
unvarying warmth. Neither day nor night, neither yesterday nor tomorrow. Shapes came and went about him.
They were regenerating him, stage by stage, as he lay in
complete unthinking tranquillity. The brain was intact but
not functioning. The rest of the man was growing back:
tendon and ligament, bone and blood, heart and elbows.
Elongated mounds of tissue sprouted tiny buds that en-
larged into blobs of flesh. Paste cell to cell together, build
a man from his own wreckage—that was no chore for the
golden ones. They had their skills. But they had much to
learn too, and this Cassiday could help them learn it.

Day by day Cassiday grew toward wholeness. They did
not awaken him. He lay cradled in warmth, unmoving,

unthinking, drifting on the tide. His new flesh was pink and smooth, like a baby's. The epithelial thickening came a little later. Cassiday served as his own blueprint. The golden ones replicated him from a shred of himself, built him back from his own polynucleotide chains, decoded the proteins and reassembled him from the template. An easy task, for them. Why not? Any blob of protoplasm could do it—for itself. The golden ones, who were not protoplasm, could do it for others.

They made some changes in the template. Of course. They were craftsmen. And there was a good deal they wanted to learn.

Look at Cassiday:
the dossier.

BORN 1 August 2316
PLACE Nyack, New York
PARENTS Various
ECONOMIC LEVEL Low
EDUCATIONAL LEVEL Middle
OCCUPATION Fuel technician
MARITAL STATUS Three legal liaisons, duration eight months, sixteen months, and two months
HEIGHT Two meters
WEIGHT 96 kg
HAIR COLOR Yellow
EYES Blue
BLOOD TYPE A+
INTELLIGENCE LEVEL High
SEXUAL INCLINATIONS Normal

Watch them now:
changing him.

The complete man lay before them, newly minted, ready for rebirth. Now came the final adjustments. They sought the gray brain within its pink wrapper, and entered it, and traveled through the bays and inlets of the mind, pausing now at this quiet cove, dropping anchor now at the base of that slab-sided cliff. They were operating, but doing it neatly. Here were no submucous resections, no glittering blades carving through gristle and bone, no sizzling lasers at work, no clumsy hammering at the tender meninges. Cold steel did not slash the synapses. The golden ones were subtler; they tuned the circuit that was

Cassiday, boosted the gain, damped out the noise, and they did it very gently.

When they were finished with him, he was much more sensitive. He had several new hungers. They had granted him certain abilities.

Now they awakened him.

"You are alive, Cassiday," a feathery voice said. "Your ship was destroyed. Your companions were killed. You alone survived."

"Which hospital is this?"

"Not on Earth. You'll be going back soon. Stand up, Cassiday. Move your right hand. Your left. Flex your knees. Inflate your lungs. Open and close your eyes several times. What's your name, Cassiday?"

"Richard Henry Cassiday."

"How old?"

"Forty-one."

"Look at this reflection. Who do you see?"

"Myself."

"Do you have any further questions?"

"What did you do to me?"

"Repaired you, Cassiday. You were almost entirely destroyed."

"Did you change me any?"

"We made you more sensitive to the feelings of your fellow man."

"Oh," said Cassiday.

Follow Cassiday as he journeys:
    back to Earth.

He arrived on a day that had been programmed for snow. Light snow, quickly melting, an esthetic treat rather than a true manifestation of weather. It was good to touch foot on the homeworld again. The golden ones had deftly arranged his return, putting him back aboard his wrecked ship and giving him enough of a push to get him within range of a distress sweep. The monitors had detected him and picked him up. How was it you survived the disaster unscathed, Spaceman Cassiday? Very simple, sir, I was outside the ship when it happened. It just went swoosh, and everybody was killed. And I only am escaped alone to tell thee.

They routed him to Mars and checked him out, and

held him awhile in a decontamination lock on Luna, and finally sent him back to Earth. He stepped into the snowstorm, a big man with a rolling gait and careful calluses in all the right places. He had few friends, no relatives, enough cash units to see him through for a while, and a couple of ex-wives he could look up. Under the rules, he was entitled to a year off with full pay as his disaster allotment. He intended to accept the furlough.

He had not yet begun to make use of his new sensitivity. The golden ones had planned it so that his abilities would remain inoperative until he reached the homeworld. Now he had arrived, and it was time to begin using them, and the endlessly curious creatures who lived back of Iapetus waited patiently while Cassiday sought out those who had once loved him.

He began his quest in Chicago Urban District, because that was where the spaceport was, just outside of Rockford. The slidewalk took him quickly to the travertine tower, festooned with radiant inlays of ebony and violet-hued metal, and there, at the local Televector Central, Cassiday checked out the present whereabouts of his former wives. He was patient about it, a bland-faced, mild-eyed tower of flesh, pushing the right buttons and waiting placidly for the silken contacts to close somewhere in the depths of the Earth. Cassiday had never been a violent man. He was calm. He knew how to wait.

The machine told him that Beryl Fraser Cassiday Mellon lived in Boston Urban District. The machine told him that Lureen Holstein Cassiday lived in New York Urban District. The machine told him that Mirabel Gunryk Cassiday Milman Reed lived in San Francisco Urban District.

The names awakened memories: warmth of flesh, scent of hair, touch of hand, sound of voice. Whispers of passion. Snarls of contempt. Gasps of love.

Cassiday, restored to life, went to see his ex-wives.

We find one now:
safe and sound.

Beryl's eyes were milky in the pupil, greenish where they should have been white. She had lost weight in the last ten years, and now her face was parchment stretched over bone, an eroded face, the cheekbones pressing from within against the taut skin and likely to snap through at any moment. Cassiday had been married to her for eight months when he was twenty-four. They had separated after she insisted on taking the Sterility Pledge. He had not particularly wanted children, but he was offended by her maneuver all the same. Now she lay in a soothing cradle of webfoam, trying to smile at him without cracking her lips.

"They said you'd been killed," she told him.

"I escaped. How have you been, Beryl?"

"You can see that. I'm taking the cure."

"Cure?"

"I was a triline addict. Can't you see? My eyes, my face? It melted me away. But it was peaceful. Like disconnecting your soul. Only it would have killed me, another year of it. Now I'm on the cure. They tapered me off last month. They're building up my system with prosthetics. I'm full of plastic now. But I'll live."

"You've remarried?" Cassiday asked.

"He split long ago. I've been alone five years. Just me and the triline. But now I'm off that stuff." Beryl blinked laboriously. "You look so relaxed, Dick. But you always were. So calm, so sure of yourself. *You'd* never get yourself hooked on triline. Hold my hand, will you?"

He touched the withered claw. He felt the warmth coming from her, the need for love. Great throbbing waves came lalloping into him, low-frequency pulses of yearning that filtered through him and went booming onward to the watchers far away.

"You once loved me," Beryl said. "Then we were both silly. Love me again. Help me get back on my feet. I need your strength."

"Of course I'll help you," Cassiday said.

He left her apartment and purchased three cubes of triline. Returning, he activated one of them and pressed it into Beryl's hand. The green-and-milky eyes roiled in terror.

"No," she whimpered.

The pain flooding from her shattered soul was exquisite in its intensity. Cassiday accepted the full flood of it. Then she clenched her fist, and the drug entered her metabolism, and she grew peaceful once more.

Observe the next one:
   with a friend.

The annunciator said, "Mr. Cassiday is here."

"Let him enter," replied Mirabel Gunryk Cassiday Milman Reed.

The door-sphincter irised open and Cassiday stepped through, into onyx and marble splendor. Beams of auburn palisander formed a polished wooden framework on which Mirabel lay, and it was obvious that she reveled in the sensation of hard wood against plump flesh. A cascade of crystal-colored hair tumbled to her shoulders. She had been Cassiday's for sixteen months in 2346, and she had been a slender, timid girl then, but now he could barely detect the outlines of that girl in this pampered mound.

"You've married well," he observed.

"Third time lucky," Mirabel said. "Sit down? Drink? Shall I adjust the environment?"

"It's fine." He remained standing. "You always wanted a mansion, Mirabel. My most intellectual wife, you were, but you had this love of comfort. You're comfortable now."

"Very."

"Happy?"

"I'm comfortable," Mirabel said. "I don't read much any more, but I'm comfortable."

Cassiday noticed what seemed to be a blanket crumpled in her lap—purple with golden threads, soft, idle, clinging close. It had several eyes. Mirabel kept her hands spread out over it.

"From Ganymede?" he asked. "A pet?"

"Yes. My husband bought it for me last year. It's very precious to me."

"Very precious to anybody. I understand they're expensive."

"But lovable," said Mirabel. "Almost human. Quite devoted. I suppose you'll think I'm silly, but it's the most important thing in my life now. More than my husband, even. I love it, you see. I'm accustomed to having others love me, but there aren't many things that I've been able to love."

"May I see it?" Cassiday said mildly.

"Be careful."

"Certainly." He gathered up the Ganymedean creature. Its texture was extraordinary, the softest he had ever encountered. Something fluttered apprehensively within the flat body of the animal. Cassiday detected a parallel wariness coming from Mirabel as he handled her pet. He stroked the creature. It throbbed appreciatively. Bands of iridescence shimmered as it contracted in his hands.

She said, "What are you doing now, Dick? Still working for the spaceline?"

He ignored the question. "Tell me the line from Shakespeare, Mirabel. About flies. The flies and wanton boys."

Furrows sprouted in her pale brow. "It's from *Lear*," she said. "Wait. Yes. *As flies to wanton boys are we to the gods. They kill us for their sport.*"

"That's the one," Cassiday said. His big hands knotted quickly about the blanketlike being from Ganymede. It turned a dull gray, and reedy fibers popped from its ruptured surface. Cassiday dropped it to the floor. The surge of horror and pain and loss that welled from Mirabel nearly stunned him, but he accepted it and transmitted it.

"Flies," he explained. "Wanton boys. My sport, Mirabel. I'm a god now, did you know that?" His voice was calm and cheerful. "Good-by. Thank you."

One more awaits the visit:
Swelling with new life.

Lureen Holstein Cassiday, who was thirty-one years old, dark-haired, large-eyed, and seven months pregnant, was the only one of his wives who had not remarried. Her room in New York was small and austere. She had been a plump girl when she had been Cassiday's two-month wife five years ago, and she was even more plump now, but how much of the access of new meat was the result of the pregnancy Cassiday did not know.

"Will you marry now?" he asked.

Smiling, she shook her head. "I've got money, and I value my independence. I wouldn't let myself get into another deal like the one we had. Not with anyone."

"And the baby? You'll have it?"

She nodded savagely. "I worked hard to get it! You think it's easy? Two years of inseminations! A fortune in fees! Machines poking around in me—all the fertility boosters—oh no, you've got the picture wrong. This isn't an unwanted baby. This is a baby I sweated to have."

"That's interesting," said Cassiday. "I visited Mirabel

and Beryl, too, and they each had their babies, too. Of sorts. Mirabel had a little beast from Ganymede. Beryl had a triline addiction that she was very proud of shaking. And you've had a baby put into you, without any help from a man. All three of you seeking something. Interesting."

"Are you all right, Dick?"

"Fine."

"Your voice is so flat. You're just unrolling a lot of words. It's a little frightening."

"Mmm. Yes. Do you know the kind thing I did for Beryl? I bought her some triline cubes. And I took Mirabel's pet and wrung its—well, not its neck. I did it very calmly. I was never a passionate man."

"I think you've gone crazy, Dick."

"I feel your fear. You think I'm going to do something to your baby. Fear is of no interest, Lureen. But sorrow—yes, that's worth analyzing. Desolation. I want to study it. I want to help *them* study it. I think it's what they want to know about. Don't run from me, Lureen. I don't want to hurt you, not that way."

She was small-bodied and not very strong, and unwieldy in her pregnancy. Cassiday seized her gently by both wrists and drew her toward him. Already he could feel the new emotions coming from her, the self-pity behind the terror, and he had not even done anything to her.

How did you abort a fetus two months from term?

A swift kick in the belly might do it. Too crude, too crude. Yet Cassiday had not come armed with abortifacients, a handy ergot pill, a quick-acting spasmic inducer. So he brought his knee up sharply, deploring the crudity of it. Lureen sagged. He kicked her a second time. He remained completely tranquil as he did it, for it would be wrong to take joy in violence. A third kick seemed desirable. Then he released her.

She was still conscious, but she was writhing. Cassiday made himself receptive to the outflow. The child, he realized, was not yet dead within her. Perhaps it might not die at all. But it would certainly be crippled in some way. What he drained from Lureen was the awareness that she might bring forth a defective. The fetus would have to be destroyed. She would have to begin again. It was all quite sad.

"Why?" she muttered. " . . . why?"

Among the watchers:
   the equivalent of dismay.

Somehow it had not developed as the golden ones had anticipated. Even they could miscalculate, it appeared, and they found that a rewarding insight. Still, something had to be done about Cassiday.

They had given him powers. He could detect and transmit to them the raw emotions of others. That was useful to them, for from the data they could perhaps construct an understanding of human beings. But in rendering him a switching center for the emotions of others they had unavoidably been forced to blank out his own. And that was distorting the data.

He was too destructive now, in his joyless way. That had to be corrected. For now he partook too deeply of the nature of the golden ones themselves. *They* might have their sport with Cassiday, for he owed them a life. But he might not have his sport with others.

They reached down the line of communication to him and gave him his instructions.

"No," Cassiday said. "You're done with me now. There's no need to come back."

"Further adjustments are necessary."

"I disagree."

"You will not disagree for long."

Still disagreeing, Cassiday took ship for Mars, unable to stand aside from their command. On Mars he chartered a vessel that regularly made the Saturn run and persuaded it to come in by way of Iapetus. The golden ones took possession of him once he was within their immediate reach.

"What will you do to me?" Cassiday asked.

"Reverse the flow. You will no longer be sensitive to others. You will report to us on your own emotions. We will restore your conscience, Cassiday."

He protested. It was useless.

Within the glowing sphere of golden light they made their adjustments on him. They entered him and altered him and turned his perceptions inward, so that he might feed on his own misery like a vulture tearing at its entrails. That would be informative. Cassiday objected until he no longer had the power to object, and when his awareness returned it was too late to object.

"No," he murmured. In the yellow gleam he saw the faces of Beryl and Mirabel and Lureen. "You shouldn't have done this to me. You're torturing me ... like you would a fly ..."

There was no response. They sent him away, back to Earth. They returned him to the travertine towers and the rumbling slidewalks, to the house of pleasure on 485th Street, to the islands of light that blazed in the sky, to the eleven billion people. They turned him loose to go among them, and suffer, and report on his sufferings. And a time would come when they would release him, but not yet.

Here is Cassiday:
nailed to his cross.

Other SIGNET Science Fiction You Will Enjoy

☐ **THERE WILL BE TIME by Poul Anderson.** Only a natural-born time traveler stood between man and a future which could destroy human civilization.
(#Q5401—95¢)

☐ **THE FALLIBLE FIEND by L. Sprague de Camp.** Could a rational, literal-minded demon survive in an irrational world of men?
(#Q5370—95¢)

☐ **THE CITY AND THE STARS by Arthur C. Clarke.** A tense story set millions of years in the future, when one man sets out to unite Earth's sole survivors, two isolated nations ignorant of each other's ways. (#Q5371—95¢)

☐ **THE WEATHERMAKERS by Ben Bova.** Harnessing weather was the goal, and the man who could perform this miracle was Ted Marrett. But the opposition he faced was almost overwhelming and his greatest opponent was the weather itself. (#Q5329—95¢)

☐ **OPERATION: OUTER SPACE by Murray Leinster.** A television producer, his secretary, and a psychiatrist find themselves trapped inside a spacecraft, being hurled far beyond the confines of the Solar System toward a planet inhabited by bizarre creatures—a volcanic world strangely similar to Earth. (#Q5300—95¢)